RETRIBUTION

RETRIBUTION

A NOVEL BY
Douglas Orahood

Archway Publishing books may be ordered through booksellers or by contacting:

Archway Publishing
1663 Liberty Drive
Bloomington, IN 47403
www.archwaypublishing.com
1 (888) 242-5904

ISBN: 978-1-4808-3285-5 (sc)
ISBN 978-1-4808-4546-6 (hc)
ISBN: 978-1-4808-3286-2 (e)

Library of Congress Control Number: 2016909722

Print information available on the last page.

Archway Publishing rev. date: 03/17/2017

DEDICATION

TO YOU, MY LOVING AND patient wife, Charlene, and our four wonderful, caring daughters, Pamela, Peggy, Holly, and Sally, our little angel and the spiritual glue that holds us all together, this book is lovingly dedicated.

ACKNOWLEDGEMENT

IT IS WITH SINCERE GRATITUDE that I acknowledge my wonderful family and friends who contributed so much to this book's evolvement over the many years it has been in sitting in my computer waiting for this day. I would also like to say a special thank you to my editor, Patti Mortensen, who took what I thought was a finished manuscript and made it worthy of my efforts to give readers a unique story of crime and punishment. Many thanks also to my photographer, Glen Young.

CHAPTER 1

THE BOY WHISTLED A SOFT, melodic tune as he left the hardwood forest and walked barefoot through the mountain meadow. Twelve-year-old Jake Tanner wore only a floppy black hat and faded blue overalls with patches on the knees and butt. Dangling from his left hand by their hind legs were two gray rabbits, blood from their nostrils leaving splattered droplets on the dusty trail. In his right hand he carried a loaded, small caliber, single shot rifle. Rattlers were a common occurrence in these lowland hills, and the boy was careful as he scanned the trail ahead for the fearsome snakes. His spirits were high; it had been a good day for hunting, and he knew his father would be pleased.

Leaving the meadow behind, the boy again entered the forest and continued following the trail as it wandered down a sloping hillside to his family's farm in the valley below. It was late afternoon on a warm fall day and the boy was in no hurry to return to the farm and the drudgery of his evening chores. Nearing a clearing through the trees, he slowed to a stop, turned around, and looked back up the trail. A small smile tugged at the corners of his mouth as the forest's serenity and kaleidoscope of autumn colors filled his eyes. *Yeah*, he thought, *today is gonna be a good day to remember when the snow comes.* Then, with a deep sigh, he turned and continued down the trail as a gentle breeze whispered through the trees, bringing with it the faint sound of voices … angry voices.

Surprised, but with more curiosity than concern, the boy stepped off the trail and moved cautiously through the trees until he could see four men standing in front of his family's unpainted, clapboard house. Scattered around the men were the smashed remains of what he recognized as his family's meager belongings. Standing a short distance away from the house was a younger-looking man holding the reins of five saddled horses. On the young man's left cheek was what appeared to be a large red birthmark.

"I'm tellin' ya, Flack, they just ain't here," said a man standing in the pile of rubbish with his back to the boy.

"Damn you, Tolman," replied a man with a bushy, whisky-colored beard, "if you say that one more time I'm gonna put a bullet 'tween your eyes."

Stunned and frightened by the man's harsh words, the boy dropped the rabbits and crept silently back into the forest's shadows, where he crouched behind a waist-high boulder. With his heart pounding in his ears, he clutched the rifle to his chest and peeked cautiously over the boulder as another man began to speak.

"Well, breakin' up all this junk ain't got us nowhere," the man said with disgust, "and you're crazy if you think I'm stayin' 'round here 'til some sodbuster comes and sees what we done. Hell, I don't even know what I'm lookin' for."

With every sensory function now screaming danger, the boy thought … Where's Pa … and Ma … Pa said they'd be back from town by now.

"If I wanted you to know what we're lookin' for, I'd have told you," Flack snarled at the man. "And don't forget, you're as much a part of this mess as the rest of us."

"Come on, Flack, you know he's right," said Tolman. "We got to …"

"I told you to shut your mouth," screamed Flack as he moved quickly to stand nose to nose with Tolman. "*We* ain't got to do *nothin'* 'less I say so. And in case you forgot, if we don't find what we've come for, we're as good as dead ourselves."

"I ain't forgot," Tolman replied bitterly while taking a step backward. "And if I live to be a hundred I ain't *never* goin' to forget. But let's face it, we've looked everywhere, and if they was here, we would've found 'em. I think Tanner was tellin' the truth when he said he burned 'em."

Tanner!! The boy thought with alarm. *Are they talking about... my Pa?*

"I don't give a damn what you think," said Flack with a dismissive wave of his hand. "But that'd be just like the bastard. Burn 'em and then he'd be the only one who'd know where ..."

"Best you leave it there," interrupted Tolman quickly. "There's others here who's got ears."

"What?" said Flack with a startled expression on his face. "Oh ... yeah ... yeah ... well, reckon I got carried away some. But we're so damn close, closer'n we've ever been, and him burnin' 'em makes me want to kill the thievin' bastard all over again."

What are they talking about? the boy thought as his eyes searched anxiously about the farm for his pa. *Ain't no way Pa would ...* and as if to complete his thought he saw the farm's two horses hitched to the work wagon behind the barn. And above the wagon, hanging from a limb of a tall oak tree, was the half-naked body of his father. His hands were tied behind his back, and he had been whipped until the flesh on his back hung in bloody strips from his body.

"Noooo ... Noooo," the boy screamed aloud in tormented agony as he slumped to the ground sobbing. *Please, God, please don't let him be dead. Oh, God, he can't be dead.*

"What the hell was that?" said Flack as he took a step backward.

"Damn, sounds like a wounded animal on the prowl," said one of the other men tentatively.

"That weren't no animal," said Tolman, reaching for the butt of his gun as his eyes swept across the hillside forest. "I told you I saw a kid hangin' 'round Tolman's wagon when me and him was talkin', and I'll bet that's him hidin' up in them trees."

Stifling his sobs, the boy's eyes opened wide in sudden recognition. *I've heard that voice before. That's the man who was talkin' with Pa in town.*" With his grief now turning to rage, the boy stood up, aimed the rifle at Tolman's chest, and pulled the trigger.

But at that exact moment Tolman saw the boy and the flash from his rifle, and as he turned to warn the others, the bullet smashed into his left shoulder with a loud thump. Staggering backward from the force of the bullet, Tolman yelled, "See there, I told you there was another one. Now we got to kill him, too."

Stunned by the blossoming blood stain on the front of Tolman's shirt, Flack and the others were slow reacting to the warning. The boy, taking advantage of their confusion, turned and sprinted back up the trail, through the meadow, and into the thick forest that lay beyond, all the while hearing horses' hooves furiously clawing up the hillside. By the time the horses reached the meadow, and raced to the edge of the forest, the boy had vanished.

"Come on out, boy!" Flack yelled. "We ain't gonna hurt ya."

"Damn it, Flack," said Tolman, wincing in pain as he rode up seconds later. "He ain't gonna come out on your say-so. You got to go in there and kill him. He knows me."

"Yeah, and you can blame your own dumb ass for that," Flack replied gruffly. "And seein' as how he don't know none of us, guess you better go in there and kill him yourself."

"But I've been shot," Tolman whined as he grasped his bloody shoulder. "You and the boys gotta do it."

"You got a problem, you take care of it," said Flack as he turned his horse and nudged it to a slow trot back through the meadow. "I ain't goin' pokin' 'round in them woods and take a bullet because that kid knows you."

The other three men looked inquiringly at each other and then turned to follow Flack.

Twisting around in his saddle, with a note of desperation in his voice, Tolman yelled at the backs of the retreating men. "Yeah, he's seen me, but now he's seen you and his dead pa. Ain't none of us goin' to be safe 'till he's dead."

The four men ignored his warning and soon disappeared down the sloping hillside. Tolman, grasping his bloody shoulder in pain and mumbling curses, turned back toward the boy and shouted, "Come on out, boy, or I'm comin' in to get ya."

Fumbling to reload the single-shot rifle, the boy's sobbing response reverberated from within the trees, "Come and get me, you murderin' coward."

Hearing the boy's insolent reply, Tolman furiously spurred his horse forward a few steps before apparently thinking better of it. Jerking the animal to an abrupt stop, he shouted, "I'm gonna kill you, boy! Ain't nowhere you can hide from me!"

Although he could see only flashes of Tolman's image through the trees, the boy rose up from his hiding place behind a fallen log and responded by firing the rifle in the direction of Tolman's voice. Tolman was opening his mouth to say something when the bullet whizzed by his head. Apparently realizing the futility of further threats, Tolman wasted no time turning his horse and spurring it back through the meadow at a gallop.

Minutes later, with the sound of hoof-beats fading in the distance, the boy crept from his hiding place and used the thick forest to circle around the meadow. Ever mindful that Tolman might be setting up an ambush, he ignored the winding path he had taken earlier and used another path leading to a small hillside cave near the side of the family's barn.

Pausing at the cave only long enough to catch his breath, he was poised to run across the open ground between the cave and the barn when a gust of wind brought the distinctive smell of wood smoke. Looking around to find the source, he was stunned to see angry, black smoke billowing out from the farm house doors and windows. At the same time he heard a whooshing sound as the tinder-dry wooden barn burst into flames.

Knowing the tree where his father was hanging was close enough to the barn to also be consumed by the growing fire, the boy ran to a stack of split wood his father had prepared for the coming winter and grabbed an ax buried in a stump. Fighting his way through the boiling smoke, he staggered to the oak tree and, with one swing of the ax, cut the hangman's rope that was tied around the base of the tree. The horses, already skittish by the roar of the fire, bolted when they heard his father's limp body drop with a thud into the bed of the wagon. The boy, in a desperate attempt to stop the horses, reached out, and with one hand grabbed what he thought was a rope dangling from the back of the wagon. Coughing and gasping from the smoke, he was dragged face down through the dust until he lost his grip and rolled over several times before coming to a stop. Exhausted, groggy, and spitting dust, he struggled to rise to his hands and knees. But his strength was gone and he collapsed.

It wasn't until sometime later, when he felt something poking him in the ribs, that he looked around and saw his sister sitting cross-legged on the ground beside to him. In her hand was a sharp stick.

"Emily!" he said with surprise as he got to his knees and looked into her face. "Where …?" But the question died on his lips when he saw the vacant expression on Emily's face and her eyes staring unseeing into the distance. "Emily … are you all right?" he asked as he raised his right hand and gently touched her cheek.

Emily, with no change in expression, slowly raised the stick and pointed it at something behind the boy. Thinking Tolman had returned and was about to kill him, the boy slowly got to his feet and turned around as cold fear crept up his spine. But instead of seeing Tolman pointing a gun at his head, he saw his mother's body, partially buried in the rubble of his family's possessions.

"Oh, God, not her too," the boy cried in anguish as he ran to his mother's side and fell to his knees. She was lying on her side, with her eyes still open, in a pool of blood that had turned dark as it seeped into the earth. She had been shot one time in the throat. Clutched in her outstretched right hand, with her finger still on the trigger, was his father's shotgun. Standing in the background a few yards away were the horses and the wagon with his father's crumpled body in the back. Trailing in the dirt behind the wagon was a bloody whip, the same whip the boy had unknowingly grabbed as a rope while trying to stop the horses.

Unable to control his abhorrence at the sight of his dead parents, the boy's stomach spewed forth the horror his mind could not toss away so easily. Sick in body and spirit, and with the remains of his retching dripping from his chin, young Jake Tanner began to scream and fling handful after handful of dirt into the air as if trying to remove the grizzly sight from his eyes. His screams echoed off the hillside as he poured out his anguish, the soulful sounds echoing back to further fuel his torment. "I swear, Papa," he screamed, "someday I'll kill 'em all. I'll find 'em and see 'em all dead if it's the last thing I ever do."

"You cut him down, Jake?" asked Sheriff Brags.

"Yes sir,"

"Yeah, well, you did good. I saw the smoke from town, and I figured I'd better come lookin'. They kill Emily too?"

"No sir."

"No! Then where is she?"

"Up in the cave," Jake replied with a nod of his head, knowing the sheriff knew about the cave. "She won't come out."

"Why not?"

"I think she was hidin' up there watchin' while our folks were bein' killed."

"You recon she's been touched by it?"

"Yes sir.

"Yeah, I've seen folks take a while before gettin' over it," said the sheriff. "Some never do. You see who done this?"

"Yes sir, I seen 'em. I shot one."

"You don't say."

"Yes sir. His name's Tolman. I seen him and Pa talkin' in town. Another one's called Flack. Don't know 'bout the other three."

"Five of 'em! And you scared five of 'em off by yourself?"

"Guess so."

"Any idea what they was after?"

"No sir. All they said was they was lookin' for somethin'."

"Well, reckon we'll find out 'fore we hang 'em. But right now we got to do right by your folks. Let's load 'em in the wagon and take 'em to undertaker Butler in town."

Five days later the farm wagon carrying Jake and Emily entered the small town of Dalton and stopped in front of the sheriff's office. Sheriff Brags walked out of his office and stood on the porch as Jake stepped down from the wagon.

"Heard you was leavin', Jake. Any idea where you're goin'?"

"No sir. Guess I'll know when we get there."

"Recon that's best, at least 'til we get them murderers hanged."

"Yes sir."

"How's Emily?"

"No change," Jake replied as he glanced at Emily sitting stone-faced on the wagon seat.

"Like I said before," said the sheriff sadly, "might take some time, maybe never. You sure you don't want to leave her here 'till she's some better? Mrs. Barbee said she'd take her in. She's the best school teacher we've ever had, and it might be good for Emily to have a woman lookin' after her."

"Please tell Mrs. Barbee thanks," Jake replied, "but I think she'll be better with me. Emily has always been shy around other folks, but we get along fine."

"Okay, I'll tell her. Heard the bank foreclosed on your pa's place. They give you anything for it?"

"The horses, wagon, and them two milk cows tied on behind is 'bout it," Jake replied with a sad shake of his head. "Weren't nothin' left but the land, and the bank says that ain't worth much without the house and barn. I traded Pa's shotgun at the mercantile for some food and a coat for Emily, and Mr. Graves at the hotel gave me a pair of boots 'bout my size that was left by a feller who died in one of the rooms. I found some cookin' pots and things after the fire, and Sam at the livery gave me a patched up tent he got in trade for some feed."

"What 'bout you, Jake?" asked the sheriff. "You got a coat for yourself? It's gonna get mighty cold 'fore long."

"No sir, it got burned up in the fire. But I'll get by."

"Well, how 'bout somethin' to shoot with other'n that old single-shot varmint rifle? These is mighty hard times, son, and there's bound to be some desperate folks out on the trail that might try takin' advantage of a couple of youngsters."

"Yes sir, I figured there might be, but I found my Pa's rifle after the fire was out. It's burnt some on the stock but it'll shoot good enough."

"I always figured on you bein' a smart one, Jake. Well, guess that's 'bout it. You be sure and … no … no … wait here," said the sheriff as he turned and hurried back into his office. A moment later he returned carrying a leather trail-coat with tobacco spittle stains down the front. "It's mostly worn out" he said as he held it out to Jake, "but it's kept me warm on many a cold night. You're welcome to it if you want it."

"Thanks, Sheriff. That's more'n generous."

"This is a poor town with poor folks, Jake. Wish we could've done better by you and Emily."

"I'm sure you've all done the best you can and I'm grateful," Jake replied as he climbed up to his seat on the wagon. "Maybe someday I can pay you back."

"Ain't no need, son. Just make your Ma and Pa proud."

"Yes sir," Jake replied steadily, "I made a promise to my Pa and I ain't never goin' to forget it." And with a flick of the horses' reins the wagon jerked forward and continued moving slowly through the town as the sheriff looked on with a sad shake of his head.

Later that evening, when a cold wind began to blow puffy white snowflakes into his dying camp fire, Jake put on the trail coat and immediately felt something heavy in an inside pocket. Reaching deep in the pocket, he found three silver dollars, the only three dollars he had ever held in his hand. *Well I'll be*, he thought with a smile, *ain't no way Sheriff Brags would accidently leave money in a coat pocket. Thanks, Sheriff, and I swear that someday I'll return 'em to you.*

CHAPTER 2

Six Years Later: February 1874

THE HORSE SNORTED CLOUDS OF frothy steam as it wandered through the snow-capped sagebrush of a west-Texas ranch. It was just before sunrise on a gloomy February morning, and eighteen-year-old Jake Tanner's chin was bobbing up and down on his chest as he dozed in the saddle. For the past two years he had been working as a range rider, monitoring the ranch owner's cattle to keep rustlers and other predators at bay. It was a job of long days and lonely nights, but it was peaceful, for the most part, and he was content to let the days and months pass as he grew into manhood. Content, that is, until his horse stumbled while climbing out of a rocky ravine and abruptly awoke him from his sleepy reverie. Although stunned by his sudden awakening, followed by annoyance with himself for dozing off, it was not the first time he had fallen asleep in the saddle. The consequences of those past occurrences, however, failed to match his astonishment upon now seeing a man lying motionless on the frozen ground a few yards away. Standing stiff legged near the man was a saddled horse, huffing and puffing and tossing its mane defensively.

Reining his own horse to a gentle stop, Jake leaned back, snatched his rifle from its scabbard near the horse's rump, and slipped silently to the ground. Standing over six feet tall with broad muscular shoulders, Jake no longer resembled the shy, skinny boy he had been six years earlier. Sheriff Brags' trail coat now fit him perfectly, and the tobacco spittle stains on the front had been washed clean by seasons past. He was considered handsome by most people, especially young women about his own age, who smiled in his direction, but the feature that captured everyone was the intense, steely look in his iron-gray eyes.

Quietly levering a cartridge into the breach of the Winchester .44, he stared at the motionless figure for several minutes before letting his eyes carefully survey the seemingly empty desert. If this was a trap set for him by Tolman, it wasn't the first and it wouldn't be the last. Satisfied there was no immediate danger, he began a wary, circular-walk around both the man and the horse. The horse's chin and chest were covered with white lather and its exhausted breathing indicated it had been ridden long and hard. On the left side of the saddle, and running down the horse's left flank, was a dark, reddish stain that appeared to be blood. The man on the ground was lying flat on his back with both arms extended outward. He was bare-headed and dressed in black clothes and a black trail-coat that was fully open, exposing his body to the frigid elements. A dried blood stain extended from the man's upper left torso to his waist and down his left pants leg. His face was very pale, and he appeared to be dead.

Jake approached cautiously and nudged the man's midsection with the toe of his boot. There was no response. Squatting down alongside the man, he twice slapped the left side of the man's face with his gloved right hand. In response came a low, guttural moan. Realizing the man was still alive, Jake stood up and carefully lowered the hammer on the rifle, a half measure to make the gun safe. Still thinking this might be a Tolman trap, he unbuckled and removed the man's gun belt and searched his coat and clothing for other weapons. Finding none, he returned to his horse, slipped the man's gun belt over the horn of his saddle, and slid the rifle back into its scabbard.

Returning to the man on the ground, Jake pulled him up into a sitting position and, after gathering his strength, struggled to lift

him up and over his shoulder. Staggering under the man's weight, he
walked to the man's horse, now standing quietly nearby, and roughly
threw the man belly-down over its saddle. To keep the man from
falling off, he used a short length of rope to tie the man's hands and
feet together under the horse's belly. Jake then grasped of the reins
of the man's horse in his right hand, mounted his own horse, and
nudged the animals into a slow trot toward a small structure barely
discernable in the distance.

Reaching what was now a clearly dilapidated shack, Jake dragged
the man inside and laid him on one of the two narrow bunks in the
tiny room. The only sound from the man throughout this rough
jostling was an occasional groan. Jake covered the man with a ragged
blanket and then rekindled a fire in the potbelly stove, tending the
flames until the stove began to radiate heat into the room.

Returning to the horses, he led them into an open lean-to shelter
attached to the shack. He left his own horse saddled but removed
the saddle and other tack from the stranger's horse. Gathering up
the man's rifle, bed roll, and saddle bags, he placed a railing across
the front of the shelter to keep the animals inside and re-entered the
shack. With the room now somewhat warmer, and needing to know
the extent of the man's injury, Jake folded down the blanket covering
the man and removed his trail-coat. Then, after unbuttoning the
man's vest, shirt, and long-johns, he was not surprised when he saw
a large, round, jagged wound just below the man's left rib cage. From
the size and shape of the wound, he guessed it had been caused by a
bullet entering the man's body from behind and exiting through the
front. By rolling the man onto his side, Jake was able to confirm his
guess by reaching around and touching the small entry wound on the
man's back. He had seen a similar wound when two ranch hands on
a cattle drive had argued during a card game, and one had shot the
other in the back. Having witnessed the medical treatment given to
the man by the trail boss, Jake knew generally what needed to be done.

Covering the man again with the blanket, he filled a metal pail
with water from his snow-melt barrel and placed the pail on the now

red hot stove. Then, using one of his gloves as a heat pad, he opened the stove's hinged door with his right hand and plunged the stove's foot-long poker part way into the flaming interior.

As the water heated on the stove, Jake busied himself by tearing one of his spare shirts into long strips and then tying the strips together end to end, leaving only the shirt's long sleeves intact. When the water in the pail was hot to the touch, he wet one of his old neckerchiefs and, while turning the man from side to side, gently cleaned the ugly wounds. A bottle of whiskey, left at the bunkhouse by the ranch owner, 'for medicinal purposes only,' was then used to cleanse both wounds. Despite being unconscious, the man groaned in pain as the alcohol burned its way into his body.

Returning to the stove, Jake removed the poker from the flames, saw that its tip was smoldering-red, and, with a grimace on his face, returned to the man on the cot and inserted the poker into the man's frontal wound. The man screamed in agony as his arms and legs flailed about like a rag doll shaken by a dog. Although accustomed to the putrid smell of burning hair and skin while branding cattle, Jake found the stench of burning human flesh nauseating. Choking down the bile in his throat, he again heated the poker in the stove and cauterized the back wound of the now delirious man.

Sweating profusely from his repulsive task, Jake sat down on the edge of his own bunk, put his head in his hands, and tried to control the dry-retching that consumed him. Knowing he must continue in spite of his queasiness, he soon forced himself to again roll the man from side to side as he placed the folded sleeves from his shirt on each wound and wrapped the strips of cloth around the man's torso to hold the make-shift bandages in place. Covering the man again with the ragged blanket, he thought, *Now he'll either live or die, there ain't nothin' more I can do.*

In the days that followed, as Jake continued to tend the man's wounds, there seemed to be little, if any, noticeable improvement.

Within an hour after Jake awoke on the third morning, though, the man opened his eyes and let out a low groan.

"Where am I?" he asked in a thick-tongued voice as his right hand reached down under the blanket toward his waist. "And where's my shooter?"

"Easy, Mister," Jake responded calmly as he stood by the stove stirring a wooden spoon within a pot. "You been shot."

"Shot?" asked the man with a bewildered expression, which faded quickly with sudden understanding. "Oh yeah, now I remember."

"You're lucky to be alive, Mister," said Jake, smiling. "Seems like the bullet went clean on through."

"Yeah ... well ... ain't the first time. How long have I been here?"

"Goin' on three days. You thirsty ... or hungry?"

"Yeah, thirsty as hell. Got any whiskey?"

"Not for drinkin'. I'm gonna need all I got to keep your wounds from festerin'. But I got fresh coffee and some two-day-old stew in this pot."

Without waiting to receive an answer, Jake filled a dented tin cup with black coffee and handed it to the man, "What do folks call you, Mister?"

"You askin' for some special reason or are you just nosey?" grumbled the man as he reached for the cup, grimacing with pain as he did so.

"Ain't neither," replied Jake in a friendly tone. "Just figured you ain't goin' no place for a spell and I got to call you somethin'."

"Oh ... yeah ... yeah ... suppose so. Well, most folks call me Billy."

"Just Billy? You ain't got no last name?"

"Yeah, course I do. But Billy is all you need knowin'."

"Well, then, I guess Billy will have to do. So, how'd you come to get shot?"

Ignoring Jake's question, Billy said, "You the one been tendin' me?"

"Yeah, thought you was dead when I found you. Glad you weren't though 'cause I don't take kindly to grave diggin' in frozen ground."

"Guess I owe you, kid."

"My name's Jake. And you ain't said how you got shot."

"It's a long story that I ain't ready to talk about. Anybody been around askin' questions like they was lookin' for me?"

"You're the only one I seen in nearly two months. Don't get many visitors."

"Ah, good … good," Billy mumbled with what seemed like relief. "And I'd be obliged if anybody does come 'round, you keep still 'bout my being here."

"Sounds like you might be expectin' folks to do you some harm. But, seein' as how I got a similar problem, I reckon I can deal with that."

"What do you mean, you got a similar problem?"

"Like you said, Billy, it's a long story."

Less than a week later Billy had recovered enough to greet Jake with a fire in the stove and a hot cup of coffee at the end of the day. Jake always fixed the evening meal, using whatever he brought back from his range wandering and his limited food supply. A jack rabbit was acceptable to Billy, but he refused to eat rattlesnake. Afterward, with each man rolling and smoking a cigarette from his own makings, they'd often talk far into the night. Jake judged Billy to be in his mid-twenties. Although thin and wiry, there was no doubt in Jake's mind that Billy would have no trouble intimidating other men if he were of a mind to. With Jake he was quiet, reserved, and strangely thoughtful. The hardness in his eyes seemed to soften as the days passed, and now and then a small smile, and sometimes even a quiet laugh, broke through the granite features of his face.

Eventually, Jake told Billy about seeing four men brutally kill his mother and father.

"I've never been able to figure out why anybody would just up and kill 'em like that," Jake lamented. "I heard 'em say they was lookin' for something, but far as I know, we didn't have no money or nothin' else worth takin'. They was murdered for nothin', Billy, … nothin' at all."

Lowering his head and shaking it from side to side, Billy said, "I'm sorry, Jake. When did this happen?"

"About six years ago, when I was twelve."

"Did … did you see who done it?"

"Yeah, I'd just come back from huntin' and I seen 'em bustin' up everything my folks owned. I hid 'fore they seen me, but I recognized one of 'em. He was a neighbor named Tolman. I shot the bastard and then run off and hid in the woods 'til they was gone. Tolman knows I seen him, and 'fore ridin' off with the others, he said he was gonna find me and kill me so I couldn't say who done it."

"So, did you tell anybody?"

"I told the sheriff, but by the time he went lookin' for Tolman, he was gone."

"So, you just let it go at that?" asked Billy frowing.

"Hell no!" said Jake angrily. "I promised my Pa that I'd find every one of 'em and kill 'em all."

"Can't say I blame you none. And you're sayin' there was four of 'em?"

"No, there was five. But the fifth one was a young feller who looked like his only job was tendin' the horses. And while I only recognized Tolman, I heard him call one of the others 'Flack.' It was Flack, Tolman, and two others who hanged my pa. I weren't there when they hanged him or shot my ma, so I can't say if the fifth feller were part of it. But I figure him just bein' there makes him guilty as the rest of 'em."

"Think you'd know any of 'em, other'n Tolman, if you ever saw 'em again?"

"Maybe … can't say for sure. But it don't matter none. I'll find Tolman and Flack and 'fore I kill 'em they'll give me the names of the others."

"You seen any of 'em since?"

"No. But I think Tolman found me 'bout two years ago. I was roundin' up strays for an outfit in Oklahoma when I heard a rifle shot and a tree limb near my head come apart. I didn't stay 'round long enough to see if it were him, but I 'spect it were. Since then I've kept on the move, still kind of hidin' out. Fact is, when I first saw you laid out like you was dead, I thought you might be Tolman layin' a trap for me. I was mighty glad when you weren't. I always figured I'd wait 'til I was full grown 'fore startin' out to find him and the others."

"Well, you still got some growin' up to do 'fore you go lookin' for men like them," said Billy. "I've met a few in my time, and right now you'd be an easy kill for any of 'em."

Three weeks later Billy told Jake that he was thinking about moving on.

"You sure you're ready?" asked Jake with concern. "Those wounds won't be healed for at least another month or so."

"Well, I don't figure on leavin' tomorrow," Billy replied with a smile. "It's got to be soon, though, 'cause my bein' here could be puttin' you in danger."

"Danger?" said Jake with a frown, "How could your bein' here put me in danger?"

"Because I'm wanted for killin' a young boy who got in the way during a gun fight," Billy confessed. "A gun fight that got me shot and chased by a posse 'til they finally gave up."

After a moment's hesitation Jake said, "I've been wonderin' when you'd tell me how you got shot."

"Yeah, well that ain't all. The truth is, Jake, I'm a gunfighter. A man people hire to kill other people, with no questions asked."

Shocked, Jake could only stare at Billy with an open mouth.

"Yeah, yeah, I know," said Billy. "And that's why I'm leavin' as soon as I can get on my horse without your help."

Jake didn't say anything for a long moment. But after his initial astonishment faded he said, "Are you goin' back to bein' a gunfighter?"

"No … hell no! It didn't make no sense then and it makes even less sense now. I'm figurin' on goin' east, maybe St. Louis, and try to find a new life, one I can be proud of."

"I know you can do it, Billy," said Jake as he held out his hand to his friend.

On a warm, spring-like morning a few days later, as they rested their horses on the crest of a hill, Billy turned to Jake and said, "You ever use a shooter?"

"Naw," Jake replied. "Never could afford one."

"Might be a good thing to have one and know how to use it if you're serious 'bout killin' them fellers."

"I know how to use my rifle good enough. Don't need no shooter."

"So you're sayin' you're gonna back-shoot 'em from a ways off and with them not knowin' why they're bein' killed?"

"No, of course not. They got to know why they're bein' killed and who's doin' the killin'."

"Well, Jake, you're probably goin' to be the one gettin' killed if you try using a rifle in a face-to-face gunfight."

"Well, I don't aim to be no gunfighter."

"You don't have to be a gunfighter to know how to use a shooter, Jake. There's things I can show you that might save your stubborn hide."

"Yeah, like what?"

"Get down off that horse and I'll show you."

Both men dismounted, and as they moved away from the horses, Billy said, "First, a man who's not a gunfighter, but finds himself faced with a fight he can't avoid, needs to stay calm. Second, he needs to know how to draw fast, shoot from the hip, and hit a target at close range."

"And what does my friend, the gunfighter, suggest?" asked Jake sarcastically.

"Tease all you want," said Billy with a stern look, "but you better listen to what I'm sayin' if you really mean to keep that promise to your pa. Them killers ain't goin' to just let you talk 'em to death."

Shocked into silence by Billy's harsh words, it took Jake a moment to realize the truth of what Billy had said. With eyes downcast, he kicked at the dirt with the toe of his boot in embarrassment and said, "Sorry, Billy, you're right. I guess it's time for me to start thinking about what needs doin'. What have you got in mind?"

"Nice to see you got my message," said Billy as the tone of his voice softened. "So here's what you need to know. In most gun fights the two men are only a few feet apart and shootin' fast from the hip. Anything much farther away than that you're better off drawin' and takin' aim 'fore shootin', 'cause it's better to hit your target with your first shot than shootin' wild from the hip and missin'. Here, I'll show you."

Untying the leather thong that held the end of his holster low on his right leg, Billy unbuckled his gun belt and then tightened it again so that the holster was now only slightly below his hip. With the gun belt in this position he retied the leather thong around his leg. "Wearin' your shooter low on your leg and *lookin'* like a gunfighter will only get you in trouble. But don't be wearin' your shooter high up on your hip like some city dude neither. Some final things to remember are: never fight when you're angry, never show fear, and look your opponent straight in the eye. Any sign of weakness will bolster the other man's confidence and maybe get you killed."

Looking around, Billy said, "See that old bird nest in that bush over there?" And in one swift, fluid motion Billy drew his shooter and fired one shot. The bird nest disappeared in an explosion of twigs and feathers.

Jake stared, open mouthed. "Damn! That's some shootin'. How'd you learn that?"

"It takes a lot of practice, Jake, first with the fast draw and then shootin' from the hip and hittin' your target every time. And remember, you'd better kill your target with your first bullet 'cause more'n likely you won't get a second chance. Now you try it a few times."

Over the next several weeks Billy continued to teach Jake his fast-draw technique and watched as Jake improved in both speed and accuracy. It quickly became apparent to Billy that Jake was a natural. Early one morning, a few weeks later, Jake woke up to find Billy gone and on his empty bunk was his black leather gun belt and pistol. From that day forward, Jake took Billy's advice and spent every spare minute of the day practicing his fast draw. It had been a long time coming, but Jake now knew the time was drawing near when he would be ready to face the men who brutally murdered his parents.

CHAPTER 3

One Year Later, June 1875

BURT TOLMAN WAS A MAN who did not take disappointment easily, and with each passing day his frustration with not being able to find and kill Jake Tanner increased. The last time he had seen Tanner was more than two years ago when a bullet from his rifle somehow missed Tanner's head. He had held Tanner in his sights for over a minute before taking the shot, enjoying the thought of being free from the fear of hanging. Equally satisfying would be to pay Tanner back for shooting him and making him a cripple. But he had waited too long enjoying the moment, and had taken the shot just as Tanner spurred his horse to chase a cow from a stand of trees. Whether the missed opportunity was the result of waiting too long, or the constant pain in his left shoulder, the last he had seen of Tanner was the top of his hat and the rump of his horse as they disappeared down the side of a steep ravine. Since then, the trail had grown increasingly cold.

"Either of you gents ever heard of a cowpoke named Tanner?" Tolman asked two cowboys nearby as he leaned against the saloon's bar. His stance was relaxed and he kept his shrunken left hand hidden in his coat pocket. This was just one of more than a hundred saloons he had visited during the past two years and asked the same question.

"Who's askin'?" came a loud, slurred reply from a table near the back of the room.

"Name's Lewis," Tolman lied as he turned around and looked at the man who had spoken. "Do you know this Tanner feller, mister?"

"I ain't 'mister' to nobody," said the man gruffly. "Name's Digger Jones. And yeah, maybe I know him. Why you want to know?"

"Personal business," said Tolman as he walked to the table and stood opposite the man. "Mind if I sit?"

"Last I heard it were a free country," Jones replied as he raised his glass in a mock salute and tossed the last of its contents down his throat.

Without further comment, Tolman used his right hand to pull an empty chair out from the table and sat down. He was dressed in a black suit with a light coat of trail dust on his shoulders and wide-brimmed black hat. His soiled white shirt was buttoned all the way to the neck and his face was covered with a dense black beard. One had to look hard into his eyes to see the hatred hidden there.

"You ain't no cowpoke, are ya?" said Jones, smiling through tobacco stained teeth while appraising Tolman with crusty, bloodshot eyes. He looked to be in his late fifties, with long gray hair spilling out from beneath his sweat-stained hat. His face was wrinkled and weathered like old leather, and his callused hands were grimy with worked-in dirt. The rank smell of the unwashed drifted from him.

"No," replied Tolman.

"Who and what are ya then?"

"I'm Reverend Walter Lewis, going about the Lord's business."

Early in his search Tolman observed that those who professed religious titles were often accorded respect and treated to free saloon drinks. Free drinks were a bonus not to be ignored, and respect was a significant benefit in obtaining cooperation from those he questioned.

"The hell ya say. Out savin' souls, are ya," said Jones with a wicked laugh.

"Yes, that is my mission in life. But right now I'm lookin' for just one lost soul."

"I take it you mean this Tanner feller."

"Yes, I surely am," Tolman replied. "And are you saying you know him?"

With a crafty look in his eyes, Jones said, "Like I said before, *Reverend*, could be. But if I *were* to know him, that information sure ought to be worth somethin'."

"Oh, why yes, of course," said Tolman, trying to control his growing excitement. "A small reward, shall we say, for your assistance in helping me locate this young man and doing the Lord's work."

"Ah, yes, praise the Lord for understandin' the ways of a poor old cowboy who's lost in the darkness of hell and damnation. Yes sir, the Lord is full of understandin' and ...."

"Yes, yes," Tolman interrupted as he turned toward the front of the saloon and yelled, "Barkeep! Bring this fine gentleman a bottle of your best whiskey."

"Yes sir, the Lord surely works in wondrous ways," said Jones brightly.

"Right," said Tolman leaning forward in anticipation. "Now tell me about Tanner. Where did you come to know him?"

"Well, I knowed a young feller named Tanner when I worked for a time at a ranch down in west Texas. The owner were a fair man but he didn't take kindly to my stealin' a few of his cows for whiskey money. Sorry to say I had to leave in a hurry when he found a few of 'em missin'."

"A young fellow you say. How long ago was that, and what was the name of the ranch?"

"Oh, I guess it were a year or so. Name of the ranch were the Rollin' K. I sure hated leavin' 'cause they feed mighty good and the owner's wife had the finest lookin' ...."

The old cowboy was still talking when Tolman tossed two silver dollars to the bartender and walked quickly from the saloon.

"That was a mighty fine meal, Mrs. Kentworth. Can't say I've eaten one better."

"Why thank you, Reverend Lewis. A man of the cloth doesn't get out this way very often."

"The Lord has called me to serve my fellow man, Mrs. Kentworth, and I just go where He directs me. I've ministered to folks in some of the biggest cities in the east and in the bleakest parts of the west. Why, I'm proud to say that I've saved souls other preachers have long ago given up on, and hope to someday travel to ..."

"And just what is it that brings you to the Rolling K?" interrupted Mr. Kentworth with a note of impatience in his voice. While his demeanor with most people was pleasant enough, Mr. Kentworth had not become the owner of a huge cattle ranch by being careless or tolerating fools. To his way of thinking, after listening to Reverend Lewis' pompous, soul-saving gibberish, the reverend was not a man to be long tolerated.

"Oh, yes, yes, of course. Well sir, I regret to say that I'm the messenger of bad news for one of your ranch hands."

"Oh my goodness," Mrs. Kentworth gushed. "I hope ...."

"Perhaps you should see to the kitchen, Gretchen," said Mr. Kentworth with a sharp edge in his voice.

"Oh my, of course, dear," she replied, apparently recognizing the tone in her husband's voice. "It has been delightful having you at our dinner table, Reverend Lewis."

"The pleasure is all mine, ma'am," said Tolman as he half stood to acknowledge her departure. "You're a lucky man, Mr. Kentworth," he continued as he sat down again.

Without responding to Tolman's compliment, Mr. Kentworth sat quietly until his wife left the room and closed the kitchen door behind her. Then, leaning forward in his chair with a look of suspicion, he said, "And just what kind of bad news are you talking about, Reverend?"

"Well, sir, I'm genuinely devastated to tell you that the parents of one of your men were drowned a few months back. And after this sorrowful event, my congregation took up a sizable collection and sent me off to fetch the man so he could return and care for his two younger brothers and three sisters."

"I see," said Mr. Kentworth as he sat back in his chair with an uneasy feeling. "And what is the name of this man?"

"Jake Tanner. I was told he works for the Rolling K."

Although his face remained composed, Mr. Kentworth's defense mechanisms were immediately alert. A few months after coming to the Rolling K Ranch, Jake had confided in Mr. Kentworth regarding the murder of his parents and Tolman's threat to kill him. From that day forward, Jake was known to everyone coming and going from the ranch as Jacob Hawkins.

"And who told you that this ... this, what's his name ... Tanner, works for me?" asked Mr. Kentworth, knowing with certainty that Reverend Lewis was really Burt Tolman.

"A man by the name of Digger Jones," Tolman said with a confident smile. "He said he worked for you some time back."

To Tolman's surprise, Mr. Kentworth immediately burst out laughing. Finally, after wiping tears from his eyes with his dinner napkin, he said, "Old Digger Jones, I should have known. I've given that old bum a couple of chances to work himself sober, but every time I do I end up losing a couple of cows. Was he drunk when he gave you this information?"

"Well, he had been drinking some. But he seemed very sure of himself."

"Yeah, I'm sure he did. And what did this information cost you, Reverend?"

"Cost me?"

"Yeah. Most times he'll tell you anything you want to know for just a drink of whiskey. But if he sees you're anxious, he'll try to sell you the whole damn saloon for the price of a bottle. Please tell me you didn't buy him a bottle, Reverend."

"Well, yes, I did press him somewhat."

Chuckling softly, Mr. Kentworth said, "Don't feel bad, Reverend. Digger Jones is well known for that sort of thing."

"So you're saying Mr. Jones lied to me, and you don't have anybody named Jake Tanner working for you?"

"That's about it," replied Mr. Kentworth as he stood up from the table. "There's no one here named Jake Tanner."

Three weeks later a covered wagon pulled by four horses and driven by two men left the ranch and headed west. Hidden in the back of the wagon was Jake's sister, Emily, and tied behind the wagon were three horses. For all appearances it was simply a range rider supply wagon. Six days later, after re-supplying the bunk houses of two other range riders, the wagon reached Jake's location. Before dawn the following morning Jake and Emily left the range rider bunk house with all their belongings, four horses, and six weeks provisions. In Jake's vest pocket was a note from Mr. Kentworth and two years wages. The note said that after Tolman left the ranch, he was followed for two weeks to make sure he was well on his way out of Texas.

Jake was now nineteen years old and ready to seek his vengeance. The only problem was Emily. After witnessing the brutal murder of her parent's, she was still so traumatized by the event that she could not speak and only functioned at a very basic level.

CHAPTER 4

Three Months Later: September, 1875

IN THE PRE-DAWN DARKNESS A sleepy young man slowly climbed the windmill's vertical ladder. Carl Murphy hated leaving a warm bed before the sun was up, and that was only one of many reasons he and his brother had fled from their abusive father. Reaching the small platform on top of the spindle-legged tower, he flopped down facing west and remained motionless as the sun slowly breached the eastern horizon. Half an hour later, feeling the sun's growing warmth on his back, he turned around to face the sun and closed his eyes as the radiant heat warmed his cheeks. A few moments later, when he opened his eyes, he was surprised by the appearance of several objects silhouetted on the distant horizon.

Scrambling to his feet, he again looked toward the sunrise, but this time saw nothing. Frowning, he was about to sit down and resume facing west when he saw the objects slowly rise above the horizon, remain visible for several minutes, and then disappear. Over the next hour he continued to observe the objects appear and disappear in an irregular pattern, each time becoming larger as they moved westward between the shallow, undulating hills and valleys of the empty Kansas prairie. The sun was fully above the horizon when he saw that the objects were two men on horseback leading two other horses with packs on their backs.

Quickly swinging his body out and over the edge of the windmill's platform, Carl raced down the ladder and ran to a nearby two-story building. Throwing the front door of the building open with a crash, he took the stairs to the second floor two-at-a-time and raced down the narrow hallway to the last door on his left.

Pounding on the door with the back his fist he shouted, "Somebody's comin', Mr. Skaggs!"

"What … what the hell you shoutin' 'bout boy?" said a gruff voice from within. "And stop all that damn yellin'."

"I said somebody's comin," Carl repeated excitedly as he opened the door and entered the room. "I seen 'em, just like you said!"

"How many?" demanded Skaggs as he flailed about wildly while trying to extricate himself from his blanket and the sagging bed. "Where the hell's my boots?"

"What's goin' on?" asked a sleepy voice from across the room.

"Yeah, who's comin'?" added a third, coarse voice. "Ain't suppose to be nobody for 'nother two days."

"Damn it, boy," shouted Skaggs. "How many are there?"

"Oh … a … just two," said Carl hesitantly.

"Two … just two?" said Skaggs worriedly, "and they's comin' from the west?"

"Ah … well … no sir, Mr. Skaggs. They ain't comin' from the west. They's comin' from the east."

"What! Damn it to hell, Carl," shouted Skaggs in a rage. "I told you plain they'd be comin' from the west, not the east."

"Yes, sir, you told me, but I thought you might what to know 'bout any strangers comin' to town, even from the east."

"Well I don't give a damn 'bout strangers comin' from the east, you moron. Now get back up on that windmill 'fore I decide you're more damn trouble than you're worth."

"Ah … yes sir, Mr. Skaggs. I'm goin'. But I sure could use somethin' to eat first."

Carl's words were followed by a cowboy boot hitting him square in the chest. Yelping in pain, he bolted through the open door as a second boot whizzed through the doorway and slammed into a wall across the hall. Coughing and clutching his chest with both hands, Carl stumbled down the stairs and out the front door of the building. By the time he staggered back to the windmill, his breathing was almost back to normal, but he winced in pain as he began climbing the ladder to the tower's platform. When he reached the top, and looked at the two riders approaching the settlement, he saw that one of the riders was leading the other rider's horse by a short rope tied to the back of his saddle.

Back in the hotel room, Skaggs grumbled to himself as he flopped down on the sagging bed. "I don't know why I bother with that stupid kid and his half-wit brother."

"I ain't no half-wit," pleaded a whiney voice from a corner of the room. "Maw said I was just slow."

"Slow hell!" roared Skaggs. "You ain't even smart enough to know how dumb you is, Bob."

"Skaggs, either shut the hell up so I can get some sleep, or I'm gonna kill both of you," grumbled someone in another sagging bed.

"Yeah, you'd like that, wouldn't you, Logan," Skaggs replied. "One thing sure 'bout washed-up gunfighters, they ain't happy 'til they put another notch on their gun butt, no matter how easy they come by it."

"The hell you say," replied Logan angrily as he sat up and faced Skaggs in the growing light. "You know I don't enjoy killin' a man 'less he's full grown. Why, hell, if I was to kill that brainless kid, it'd be no different than shootin' a skunk. Just not as much stink afterward."

"Well, I don't want him dead just yet," said Skaggs. "He might come in handy some day."

A fourth figure, curled up on the floor and tied to the railing of Skaggs' bed, was awake but remained silent.

As Jake reined his horse to a stop outside the settlement, the other three horses came alongside and also stopped. Resting easy in the saddle, he used his gloved right hand to tip his hat back and wipe his forehead with the tattered neckerchief tied loosely around his neck. Thick black hair spilled out from under his hat and the bushy mustache under his nose matched the black stubble on his cheeks. Spidery wrinkles at the corners of his eyes added to his weathered complexion. The rider on the horse next to him was slumped forward in the saddle as if asleep. It was only when the horse became skittish and abruptly side-stepped that the rider awakened and her long, dark-blue skirt puffed out in the breeze.

Reaching into a vest pocket, Jake removed a sack of tobacco makings. With practiced ease he rolled and lit the cigarette with a wooden match taken from another pocket. As smoke from the burning tobacco drifted skyward, his eyes moved up the windmill until they came to rest on Carl. A moment later, and with an air of dismissal, he looked toward the group of buildings making up the settlement. It was typical of many other towns he had seen on the empty western plains, former stagecoach stops left to fend for themselves after the ever-expanding railroads passed them by.

Something's wrong here, Jake thought as he pinched out the cigarette between his gloved thumb and forefinger. *Folks ought to be moving around by this time of the mornin', and they ain't. Except for them four horses tied to a railing in front of the hotel, and that kid up on that windmill watching us, this looks like a ghost town. Yeah, this town's got trouble and we should just keep moving on. But … damn, we've got troubles of our own and ain't got no choice.* With a disgruntled frown on his face, Jake gently spurred his horse forward and the other horses quickly fell into line. The woman said nothing and continued to sit upright with her hands clasped tightly on the saddle horn.

Entering the settlement, the muted flopping of the horse's hooves were the only sounds echoing between the buildings. Approaching a blacksmith's shop on the far edge of the settlement, Jake turned his horse to face the building's hitching rail. The other horses followed as Jake dismounted and tied his horse's reins to the railing. But when the woman's horse came to a stop, the woman suddenly began struggling as if trying to dismount but was somehow constrained.

Moving quickly to the woman's side, Jake worked to remove the three short lengths of rope used to tie the woman's feet to the saddle's stirrups and her hands to the saddle horn. Once the constraints were removed, the distraught woman dismounted and hurried to sit down on a wooden bench in front of the building. Jake, gently taking the woman's trembling hands in his own as he sat down beside her said, in a soft, reassuring voice, "It's all right, Emily. We'll just stop here for a little while. There ain't no need to be afraid."

Silent moments passed as Emily's trembling subsided. Then, gently brushing a strand of hair from her angelic face, he said, "I need to leave you here for a few minutes while I talk to the blacksmith. You won't be afraid, will you?"

Emily shook her head slowly from side to side, but Jake could see fear building in her eyes. "I promise I won't be long," he said, as his jangling spurs marked his progress to and through the building's open doorway. Emily remained seated on the bench with her hands twisting nervously in her lap.

Sitting at a small table in the shop's damp, smoky haze was a man using a pencil to make scratching noises in a ledger. His grimy hands and the blackened leather apron tied at his waist left no doubt as to his blacksmith trade. Although bare-headed, his face remained hidden in the partial darkness as he bent to his task. He must have known by the sound of Jake's spurs that someone had entered his shop, and, without looking up, simply motioned with his left arm for the intruder to enter.

Ignoring the blacksmith's wave, Jake remained standing just inside the shop's entrance and said in a deep voice, "You the one I need talkin' with 'bout puttin' up my animals?"

"Ain't no other," replied the blacksmith in a gruff voice as he stopped writing and looked up at his prospective customer. Because of Jake's deep voice, the blacksmith was not surprised to see the tall, broad shouldered man standing in the shop's doorway. "As long as you got twenty cents a day for each of 'em, feed included."

"That the amount for keepin' 'em stabled rather'n in your corral out back?"

"Nope. Stabled will cost each of 'em another five cents a day."

"Sounds reasonable," replied Jake as he stepped farther into the shop while digging into a vest pocket. "And how's the hotel for stayin'?"

Interested now that he had a paying customer, the blacksmith's demeanor changed to a friendly, soot-smudged smile as he said, "Rooms are clean ... and the food ain't half bad neither. Eat there myself most days."

"Much obliged," Jake replied as he laid two silver dollars on the table and turned to leave. "Figure I'll be stayin' a couple of days."

"Just be careful," said the blacksmith, as he once more began scratching in the ledger.

Stopping and turning to look back at the blacksmith, Jake said in a wary voice, "Why the warnin', mister?"

Lowering his voice to a confidential whisper, the blacksmith said, "Because there's some outlaws stayin' at the hotel."

"Lots of outlaws here 'bout," said Jake. "They been causin' trouble?"

"Guess you could say that," confided the blacksmith. "A homesteader from here-'bouts ' told me he was on the train from Dodge City when it stopped for water 'bout three miles north of here. Says this bunch of outlaws boarded the train, robbed all the passengers, and then forced a young woman off the train. They killed one of the two men escortin' her without so much as a howdy, and beat the other near to death 'fore sendin' him off on horseback to tell her pa to come get her, along with five thousand dollars or she's dead."

"When did this happen?"

"Near as I can figure, yesterday mornin' 'bout this time."

"You got a sheriff?"

"Had one ... 'til yesterday."

"They killed him?"

"Yeah, good man too. Had himself a pretty little wife and two young boys. One of them outlaws, the one they call Logan, shot him dead 'fore his gun ever cleared his holster."

"Guess that's why I ain't seen nobody 'round."

"Can't nobody blame 'em. Folks is scared. They figure there's sure to be more shootin' when the girl's father gets here. People in town and sod busters out yonder don't want no part of that, them havin' families and all. There's just me, my barkeep at the saloon, and Miss Martha at the hotel. We all been told to stay put by a man them others call Skaggs."

"Those four horses out front of the hotel theirs?"

"Yeah, them poor critters been standin' out there since them buzzards come to town. They'd all be dead or crazy by now if I hadn't moved 'em over to the water trough a couple of times and give 'em some feed. It just ain't right treatin' animals that-a-way."

"How many of 'em are there?"

"Four, far as I know. The one called Skaggs, two loud-mouth youngsters, and Logan."

"That one of 'em sittin' up on the windmill?"

"Yeah, one of the youngsters. Keepin' an eye out for the girl's father most likely."

"Well, appreciate the warnin'," said Jake over his shoulder as he turned to leave.

"Say, hold on, mister," called the blacksmith. "Should I need to know, me bein' the undertaker here 'bouts, what's your name?"

Turning back toward the blacksmith, Jake hesitated for a moment and then said, "Jacob Hawkins. But if anybody comes askin', I'd appreciate your sayin' you ain't never heard of me. That any problem for you, Mr. ...?"

"Mayfield, Willard Mayfield. And I suppose it wouldn't do any good askin' why I ain't never heard of you."

Deciding the less said the better, Jake replied, "Best we just leave it at that."

"You ain't wanted by the law, are you, Mr. Hawkins?"

"No, I ain't wanted by the law," Jake replied with a smile tugging at the corners of his mouth.

"Then you got my word, Mr. Hawkins, I ain't never heard of you."

Returning to the roadway, Jake glanced up at the windmill and saw that the boy was now looking off to the west toward Dodge City. Frowning, he turned and walked to where Emily was sitting on the bench and sat down beside her. Removing the glove from his right hand, he used the tips of his fingers to gently lift her chin and look into her deep brown eyes.

"We're goin' to stay here a couple of days, Emily," he said softly. "It ain't the best place, but we can't go on 'til you get some rest."

In response, Emily moaned loudly and began beating her fists on Jake's chest. Grabbing her wrists and holding them tight, Jake continued talking softly, "We've been on the trail for over a month, Emily, and you're too exhausted to go on. We'll get a room here at the hotel, stay a day or two, and leave when you're up to it."

Emily shook her head violently and struggled to release Jake's grip on her wrists.

"Please, Emily," said Jake trying to calm her. "You're so tired that if I hadn't tied your feet to your stirrups you'd have fallen off a half dozen times last night. I'm used to this kind of life, but you're not. And if you don't get some rest … well … it could be bad for both of us."

As Emily's shoulders slumped in apparent acknowledgement, Jake stood up, pulled Emily gently to her feet, and together they made their way across the roadway and entered the hotel's deserted lobby. Seeing no one, Jake walked to a high counter near the front and saw a book with the words, Guest Registration, printed on the cover. Near the book was a small bell that Jake punched, producing a high pitched ring that caused Emily to cover her ears and cower.

Realizing his mistake, Jake turned and held Emily close while saying, "I'm sorry, Emily, I had no idea it would ring so loud. Please … don't be upset."

Unnoticed by Jake, someone was watching through a small slit between the curtains mounted on the wall behind the registration counter. It was only after Emily calmed down that a petite, middle-aged woman pushed through the curtains and asked, "Can I help you, sir?"

Turning back toward the counter as he snatched his hat from his head, Jake replied, "I'd be pleased if we could have a room, ma'am."

"Of course," the woman replied pleasantly as she turned the registration book to face Jake and said, "Please sign here. Rooms are seventy-five cents a day."

Jake leaned over the book and wrote a name in the place indicated while the woman looked at Emily with obvious concern.

"Is your wife ill, mister?" she asked. "She seems a might …."

"She just needs some rest, ma'am," interrupted Jake. "We've been on the trail a while."

"Oh, yes, of course," replied the woman. "Please forgive my asking. Is that all you'll be needing?"

Quickly realizing that if Tolman were to suddenly appear, and ask about a single man named Tanner, no one would think twice about a man with a wife. "Well, my … my missus could use a hot bath, ma'am."

Turning the registration book around so she could read his name, the woman handed Jake a key with a small metal tag attached and said, "Your room is the first one on the left at the top of the stairs, Mr. Hawkins. The wash room for ladies is just across the hall and I'll have a hot bath ready for her within the hour."

"Thank you, ma'am," said Jake as he turned around, took Emily by the hand, and together walked toward the stairs.

Once settled in their room, Jake insisted that Emily rest while he took care of the horses. Minutes later, when she was fast asleep on the bed, he left the room and locked the door from the outside. He was about to turn and go down the stairs when he heard the muffled voices of men arguing, followed by a shrill scream. The scream was quickly silenced by the sound of a slap on bare skin and a body hitting the floor. Reacting to the sounds, Jake took several hurried steps down the hall before realizing he was outnumbered four to one, assuming the scream came from the kidnapped young woman. As silence continued to fill the hallway, Jake swallowed hard at his hesitation to interfere and turned toward the stairs.

At the bottom of the stairs, Jake turned and saw the petite woman still standing behind the registration counter. "Beggin' your pardon, ma'am," he said in a quiet voice. "Mr. Mayfield at the blacksmith shop says some outlaws kidnapped a young woman and they're holdin' her here in the hotel. Are they the ones down at the far end of the upstairs hallway?"

"Why ... yes ... yes, I'm afraid so," replied the woman sadly. "They also killed our poor sheriff."

"Yeah, I heard about that too. Have they hurt you any, ma'am?"

"No, but I've been careful not to give them any cause."

"What about the girl?"

"Well, so far they don't seem to have hurt her none too bad, but I'm afraid that with all their drinking, that could change. The young ones have been eyeing her and pleading with the one named Skaggs to let them take advantage of her. I don't think there's much anybody can do if they get their way."

"You're probably right, ma'am. Guess the best we can do is hope it don't come to that."

CHAPTER 5

IT WAS LATE AFTERNOON WHEN Jake and Emily left their room and descended the thread-bare carpeted stairs to the hotel's main floor. Looking through an open archway into the dining room, Jake saw the woman who had greeted them earlier in the day. Her back was toward him as she cleared a table of dirty dishes. "Evenin', ma'am," he said pleasantly. "We'd appreciate gettin' …"

At the first sound of Jake's voice, the dishes in the women's hands crashed to the floor as she cowered and raised both arms in a protective manner over her head.

"Beggin' your pardon, ma'am," said Jake as he took a hesitant step forward. "I didn't mean to scare you."

"Oh … oh my goodness," said the woman as she peeked at Jake between her crossed arms while still cowering. "I … I thought you were one of them."

"One of them?" repeated Jake.

"Yes … well … please, never you mind," stammered the woman while lowering her arms and regaining her composure. "Ah … well now, what was it you were asking, Mr. Hawkins?"

"I was 'bout to ask if we could sit for a meal," replied Jake. "But maybe this ain't a good time."

"Oh no ... I mean yes, please come in and ... and sit down over there," said the woman while pointing a shaky finger toward a round table with two spindly chairs.

"Thank you, ma'am," said Jake, as he and Emily walked to the table indicated by the woman. "Ma'am, are you sure you're all right?"

"My name is Martha, Mr. Hawkins, and yes, I'm fine now. It was them outlaws who scared me out of my wits. I fixed them a meal like they wanted, but after eating they just got up and started walking out. That's when I made the mistake of asking them for payment, and the one called Logan grabbed me by the back of my hair, put a knife to my throat, and said if I didn't do as he said, he'd cut my throat and burn down my hotel. And I believe he would, too."

"What about the girl? Was she with 'em?"

"Yes, but they wouldn't give her anything to eat. They just took pleasure teasing her by dangling food scraps in front of her face and then pulling them away when she went to reach for them. Her eyes are all red, from crying no doubt, and she's got an ugly bruise on the side of her face. They got a rope tied around her neck and one of them always has hold of the end. They jerk her around with the rope if she don't move fast enough."

"Where are they now?" Jake asked in a hard, even voice.

"Gone ... over to the saloon I guess," Martha replied. "At least that's where they were talking about going".

With a face full of anger, Jake suddenly turned around and started to leave the room.

"You're ... you're not going over there are you?" said Martha with alarm as she reached out and grasped his arm.

"Yes, ma'am, seems like I've got a sudden thirst for whiskey." Without another word he shook Martha's hand off his arm and continued walking out of the room, leaving Emily staring after him in dismay.

It was with clenched fists and eyes blazing that Jake left the hotel and walked briskly across the road toward the saloon, but as he stepped up on the saloon's wooden walkway, he paused, suddenly remembering Billy's warning about never getting in a fight when angry. After taking several deep breaths to calm himself, he pushed his way softly through the saloon's chest-high swinging doors and strolled over to a battered bar with a brass handrail. Willard, the black-smith, was standing behind the bar polishing a chipped glass with a dingy rag.

"What can I get you, Mr. Hawkins?" Willard asked in a hushed voice.

Jake could see Willard's eyes looking past him to the back of the room where several men were arguing heatedly. Apparently his entry into the saloon had been unobserved.

"Whiskey," Jake replied in an equally quiet voice.

Looking into the large, image-distorting mirror on the wall behind the bar, Jake could see four men sitting around a table. The girl, sitting crumpled and dejected on the grimy floor next to the table, looked exhausted and disheveled in a soiled, dark-green dress with a small bustle. A coarse rope was looped tightly around her neck. Sitting next to her in a chair, holding the end of the rope in his hand, was the boy Jake had seen earlier on the windmill tower.

Willard set the glass he had been polishing on the bar in front of Jake and poured a small splash of whiskey into it as he continued to whisper, "That's Skaggs sittin' with his back to you. Logan's the mean-lookin' one on Skaggs' left. The older boy is Carl and the younger one is his brother Bob."

"That's 'bout what I figured," Jake replied.

"You don't look like a drinkin' man to me, Mr. Hawkins. You thinkin' 'bout tryin' somethin'?"

"Can't say, but I had to see it for myself."

"Looks bad and could get worse if they keep drinkin' the way they is," said Willard. "Makes a man sick to think he can't do nothin', least not with the odds against him. I'm here only 'cause my bartender got scared and quit. I was gonna close up so they couldn't keep drinkin', but Logan said if I did it'd be the last thing I'd ever did."

Jake said nothing in return as he raised the glass to his mouth but only wet his lips. *Willard's right*, he thought, *four against one ain't a fight anybody can expect to win.*

"You willin' to back me up if it comes to that, Mr. Mayfield?" Jake asked.

"Call me Willard, and what've you got in mind?"

"Ain't sure. Guess I'll figure it out if and when it comes to that."

"Well, I ain't got no family to speak of," said Willard. "And I'd have a hard time livin' with myself if I said no, so count me in."

As Jake watched in the mirror, the conversation around the table in the back of the room became even louder. Suddenly, Skaggs slopped the last bit of whiskey from a bottle into his glass and then threw the empty bottle against the wall, showering the floor with shards of broken glass. "All right, you horny bastards!" he exploded in anger. "Go ahead and take your pokes. But I'm warnin' you, I don't want her pa seein' her all busted up 'fore we get his money."

Hearing this, the young woman screamed in terror and scampered on her hands and knees away from the table.

Laughing at her antics, Logan stood up and said, "Well, boys, reckon I'll take my turn with her 'fore you whore-beaters spoil her so bad she won't be worth havin'. Come on, little girl, let's go have some fun."

But before Logan could take the rope from Carl, the girl jumped up and started to run screaming toward the saloon doors. It was only at the last second that Carl was able to hold on to the rope and give it a jerk, causing the girl's feet to come out from under her as she crashed to the floor on her back. Gasping for air as the noose around her throat tightened, she instinctively rolled over and rose to her knees, her fingers clawing at her throat to loosen the noose as the four men laughed.

"Looks like we got us fighter boys, just the way I like 'em," said Logan.

"Now hold on," said Carl as he looked across the table at Skaggs. "Me and Bob been the ones askin' for her, Mr. Skaggs. Seems like we should get her first."

"Tell you what, Carl," said Logan with a menacing smile, "Let's fast-draw and whoever wins gets her first. Course the loser is gonna be dead so it won't matter much to him. How 'bout it, Carl?"

"Ah, come on, Logan. Ain't no way that would be a fair fight. You told us you already killed more'n a dozen men. Let's cut cards for her, high card wins."

As his right hand reached for the butt of his gun, Logan looked fiercely at Carl and said, "I ain't cuttin' no damn cards with you sorry turds. So either get off your butts and draw your shooters or shut the hell up."

"Enough!" yelled Skaggs as he slammed the palm of his hand on the table. "Just get the hell on with it, Logan. These no-account, snot-nose boys can wait their turn."

"Ah, Mr. Skaggs, that ain't fair," whined Carl. "Bob and me …."

Flashing out like a snake striking its quarry, Skagg's fist hit Carl's nose with enough force to cause him and his chair to fall over backwards. "If you don't shut up I'm gonna kill you myself!" raged Skaggs.

Howling in pain as tears streamed down his face, Carl rolled around on the floor clutching his nose. Blood covered his hands and spilled down the front of his shirt. The shattered glass on the floor from the broken whiskey bottle increased his pain as it sliced gashes in his back.

"How 'bout you, Bob?" Logan teased. "You want to draw against me."

"Ah, no … no sir, Mr. Logan," Bob replied submissively. "I'll take my turn after you and Carl. I been gettin' last pickings all my life. Won't hurt me none to wait."

"Now that's 'bout the smartest thing I've ever heard you say, Bob," said Logan with a small smile. "Maybe you ain't so dumb after all."

"I ain't dumb," mumbled Bob as he leaned over and turned Carl's chair upright. "I just think slow. Ain't that right, Carl?"

"No, that ain't right," said Carl as he sat down at the table and used his shirttail to stop the flow of blood from his nose. "Like it or not, Bob, you're 'bout as dumb as the dumbest jackass I ever seen."

"Well," replied Bob with a smirk on his face, "at least I ain't dumb enough to get my nose busted."

Ignoring Carl and the rope he was holding, Logan grabbed the cringing girl by the hair and said, "You can sit here and listen to these boys bawl all night if you want, Skaggs, but I'm takin' my turn with the girl and …."

"The hell you are!" roared Jake with disgust as he turned around and faced Logan.

"What?" snarled Logan with surprise as his head snapped around to look at Jake. "And who the hell are you?"

"Name's Hawkins," Jake replied evenly. "Best you take your hands off the girl and let her be."

"Well, well, look here boys, seems like we got ourselves a real live hero," said Logan as he turned with a smile to his companions. "Let her be," he mimicked in a high, whiney voice as he turned with a scowl to face Jake. "Well now, *cowboy*, suppose I don't want to let her be. What are you gonna do, call your momma?"

"Guess you'll just have to find out," said Jake.

Skaggs and the two boys jumped up from the table, spilling their chairs backward across the floor in their haste, and moved away from Logan. Out of the corner of his eye, Jake saw Willard move away from where he was previously standing behind the bar.

The room was deathly quiet as each man stared unblinking at the other.

"Draw your shooter, cowboy, or I'll kill you where you stand!" roared Logan.

"Ain't no need for gun play," replied Jake calmly as his stomach tightened into a knot. "All you and your trashy friends got to do is release the girl and go about your business."

"You hear that, boys?" said Logan, laughing as he turned to look at Skaggs and the others. "He called you boys trashy."

"Kill him!" yelled Skaggs with clenched fists.

"Oh, I'll kill him soon enough," said Logan with a grin. "I'm just testin' his nerve. You ready to die, cowboy?"

Jake stared, unflinching, into Logan's eyes. "Don't reckon I am. And don't reckon you are neither. So maybe you boys should ride on out."

"You cocky bastard! You're the one who's gonna be ridin' out," seethed Logan as the fingers on his right hand fluttered near the butt of his gun, "Folded over your saddle face down. Now draw, damn it!"

Jake did not move. He had purposely baited Logan into being angry in the hope that Billy was right when he said that in a gunfight an angry man was prone to miss. To add one more insult to further inflame Logan's anger, he said, "I feel sorry for you, Logan, you're nothing but a yellow-bellied coward who preys on the weak and helpless. You ain't good enough to face a real gunfighter."

"You don't say," said Logan with a snarling smile on his lips as his hand flashed toward his pistol.

But Jake's hand moved faster as he drew his pistol and fired from the hip. The deafening explosion from both guns rang out almost as one. Jake's bullet hit Logan square in the chest, lifting him off his feet and backward until he lay flat on the floor. A sputtered cough spilled blood from his mouth while his spurs gouged the floor with his jerky leg twitches. Just as quickly, from somewhere close behind, Jake heard and felt the blast of another pistol. Swinging around defensively, he saw Willard standing behind the bar holding a smoking pistol aimed at the back of the room. At the same time he heard a groan and a chair breaking, followed by the thud of another body hitting the floor.

A shrill scream erupted from the girl as she scurried under a table and covered her ears with her hands. Jake glanced at her and then shifted his eyes to Skaggs, who was now rolling around on the floor with both hands pressed against his stomach, his pistol and the shattered chair against which he had fallen lay nearby on the floor. Carl and Bob stood in wide-eyed disbelief in the back of the room. Hesitantly, they raised their hands over their heads.

"Drop them gun belts 'less you want to die!" shouted Willard, and with trembling hands Carl and Bob unfastened their gun belts, letting them drop to the floor.

Jake, with a strange weakness in his knees, stumbled to where Logan lay on the floor and kicked away the man's pistol. Kneeling down along the side of the man he had just killed, he was awestruck that, even in death, Logan's eyes showed surprise that he was not as fast on the draw as he believed. Slowly shaking his head at the sorrowful waste of a life, Jake stood up and absent mindedly used his left hand to touch a burning place on the side of his neck. It was only when he removed his hand, and saw it covered with blood, that he realized Logan's bullet had come within an inch of ending his life. Feeling faint from his near-death experience, he grasped the arm of a nearby chair and sat down heavily while using the neckerchief around his throat to stem the flow of blood.

Skaggs was cussing and yelling in pain as he rolled around on the floor, leaving smeared blood stains on the bare wooden planks.

Watching Skaggs struggling in obvious pain, Willard said with a chuckle, "Guess the law won't be hangin' you after all, Skaggs. But then again, hangin' would be a blessin' compared to dyin' like you're doin'."

Hearing the gun shots and screams from where she was standing in front of the hotel, Martha raced across the road and burst into the saloon. Glancing quickly around the room, she saw the two outlaws on the floor, Willard pointing a pistol at the two boys cowering in the back of the room, and the girl crouched and sobbing under a table. With calm assurance, she went to the girl, coaxed her out from under the table, and gently removed the rope from around her neck. Sitting her in a chair, she looked at Willard and opened her mouth as if to ask for an explanation, but before she could utter a word, she followed Willard's gaze to Jake. Seeing the bloody neckerchief Jake was holding against his neck, she dropped to her knees, pulled up the girl's dress, and ripped off the bottom ruffle from her petticoat. With surprising agility she raced to Jake's side, removed the now blood-soaked neckerchief from his hand, and pressed the folded ruffle firmly against the wound. "Quick," she shouted to the girl, "tear off another one and bring it to me!"

Still shaking, but no longer crying, the girl did as she was told and hurried to where Martha was standing next to Jake. Holding the first ruffle in place over the wound, Martha wrapped the second ruffle around Jake's neck several times and tucked the end under the folds. The flow of blood was already beginning to slow.

Jake, about to thank Martha, was surprised when the girl suddenly dropped to her knees in front of him, ripped off another ruffle, and began to wipe blood from his left hand. Slowly, she raised her eyes and looked at Jake with profound gratitude. Although bruised with tear stained cheeks, she was the most beautiful woman he had ever seen.

"Mr. Hawkins," called Willard from across the room. "You hurt bad?"

Hearing no response, but seeing Jake sitting calmly, Willard shouted at Carl and Bob "Get down on your knees." Visibly shaken, the two boys scrambled to do as they were told. One by one Willard bound their hands behind their backs and sat them on the floor with their backs to the wall.

Skaggs, his clothes now covered with blood, continued to roll around on the floor grasping his stomach and crying out in anguish, "Somebody get a doctor."

"Ain't no doctor," said Willard. "And even if there were, I wouldn't want him wastin' his time with you. You and Logan got the bullets you was savin' for this poor girl and her father. And now you can both go to hell."

"Mr. Hawkins," said Martha as she leaned close to Jake and looked into his face, "are you all right?"

Reluctantly, Jake tore his eyes from the girl and stammered, "Oh … yeah … guess so."

"If I live to be a hundred, I don't think I'll ever see anything like this again," said Willard as he walked to where Jake was sitting. "Can't be no doubt you saved this girl and her father from them killers, Mr. Hawkins."

Returning his gaze to the girl's captivating face, Jake said softly, "Didn't plan on killin' anybody."

"Maybe you didn't plan on it, Mr. Hawkins," said Martha, "but I saw the look on your face when you left the hotel, and I knew you weren't the kind of man who could ignore a young girl being mistreated."

Turning to Martha and Willard, Jake said, "I'd appreciate you folks callin' me Ja ... Jacob. And you all should be praisin' Mr. Mayfield, 'cause he's the one that kept Skaggs and the others from doin' me in."

Apparently exasperated by all the talk, Martha said, "I need to get this man over to the hotel so I can clean his wound. Can you walk, Jacob?"

Rising unsteadily from the chair, Jake replied, "Yeah, sure," and walked out of the saloon with Martha by his side. The girl followed demurely behind.

In the hotel kitchen Martha sat Jake in a chair and cleaned his wound with a soft cloth moistened with hot water from a kettle on the stove. "I'm sorry, Jacob, but the only thing I got to put on this wound is a cure-all, snake-oil I bought from a peddler passing through."

Jake wanted to flinch with pain each time Martha used her fingers to spread the ointment on the wound, but he willed himself to remain still and poker-faced. Only a slight twitch at the corner of his mouth betrayed his discomfort.

The girl stood in the doorway to the kitchen watching as Martha ripped an old flour sack into long strips and applied them as a new bandage. Jake tried to ignore the girl's stare, but his eyes continued to seek her out. Her soiled and bedraggled dress revealed a trim figure, and the delicate skin on her hands and face gave evidence of a refined life style. Long, wavy, blond hair framed her face and added to the beauty of her deep-blue eyes. Her calm demeanor convinced Jake that she possessed a subdued quality of self assurance and boldness.

Overcoming his shyness, he looked directly at the girl and said, "My name's Jacob."

"Yes, I know," she replied. "My name is Elizabeth, but everybody calls me Beth. I ... I don't know how to thank you for saving me from those horrible men, but I know my father will be very grateful and pay you well."

"No thanks needed," Jake replied with a sober expression. "And I ain't takin' money from your father neither. I guess ---." Suddenly, Jake remembered that he had left Emily standing in the hotel's dining room when he rushed out. "Where's Emily?" he shouted excitedly as he jumped to his feet.

"Oh my," said Marth, concerned. "The last time I saw her she was still standing where you left her. I forgot all about her when I heard the shooting."

"I've got to find her," Jake said as he rushed from the room, almost knocking Beth down as he bolted through the door way.

"Who's Emily?" asked Beth as she regained her balance.

"His wife," replied Martha. "She's a quiet, frail little thing that needs looking after."

"Oh," said Beth in a voice that seemed to be tinged with disappointment.

"Emily, Emily, where are you?" Jake shouted as he rushed into the dining room. Not seeing her, he turned and ran up the stairs to their room, where he found her cringing and sobbing under the bed.

"I'm so sorry, Emily." Jake pleaded, taking her hand and helping her out from under the bed, "but I just couldn't bear hearin' 'bout how they was treatin' that poor girl. It was like she was you, and I ain't never goin' to let nobody hurt you."

Emily, drying her eyes as she sat on the bed, whimpered softly but said nothing.

"But the problem now," Jake continued with a sigh as he sat down beside her, "is that I had to kill a man to save the girl from terrible harm. And now there's goin' to be talk, talk that could give Tolman a trail to follow. So somehow, between now and tomorrow morning, I've got to make sure that don't happen."

CHAPTER 6

ASSURING EMILY THAT SHE WAS safe, Jake left her in the
room and returned to the saloon, where he saw Willard struggling
to drag Logan's body out the back door. A quick glance at Skaggs,
unmoving on the floor, told him that he was also dead. Stifling his
discomfort at seeing the man he had recently killed, Jake hurried over
to Willard and started lifting Logan up by his legs as he said, "Might
be easier if we worked together."

"Yeah, thanks," Willard replied as he grasped Logan under the
arms and together they carried the body through the door way. "Got
them two boys locked up in that old shed over there," he continued
with a nod of his head. "Figure the judge in Dodge City will hang
'em soon enough."

"Yeah, more'n likely," Jake replied with a sigh. "Sure is a shame
when youngsters get mixed up with killers like Logan and Skaggs.
Ain't much to look forward to except bein' killed or spendin' the rest
of your life in some filthy prison."

"Now don't you go feelin' sorry for 'em, Jacob. They could've left
any time they had a mind to. Nobody was forcin' 'em to stay with
them varmints."

"True," replied Jake, as he and Willard struggled up a slight
incline toward some grave markers at the top of a nearby rise. "But

maybe they didn't have no place else to go. Maybe Skaggs and Logan were the only ones who'd take 'em in."

"There's lots of maybes in this world, Jacob. But nothin' can excuse these boys from fallin' in with bandits and killers and not havin' the sense to see it. No sir, I think these boys saw a way to get rich without much effort and take terrible advantage of a young, innocent girl."

"Reckon you're right," grunted Jake, trying to get a better hold under Logan's knees. "You plannin' on puttin' up markers after we put Logan and Skaggs under?"

"Probably should, but I ain't," replied Willard. "We got a nice, peaceful place here, and I ain't anxious to have gawkers and newspaper folks nosin' around makin' up stories."

"Yeah, they do tend to exaggerate some," said Jake, "but word of a train robbery, a kidnappin', and a killin' is sure to get somebody's attention. Then they'll be spillin' in here like rain off a tin roof."

"Damn, you're right, Jacob, and there ain't nothin' we can do to stop it."

After a moment of silence, as the men continued stumbling their way up the inclined pathway with Logan's dead weight between them, Jake said, "Do you remember my askin' you to say you'd never heard of me?"

"I remember, and I figured your name weren't Hawkins neither. You got some special reason for all this secrecy?"

"Yeah, but now ain't the best time for bein' truthful."

"There's always time for tellin' the truth, Jacob. Maybe I can help."

"You can help by just sayin' you never heard of me."

"Yeah, I could do that. But, seein' as how I saved your life, maybe I've earned the right to know why you just happen to be hidin' out in my town and ending up savin' it from the killin' of innocent folks."

Jake did not respond as he and Willard entered the graveyard and stretched Logan's body out on a bare patch of ground. "Well, you gonna tell me?" asked Willard as he stood upright and stretched his back.

Hesitant, but knowing he owed Willard an explanation of some kind, Jake said, "Well, 'bout the best I can say is that there's a man lookin' to kill me."

"Damn, Jacob!" Willard said with surprise, "What did you do, kill one of his kin folk or somethin'?"

"No, I've never killed anybody. Oh, yeah … well, at least not 'til today."

"Then why does he want to kill you?"

"Because I saw him and four others kill my ma and pa."

"What the hell!" said Willard as he looked aghast at Jake.

"I told you I think it's best if that's all you know."

"Yeah … yeah … I see what you mean. I can't be tempted to say something if I don't know nothin'. But how am I goin' to explain a dead gunfighter and Skaggs? And what am I goin' to do about them two boys?"

"I've thought some 'bout that," said Jake with a sly look on his face. "Suppose you were to say that a stranger came to town, stopped at the saloon for a drink, got to arguing with Skaggs and Logan about takin' his pleasure with the girl, and then killed 'em both. After that, he lost his taste for the girl and rode off without you even knowin' his name."

"But them boys seen it, and Martha and the girl, too."

"Yeah, and tonight might be a good time to let them boys think they escaped a hangin'. After all, we don't know if they ever killed anybody, and maybe this'll teach 'em a lesson. I'd venture to say there ain't nothin' like almost gettin' hanged to make a boy think 'bout changin' his ways."

"Jacob," said Willard with admiration, "you're 'bout the most crafty feller for fixin' problems that I've ever come across, and this might be what them boys need to set 'em straight. Yes sir, it just might work, and I know Martha and the girl won't be a problem once they know everything."

"I agree," said Jake, "with these fellers buried I don't think anybody will be anxious to dig 'em up just to take their pictures, and with no bodies, no pictures, no young boys, and the girl bein' alive, there just ain't a whole lot to this story."

"Sounds like a really good plan, Jacob. Okay, let's go get Skaggs up here and then start digging. After it gets dark, I'll take them boys some supper and let 'em think they've escaped, along with their broken down horses. I can already see 'em high-tailing out of Kansas like the devil was after 'em."

The following morning Beth was serving breakfast to Willard when Jake entered the hotel's dinning room. She was wearing a simple, form-fitting, white cotton dress with a pattern of small yellow and orange flowers. Gone were the petticoats, the tear stained cheeks, and red rimmed eyes. Her once matted and disheveled hair was now woven into a glimmering, loosely-tied braid that extended down her back. She smiled shyly at Jake and then turned back toward the kitchen. The bruise on her cheek was the only reminder of what she had been through during the past few days.

"Mornin' Willard," said Jake as he walked to where Willard was sitting at a table chewing on a piece of beefsteak.

"Mornin', Jacob. Martha tells me your missus ain't feelin' well."

"Yeah, we been on the trail for a while and she needed to get some rest. I think we'll be ready to move on tomorrow. You want some company for breakfast?"

"Sure, take a seat," Willard replied spearing another bite sized piece of steak with his fork. "It'll be nice having company at breakfast for a change." Both men were silent as Willard smothered a large biscuit with butter and took a bite. Jake was about to say something when Willard said, "So how long you goin' to keep this up?"

"Keep what up?"

"Your lettin' this killer chase you around the country and wearin' out your missus. Seems like you got to take a stand sometime, and from what I saw yesterday, I'd say you're more'n up to the job."

"And what job would that be, Mr. Mayfield?" asked Beth with a smile as she refilled his empty coffee cup.

"Oh, why … why … no job at all, really," said Willard, momentarily flustered. "I … I was offerin' Jacob a position runnin' my … saloon. But he turned me down sayin' he and his missus are movin' on tomorrow."

"What! Oh no … no, you can't" said Beth as she turned to face Jake. "I mean … please … my father will be here soon and I want him to meet you. You saved my life, Mr. Hawkins, and my father's life as well. And I know he will want to at least thank you."

"No thanks are necessary, Miss Elizabeth, and please call me Jacob."

"I will if you stop calling me *Miss Elizabeth*," Beth replied with a radiant smile.

"It's a deal," said Jake, returning her smile with one of his own. "You look like you're feeling much better today, Beth."

"It's truly wonderful what a bath and clean clothes can do for a girl," said Beth as she twirled around once. "Martha brushed my hair and gave me this dress to wear."

"All right, you two," said Willard with a smug grin of his own. "If you can stop flirting with each other for awhile, I'm sure *Mr. Hawkins* could use some breakfast before he wastes away before our very eyes."

"It will be my pleasure, *Mr. Mayfield*," giggled Beth as she curtseyed and then rushed to the kitchen.

Willard smiled knowingly at Jake and said, "You better mind your manners, Jacob. I think that young lady has eyes for you, wife or no wife."

"Naw, she's just grateful for bein' free from her tormentors," said Jake.

"Maybe. But you still haven't answered my question."

"What question?"

"About takin' a stand."

"You're a nosey old goat, aren't you?" said Jake with a chuckle.

"I figure my savin' your butt gives me the right, don't you think?" Willard replied.

"Yeah, guess it does. So, to answer your question, I'll make my stand when I find a safe place to leave my missus."

"And then what?"

"What do you mean, 'and then what'?"

"I mean, what are you going to do when you find these men?"

"Why, I'm goin' to kill 'em," replied Jake, as though any other answer would be unthinkable.

Willard stopped eating and looked hard at Jake for a moment, then continued eating silently.

"What?" said Jake with a hint of anger. "Are you sayin' I don't have the right? Those *bastards* killed my folks and I don't even know why, or if there is a why."

"No, I ain't sayin' you don't have a righteous cause against them killers. But to my way of thinkin', that'll make you a killer just like them, and probably get you hanged for takin' the law into your own hands. Think about it, Jacob, there's got to be a better way."

Lowering his eyes to the table, Jake's anger softened. "Maybe you're right, Willard, but I don't know any other way. It happened a long time ago and … well … I was the only witness. Even now, if I went to the law, it would just be my word against theirs. And I can't let 'em get away with it, Willard, I just can't."

"No, reckon you can't. But there's got to be another way, and it's up to you to find it 'fore you become a wanted killer yourself. Would your ma and pa want that?"

After finishing his breakfast, Jake took a breakfast tray for Emily up the hotel stairs and knocked softly on her door. Emily slowly opened the door only wide enough to peer out with one eye. Seeing Jake, she opened the door and let him in, but did not speak. She was fully dressed and had taken the time to make the bed. The bed roll he had left on the floor where he slept was rolled up and placed on the end of the bed.

"You're looking much better, Emily," he said, placing the tray on a table near the bed. "Look, I've brought you some breakfast. And maybe, after you've eaten, we can take a walk. Would you like that?"

Emily, standing rigid in the middle of the room, shook her head from side to side as a dark forbiddance filled her face.

"Okay, it's all right," said Jake. "We don't have to go out if you don't want to. Come, sit down, and have something to eat. If we're going to leave tomorrow, you have to get your strength back, and to do that you have to eat."

Suddenly, Emily's hands became fists and she began to beat them against the sides of her head while moaning and rocking from side to side. Rushing to her, Jake pulled her arms down to her sides and crushed her with a firm bear hug. Whispering in her ear he said, "It's all right, Emily, really it is. If you don't want to leave tomorrow, we won't. I promise."

Slowly, Emily's struggling against his hug stopped and she became calm again. "But we do have to leave sometime," he said softly, leaning back and looking into her eyes. Then, releasing her, he gently placed the palms of his hands on her cheeks and said, "You know we can't stay here very long. You know that, don't you?"

Emily nodded her head slowly up and down as a tear from each eye trickled down her cheeks and wet his hands.

Jake, still holding her face in his hands, kissed her gently on the forehead and then on the tip of her nose. "That's my girl," he said with a smile. "Now, come and have some breakfast and we'll talk about better times." Jake knew, though, that he would be the only one talking, because Emily had not spoken since the day their parents were murdered.

It was early afternoon when Jake left Emily sleeping and descended the hotel stairs. The weariness that always came after caring for Emily, and his fitful sleep last night, weighed heavily on his shoulders. Seeing two comfortable-looking, high-backed chairs sitting empty on the hotel porch, he sat down in the one nearest the hotel's open doorway. Within minutes he was almost asleep, when he heard a footstep nearby and jumped up, reaching for his gun.

"Oh my goodness," said Beth when she saw the startled look in Jake's eyes. "I didn't know you were asleep."

"What! ... Oh, no," said Jake, struggling to take off his hat. "I was ... a... just restin' a bit, that's all."

"Well, if you're sure I won't be a bother, may I sit down?"

"Why ... yes, yes of course."

After sittin down, and squirmed a bit to get comfortable, Beth turned to Jake and said, "All last night, and again this morning, I've tried to find the right words to thank you for risking your life to save mine. I'm at a loss, because words just don't seem to be nearly enough. All I can say is that I'll be forever in your debt, and I hope that someday I'll be able to do something for you that will truly show my gratitude."

Facing away from Beth to hide the growing warmth on his cheeks, Jake could only mumble, "It weren't nothing, really."

"Why, Jacob, I do believe you're blushing."

"I ain't neither. Just got somethin' in my eye."

"Well, I think it's cute," said Beth smiling.

With his face still turned away, Jake replied more strongly than he intended, "It ain't cute. It's a damn nuisance that comes and goes with a mind of its own."

"Oh, I'm sorry," said Beth in a contrite voice as she reached out and touched his arm. "I didn't mean to make you upset. Please forgive me."

Turning back to face Beth, Jake said, "I'm sorry too. It's just that I get ... well, embarrassed when ... well, you know."

"Yes, I can see that might be a problem for a man. But I kind of like it. It shows your gentle nature."

Several moments passed in silence as Beth tried to think of something to say to change the subject. Hoping she wouldn't offend Jake by asking, she ventured, "I hope your wife is feeling better."

"What? Oh, yeah ... yeah, I think she's feeling much better today."

"I'm glad," said Beth. "Although I have not met her, I'm sure she is a wonderful woman."

"Yes, a wonderful woman," repeated Jake with an obvious lack of enthusiasm.

"You sound sad," said Beth with a look of concern. "I hope I haven't said something wrong again."

"No, not really," Jake replied as he tried to mask his weariness. "It's just been a very ... well ... difficult time."

"Yes, it certainly has. Mr. Mayfield told Martha and me about ... well ... the things you and he talked about yesterday. You know, about a stranger coming to town and killing Logan and Skaggs. He told us why you wanted it that way, and I certainly understand. It must be awful to be running away from someone who wants to harm you, especially having a wife and all."

Jake turned slowly and looked at Beth for a long moment. "Would you like to go for a walk?" he finally asked.

Beth hesitated as she slowly rose to her feet, "Well ... okay ... I guess so."

Hearing Beth's consent, Jake stood, took one step down from the porch to the roadway, and turned to wait for Beth to join him. Beth, though, was still standing on the porch with an uncertain look on her face. Taking one step forward, she leaned down to Jake and whispered, "Are you sure this will be all right with your wife?"

Turning his head from side to side to make sure no one was near, Jake said in an equally hushed voice, "She ain't my *wife*."

"What?" gasped Beth, quickly standing upright. "What are you saying?"

Still talking in a hushed voice, Jake said, "I said she ain't my wife. She's my *sister*."

"But ... why did you tell everyone she was your wife?"

"I didn't. Everybody just figured she was. And I thought it would be better that way."

"Better what way?" asked Beth, as she stepped down from the porch to the roadway and stood looking into Jake's eyes. "I don't understand."

"Do you see those trees out yonder?" asked Jake turning his head and nodding toward to a small grove of cottonwood trees just outside the settlement.

"Yes, of course."

"Well, if you'll walk with me, I'll try to help you understand."

For several seconds Beth stood and looked at Jake, uncertainly. "All right, but you must promise to tell me everything."

The shade of the trees was cool and refreshing, but, as they settled themselves on the soft ground, crushing a patch of prairie grass beneath them, Jake found himself struggling to keep his promise. Talking openly about himself with anyone had always been difficult, and, as the minutes passed in silence, he could see that Beth was also becoming fidgety.

"I'm not sure where to start," he finally said.

"Well, why don't you start by telling me about your sister? Martha told me that she... well ... has been acting strangely."

"I guess that's a good way to put it," Jake replied with a sigh. "Fact is, she ain't quite right in her mind."

"Has she always been that way?"

"No. She was once a smart little girl. Smarter'n me, really."

"So what happened?"

Hanging his head and speaking so softly that Beth could barely hear him, Jake said, "I think she was watchin' when our folks were tortured and murdered. She was only ten at the time, and ever since then she's never talked or been right in the head."

"Oh my Lord," said Beth with astonishment. "But why ... why would anyone do such a horrible thing?"

"I don't know why they done it, and the only reason Emily wasn't killed was because she was hiding in a hillside cave we used to play in."

"Why weren't you killed?"

"Because I was out huntin', and by the time I came back, it were pretty much over."

Jake continued telling Beth about recognizing Tolman, shooting him, and then escaping into the woods. He also told her about

Tolman's threat to kill him and Tolman's visit to the Rolling K ranch just three months ago. "Me and Emily have been on the move ever since, and that's why I asked Willard and Martha to lie about our bein' here."

"And this man is looking for both of you?"

"No, just me. Like I said, he and the others don't know about Emily."

"So what are you going to do?" cried Beth.

"Well, as soon as I can find a safe place to leave Emily, I'm goin' to find these men and kill 'em."

"Oh, Jacob, you don't really mean that."

"Of course I do. Why wouldn't I?"

"Because that would be wrong. That would make you … well … just like them."

"Yeah, I know," Jake replied impatiently, "and don't think I haven't thought 'bout it. But before I buried my pa, I swore that I'd kill every one of 'em, and I mean to do just that."

Beth was quiet for several minutes. Finally, looking deep into his eyes, she said, "May I ask you a personal question?"

"Okay, sure, go ahead."

"How did you feel after you killed Logan?"

"What? What do you mean, how did I *feel*?"

"I mean, how did you *feel*? Did you feel good, did you feel bad, do you regret having to do it, or have you even thought about it? I'm sorry, Jacob, but, as I have been listening to you, I have also been trying to determine for myself what you might or might not be feeling about the man you killed yesterday. So far I haven't a clue. So tell me, did you then, or do you now, have any feelings one way or the other? Or doesn't it bother you at all? Or … oh my gosh."

"What?"

"It just occurred to me that maybe Logan wasn't the first man you've killed. Is that what I'm failing to understand? Is that why you don't appear to be feeling anything?"

"Now wait a minute," said Jake defensively. "What makes you think that because I don't show my feelings I'm some sort of monster?

The fact is that Logan *was* the first man I've killed, and while I don't feel good about it, I keep telling myself that it was either him or you."

"Me?"

"Yes, you. You may not know it, but me and Willard were sure that when your father arrived, you were both goin' to be killed. Not to mention what Logan and them boys had in mind for you. Do I feel bad about havin' to kill him? Yes. Would I do it again? Yes. Do I look forward to killing the men who murdered my folks? Hell yes. And if you're askin' how I *feel* right now, the simple truth is that I'm just plain tired of runnin', and killin' Logan showed me that I'm ready to do what I promised my pa I'd do."

"Oh, Jacob. I had no right to …"

"No, no, it's okay," said Jake, calming himself. "I guess I'm just … well … a might … I don't know …"

"Sensitive."

"Well, that ain't the word I would use," said Jake. "But, yeah, I guess so."

Smiling, Beth said, "That word *is* a bit feminine isn't it?"

"Yeah, but it seems to fit."

Beth was quiet for several minutes, but Jake could see that there was still something on her mind. Taking a deep breath, she said, "Please forgive me for bringing it up, but what exactly did you promise your father?"

"That I'd kill 'em all. That I'd see 'em all dead."

"Are you sure that's exactly what you said?"

"As best as I can remember. Why?"

"Well," said Beth thoughtfully, "that sounds like two *different* promises to me."

"What do you mean, two *different* promises? Dead is dead, no matter how you twist it."

"I'm not trying to twist it, Jacob. It just seems to me that if you find these men, and kill them, then you are no better than the very worst of them. But if you find them, and a judge sentences them to hang, then won't you see them dead like you promised your father?"

"Well, yeah ... I guess so. But how can I do that? Me and Emily were the only ones who saw it, and she can't talk. And even if I did what you're sayin', it would be my word against theirs, and they sure ain't goin' to admit they done it."

"No, I'm sure they won't," said Beth as she lowered her eyes, "and that's the hard part for you, finding a way to bring them to justice instead of killing them. Perhaps not for murdering *your* parents, but for some other equally horrendous crime. I don't know why, Jacob, but I feel certain that these terrible men, having robbed and killed before, will rob and kill again. And if, when they do, you find them and turn them over to a sheriff to stand before a judge, they will be made to pay for their crimes with their lives. And if so, won't you then be able to *see them dead*?"

Jake sat quietly for several minutes thinking about what Beth had said. Her words made sense and sounded strangely similar to what Willard had said just a few hours earlier. Had Beth indeed found a way for him to keep his promise to his father without having to kill the men himself? Maybe, but the unanswered question was, would doing so satisfy his fervent need for vengeance? Yet, as he had just said to Beth, 'dead is dead, and if the capture and subsequent hanging of these murderers came about as a direct result of his efforts, then surely vengeance would be his.

"I suppose I could try it your way," he finally said, "but what if I can't bring 'em in without a fight? Suppose some of 'em resist and I have to kill 'em?"

"I saw what happened yesterday with Logan, Jacob. And I saw how you tried to avoid having to kill him. But when he drew his gun, you had no choice but to protect yourself. I'm sure that anyone else under the same circumstance, if they were able, would have done the same thing. No one can fault you for protecting yourself."

"Then you're sayin' that if I have to kill some of 'em in self-defense, you wouldn't hold it against me?"

"Yes, I believe I am. But why is it important that I wouldn't hold it against you?"

"Because ... I'd like to come callin' sometime. But 'fore I do, I'd like to know if I'd be welcome."

"Why, Jacob," said Beth with a broad smile, "are you saying you want to see me again?"

Blushing, Jake replied with a sheepish grin, "Yeah, guess that's what I'm trying to say. I just ain't any dang good at it."

Beth looked into Jake's eyes and in a soft, warm voice said, "Well, I think you're saying it just fine. And yes, you will always be welcome."

CHAPTER 7

"MORNIN'," WILLARD CALLED OUT AS he saw Jake enter the blacksmith shop.

"Mornin'," Jake replied, walking to where Willard was puffing air into the forge's coals with a large over-head bellow. "Lots of folks are out and about. Are they askin' questions you're havin' trouble answerin'?"

"No, but they seem disappointed that our mysterious stranger ain't around so they can buy him a drink."

"Then they're acceptin' our story?"

"Yeah, *they* are. But I hope this dies out 'fore some nosey newspaper people get wind of it, 'cause then it won't matter what I tell 'em. They'll just sniff around 'til they find somethin' worth exaggeratin'. More'n likely they'll ignore our story 'bout a stranger wantin' the girl for himself, and call him a hero for savin' her from a fate worse than death."

"I actually like that story," said Jake. "I'm sure folks in the east will sleep better knowin' gentlemen like that are roamin' the west lookin' to save maidens in distress."

Willard started laughing and continued until he was weeping and choking. "Damn, you do have a sense of humor, Jacob. Let's hope we're both laughin' when this is over."

"Well, me and Emily, and the girl and her father, should be leavin' in the next day or so, and if everybody keeps to the same story, it should turn out okay."

"Yeah, reckon you're right."

Suddenly a male voice from outside the shop shouted out in alarm, "Rider comin'!"

This announcement was quickly followed by a multitude of equally alarmed voices urging everyone to go inside. Jake and Willard looked at each other with surprise; then both ran toward the front of the shop and into the street. Nearby a man was standing in the roadway, looking and pointing toward a horse and rider approaching the settlement from the north. Even from this distance Jake could see the man was well-dressed and mounted on a beautiful, chestnut-colored horse.

As the horse and rider continued moving slowly forward, Jake and Willard began walking hurriedly along the roadway toward the intruder. Reaching the edge of the settlement, the man reined the horse to a stop and looked back in the direction from which he had come. Sensing the man's uncertainty, Jake and Willard also stopped, looked down the roadway past the man, and saw a large group of riders about a quarter of a mile away. As they watched, the group of riders moved forward at a slow trot until they were only a few yards behind the well-dressed man. They stopped. After a brief pause, a tall, heavyset man, dressed in a black suit and a black, flat-brimmed hat, left the group and rode forward until he stopped alongside the well dressed man. He was clean shaven with curly brown hair peeking down from under his hat and over his ears. His piercing, light brown eyes stared curiously at Jake and the pistol on his hip.

"You the one called Skaggs?" asked the well dressed man in a demanding voice as he looked at Willard.

"No sir," Willard replied. "My name's Mayfield. Who are you, sir?"

"Name's Owens," said the well dressed man. "And the gentleman next to me is United States Federal Marshal, Frank Farnsworth. We've come about …"

At that instant Jake heard a high pitched scream and turned to see Beth running and yelling, "Papa … Papa."

Mr. Owens quickly spurred his horse forward past Jake and Willard and raced toward Beth. Approaching her, he jumped down from the horse before it had even stopped and gripped her in a fierce embrace.

"Oh, Papa, I knew you'd come."

A day late, thought Jake, *but probably just as well.*

Less than an hour later, Beth, Mr. Owens, Jake, Willard, and Marshal Farnsworth were sitting around a table in the hotel dining room. As Martha served coffee, Beth told her father about her abduction from the train and her treatment by Skaggs and the others. When she finished, she turned and looked at Jake and said, "Mr. Hawkins saved my life, Papa, and maybe yours, too. If it weren't for him …."

"That right, Mr. Hawkins?" interrupted Marshal Farnsworth with a skeptical scowl on his face. "You killed all four of these outlaws yourself?"

"No sir, only the one called Logan. Mr. Mayfield killed Skaggs and …."

"Maybe it'd be best if I told you, Marshal." Willard interrupted. "I think Mr. Hawkins is a might too modest to tell it straight out."

Over Jake's objection, Willard spared no detail in telling the marshal all that transpired from the time Jake arrived in the settlement until they buried Skaggs and Logan. He also told him the story he and Jake had fabricated about the shooting and why it was important that Jake's name never be mentioned. Jake sat in silence, his cheeks burning with embarrassment, while Willard told of his heroics.

Looking from Willard to Beth as if seeking corroboration, the marshal said, "Is that what you recall, Miss Owens?"

"Yes, exactly," Beth replied, smiling at Jake.

"So, Mr. Hawkins," said the marshal, "you say you're a man on the run, but not from the law. That being the case, I guess I won't find a wanted poster for Jacob Hawkins when I get back to my office, now will I?"

Jake hesitated a moment while he considered his response. He wasn't worried about the marshal finding a wanted poster for Jacob Hawkins, although that could turn out to be an untimely coincidence. His real concern was, could he trust all these people with the truth? "My name ain't Jacob Hawkins, Marshal," he blurted out. "It's Jake Tanner."

"What!" cried Beth as she and Martha shared a look of surprise. Willard sat quietly, a small smile playing about the corners of his mouth.

"I'm sorry, Beth," said Jake with concern as he leaned toward her. "I didn't want to deceive you. Fact is, I weren't plannin' on tellin' any of you my real name 'cause I didn't want any of you gettin' hurt ... or maybe even killed."

"What's the name of the man tryin' to kill you, Mr. Tanner?" demanded the marshal. "And what's this all about?"

Once again Jake sat quietly before answering, taking time to ask himself how much, if anything, he should reveal. Reluctant as he was about letting others know his business, he had a gut feeling the marshal was someone he could trust. "His name is Burt Tolman, and he's been tryin' to find me while posing as a preacher named Walter Lewis."

"Well now, that sounds mighty interestin'," said the marshal. "But the question that comes to my mind is, what did you do to this man to make him want to kill you?"

"He didn't do anything!" cried Beth angrily as she stood up, taking offense with the marshal's accusation. "When Jake was a young boy, he saw Tolman and four other men murder his mother and father. Jake shot him and then ran off and hid before Tolman and the others could kill him. Ever since then, Tolman has been trying to kill Jake so he can't identify him and the other men."

"What?" exclaimed Beth's father as he looked at his daughter. "How in the world could you possibly know all this?"

Beth stood still for a moment, looking first at her father and then the marshal, before saying, "Because Jacob ... I mean, Jake, told me and I believe him."

The room was silent while everyone, except Jake and Willard, looked from face to face in amazement.

Even the marshal seemed surprised and said, "Is what she sayin' right?"

"Yes sir," Jake replied, uncomfortable with Beth's coming to his defense. "At least that's the sum of it."

"Well, the sum of it ain't quite good enough, Mr. Tanner. Me and you got a lot more to talk about."

Several hours later, after Jake told the marshal in detail how his parents were tortured and killed, and about Tolman's efforts to find and kill him in the seven years since, the marshal said, "You got anything to prove what you're saying?"

"Only this," replied Jake, reaching into a vest pocket and handing the marshal Mr. Kentworth's note about Tolman's visit to the Rolling K Ranch. The marshal read the note carefully and then handed it back to Jake with an approving nod of his head. "That's about as much proof as a man can ask for, Mr. Tanner, but it has me wondering about the other men who murdered you folks. Do you know any of their names?"

"Only one. I heard Tolman call one of 'em, Flack."

"Well now, how about that?" said the marshal, smiling as he leaned back in his chair. "His first name wouldn't be Roy would it?"

"Can't say, I only heard him called, Flack."

"Well, well, well, Roy Flack and his gang of murdering cowards. Hell, me and every lawman west of the Mississippi have been tryin' to hang him and his gang. I first came across him a few years after the war when he was leadin' a gang of confederate misfits, outlaws like Jack Morgan, Gil Tucker, Dan Upland and, worst of all, the O'Leary brothers. I heard tell Flack and the others weren't happy with the way the war ended and decided to make a war of their own by robbing and killing innocent folks. Now you're saying you saw Flack, this man Tolman, and three others kill your folks about seven years ago?"

"Yes sir, 'bout then."

"Yeah, that sounds about right. You got any idea why they done it?"

"No sir. I've never been able to figure that out. The only thing I do know is they were lookin' for somethin' that only Flack and Tolman seemed to know about, and that whatever it was they never found it."

"Did your folks have any gold or silver or anything of value or importance that these killers might've been after?"

"Not that I know of. My pa was a farmer, Marshal, and worked hard just tryin' to keep food on the table for his family."

"Your pa ever serve in the Confederacy?"

"He never said so. Do you think that might have somethin' to do with them killin' my folks, them bein' Confederate outlaws and all?"

"Hard to say, son. And they never found anything?"

"No sir, not that I could see."

"Okay, what do you know about this man, Tolman?"

"Not much. The only time I'd seen him, other'n when I shot him, was when me and my pa went to town to get our horse shod. I went to get some candy, and when I come back, I saw my Pa and Tolman arguin'. Tolman looked putout, and 'fore walkin' away, he shook his fist in my Pa's face and said it weren't over. When I asked my Pa what it was 'bout, he said it were nothin'."

"I see," said the marshal thoughtfully. "Think you'd recognize any of these men if you saw 'em today?"

"Probably. Can't say for sure, other'n Tolman and maybe Flack. Marshal, are you sayin' that these other men, Morgan, Tucker, the O'Leary's, and maybe some others are the ones who killed my folks? 'Cause if they are, I mean to find 'em and make 'em pay with their lives."

"Could be, Mr. Tanner, at least some of them. But men in gangs like Flack's don't usually stay together very long. They come and go, some get killed or captured, others join up, and a few get tired of the robbin' and killin' and drift off to new lives."

"But they could be the ones."

"Yeah, at least some of them. So if you're planning to find these men, and kill them, you had better make sure they're the right ones, and then plan on getting hanged yourself for takin' the law into your own hands."

Thinking back to his earlier conversations with Willard and Beth, Jake looked sternly at the marshal and replied, "I ain't no killer, Marshal, and I'm only interested in findin' those who done the killin' and see 'em hanged by the law."

"Well now, I'm mighty pleased to hear that, Mr. Tanner. You're young, but from what I've seen and heard, you just might be the man I've been looking for."

Confused, Jake said, "Guess I'm not followin' you, Marshal. Why would you be lookin' for somebody like me?"

"Because I need a deputy with your abilities, Mr. Tanner. A Deputy United States Federal Marshal to help me keep the peace in the states and territories assigned to me. And I'm particularly interested in a deputy who's seen Flack and has a personal interest in seeing him and the rest of his gang hanged. Are you interested?"

"I hope you're jokin', marshal, 'cause I ain't no lawman, ain't never thought about bein' one, and don't have the time or need to be chasing outlaws all over the west. The only thing I want to do is what I said I was goin' to do; find my folks' killers."

Smiling broadly for the first time, the marshal said, "Who says you can't do that and help me round up trouble makers at the same time, Mr. Tanner, and with the law standing behind you making it all nice and legal. Think about it, and let me know before I leave town tomorrow."

CHAPTER 8

WHILE JAKE AND MARSHAL FARNSWORTH were talking, Beth climbed the hotel stairs and knocked softly on Emily's door. After waiting an anxious moment, and then knocking again, the door opened only wide enough for Beth to see one of Emily's eyes peering out. Emily, seeing Beth, closed the door abruptly.

Undeterred, Beth knocked on the door again and said in a gentle voice, "Emily, my name is Beth, and I would like very much to talk with you." Hearing no response, Beth knocked a third time and said, "It's important, Emily, really it is. Please let me in."

Again hearing no response, Beth was about to turn away when the door opened as before.

"Hello, Emily. My name is Beth, and your brother Jake is my friend. May I come in?"

Emily did not respond, but did not close the door.

"I know you don't know me," said Beth, "but if Jake tells you it's all right, will you let me in?"

Emily stared at Beth for a few seconds before making a slight up and down movement with her head as she closed the door.

Beth's emotions were a combination of hope and concern as she retreated down the stairs and into the hotel's dining room -- hope that Jake would help her talk to Emily, and concern about whether she was doing the right thing. Not seeing Jake or the marshal where they had been talking, she went into the kitchen and found Martha putting a pan of bread dough in the oven of a large, wood burning stove.

"Have you seen Jake?" Beth asked with a sigh. "I really need to talk to him."

"He and the marshal just left," replied Martha. "I don't know where they went, but the saloon might be a good guess."

When Beth walked out the front door of the hotel, she saw Jake and Willard sitting on the bench in front of the blacksmith shop. As she crossed the road, she heard Jake saying something about Marshal Farnsworth, but when she approached they stopped talking and stood up to greet her.

"I'm sorry to bother you, Jake, but can I speak with you for a few minutes in private?"

"Of course," Jake replied as Willard hurried into his shop. "Please sit down."

"Thank you," said Beth as she sat down and nervously began smoothing her skirt while trying to decide how to say what was on her mind. Taking a deep breath, she said, "Do you remember me saying that someday I would like to do something for you in return for saving my life?"

"Yeah, I remember, but it ain't necessary. Sometimes things happen and then they best be forgotten."

"Well I will never forget. Not in a million years. And I've thought of something that I think will help you and be a blessing to me."

As a frown of confusion crossed Jake's face, he said, "I'm not sure I understand what you're sayin'."

"You will soon enough. But first, you've got to convince Emily that I only want to talk to her."

"Why would you want to talk to Emily? I can barely talk to her without gettin' her upset."

"Please, Jake. Just let me try."

A few minutes later Jake knocked on Emily's door and said, "It's me, Emily." The door opened as before, but when Emily saw Beth, she opened the door just wide enough to let Jake enter the room.

"It's all right, Emily," said Jake in a gentle voice as he held the door open with his hand. "Beth is my friend, and I want her to be your friend, too. She wants to talk with you 'bout somethin'."

Emily, to Beth's surprise, looked from Jake to Beth, and then back to Jake with only a slight look of wariness as she backed into the room and sat on the edge of the bed. Noting Emily's calmness, Beth said, "Jake, why don't you go and continue your conversation with Willard. Emily and I will be fine."

"Are you sure, Emily?" said Jake, his concern plainly evident to Beth.

Emily nodded her head slowly as she watched Beth enter and sit down on the only chair in the room. Jake took one more look at each of the young women before walking from the room and closing the door.

Beth, unsure how she should begin, smiled warmly at Emily and said in a halting voice, "Do you … understand everything Jake says to you?"

Emily, noticeably wary, answered Beth's question with a slight nod of her head.

Taking a deep breath, Beth said, "Jake has told me how both of you have been moving from place to place for a long time, and I'm not going to say anything more about that because I don't want to upset you. I think, though, and I believe you know, that this cannot go on much longer. Am I right?"

Emily stared at Beth for a long minute but did not shake her head in disagreement.

Knowing that the next few things she was going to say would be critically important, Beth said, "I know you love Jake. And I know he loves you -- but for what he needs to do now, and where he needs to go, it's impossible for you to follow him any longer."

Emily's face was suddenly fearful, and she started to stand up.

"No, no, it's all right," said Beth soothingly. "I don't want him to leave either. But he's a man now, and has a man's work to do. All we can do is love him and let him go. He won't be far, I promise, and while he's gone, you can live with me in Dodge City, and we'll become the best of friends. I've never had a sister, Emily, or even a brother. My mother died when I was very young, and I've always wanted a sister to love and to share my life." Then, almost afraid to breathe, she asked, "Will you be my sister, Emily?"

When Beth came down stairs from Emily's room, she saw Jake sitting in the hotel's dining room, nervously fidgeting with the brim of his hat. After hesitating a moment to build up her courage, she entered the room and walked to where Jake was sitting. "May I sit down?" she asked.

"Of course," he replied, smiling and standing up as she seated herself. "I hope you're goin' to tell me what's goin' on with you and Emily."

"I don't know if anything is going on," said Beth with a sigh. "She just sat there looking at me, and I'm not sure what's going on behind those brown eyes."

Wearily, Jake said, "I know, it's been like that for a long time, and I ain't sure it's ever goin' to be any different. I guess you know that now."

"I know she's very disturbed, and that the life you've been leading is not helping her. She needs a permanent home, Jake, and people around her who love her and are willing and able to help her get better."

"Yeah, she had that for a while at the ranch. She and Mrs. Kentworth worked together in the kitchen and I thought …. But then Tolman found us and … you know the rest."

"Yes," said Beth excitedly, "and that's exactly what I'm talking about. Emily needs a home where she doesn't feel afraid, a home where she can be happy and have a life of her own."

"I know, I know, and I agree. But what can I do? I've been tryin' to figure somethin' out for a long time, but so far I haven't come up with anything."

Well," said Beth with a happy smile, "I think I have just solved your problem. I know a home where she will be happy, have her own life, and where someone will love her as much as you do."

"Yeah, and where and who would that be?" said Jake with a touch of sarcasm.

"With me," said Beth.

"Sounds like you and Beth had an interesting conversation," said Jake as he entered Emily's room. "Do you like her?"

Emily, sitting on her bed and slowly brushing her hair, surprised Jake by smiling and nodding her head in an animated manner he had not seen in a long time.

"Are you sayin' you want to live with Beth?" he asked with astonishment.

Nodding her head again, she shocked Jake even more when she said, "Sis …ter."

Beth's father had an uneasy feeling as he listened to Beth tell him about her conversations with Emily and Jake. Since the death of his wife twelve years before from a drunken cowboy's stray bullet, he had become especially protective of Beth. Letting her travel on the train to visit his sister in Kentucky had been the hardest thing he had done since his wife's untimely death. The fact that the two trusted men he had sent to protect her during her trip had failed to do so made him increasingly wary for her welfare.

"Are you sure you know what you're doing?" he asked, looking at Beth with concern. "It's obvious that she is a very troubled young lady who may never be normal. I know you feel you owe a debt to Mr. Tanner, but have you thought about the consequences if she *never* gets better or, God forbid, Mr. Tanner gets himself killed? You … well … could be saddled … no, no, that's not right. What I mean to say is that caring for her could become a life-time job, and you need to understand that."

"I've thought about all that, Papa, but if it weren't for Jake I don't think I would have a life at all. I know it sounds as if I'm only doing this for that reason, but I'm not. I truly believe that with love and caring, Emily will get better."

"All right, all right," said Mr. Owens, holding up his hands in mock surrender. "You know I can't refuse when you've got your mind made up. So, of course, she's welcome, and Mr. Tanner too, anytime."

The following morning Jake repeated the oath of office becoming a United States federal marshal and Marshal Farnsworth pinned a shiny silver star on his vest.

CHAPTER 9

Two Years Later: August 1877

"YOU DID A GOOD JOB bringing in Mexican Joe," said Marshal Farnsworth as Jake took a seat opposite the marshal's battered desk. "Did he say why he killed those two cowboys from the Double Bar O ranch?"

"No, I'm afraid his English is worse'n my Spanish. But I did find those boys' horses and that fifty dollar gold piece that come up missin'. With that and the ranch foreman 'bein' a witness to the killin', I don't think Judge Baker will have any trouble hangin' him."

"Good, that sly old fox has been a thorn in my side for too many years," said the marshal as he leaned back in his chair. "I thought I had him a couple of times but he's slippery'n axle grease. All together, I figure he's killed more than a half dozen men for the change in their pockets. It's about time he caught the end of a rope."

"Yes sir," said Jake, nodding his head in agreement as he waited for the marshal to give him another assignment. The marshal, however, was now gazing out the grimy window of his Dodge City office in what appeared to be quiet contemplation.

Assuming this was a sign of dismissal, Jake was about to stand up when the marshal leaned forward abruptly, looked at him with a serious expression, and said, "You been with me how long now, Jake, 'bout two years?"

"Yes sir, that's right."

"And from what I've seen in that time, you're one of the best deputies I've ever had. You've brought in some mighty tough characters, with havin' to kill only only one, and I know by experience that he was by far the orneriest one of the bunch. That being said, I'm goin' to give you some information that I think will interest you. Mind you, it might be a false trail, but I figure you've earned the right to take a few days and check it out."

"Check what out?" said Jake, sitting upright with interest.

"The jail in Wichita, Kansas. I just read in their newspaper that they have a man named Tom O'Leary sittin' in their jail, accused of killin' a county sheriff. The paper doesn't say anything about him having a brother named Jim, or that they were riding with Flack when your folks were killed. But if I were you I'd …"

"I'm on my way," said Jake as he jumped to his feet and started to turn toward the door.

"Now hold on … just hold on a minute," said the marshal harshly, "and sit your butt down in that chair."

Stunned by the marshal's words, Jake sheepishly turned around and sat down. "Yes sir," he mumbled. "Guess I wasn't thinkin' straight."

"You guessed right," said the marshal firmly. "Only a fool goes charging off without a plan and ends up gettin' nowhere or maybe killed."

"Yes sir,"

"Look, Jake, what I'm trying to saying is that you need to go to Wichita and keep your eyes and ears open, find out if the O'Learys were with Flack when your folks were killed, and what they were looking for. If I were you, I'd be thinking that the best way to get answers to these questions is to get them from Tom before they hang him. Then maybe, just maybe, you can also find a trail to track down Flack, Tolman, and the others. The trial starts in five days so you better get going."

"Yes sir," said Jake as he again stood to leave.

"One more thing before you go," said the marshal, "when was the last time you and Emily spent some time together?"

"Been a couple of months, I guess," answered Jake. "Maybe longer. You've been keepin' me a might busy."

"Yeah, I figured as much," said the marshal with a smile. "Best you go see her 'fore you go."

"Like you said, Marshal, I've only got five days to find some answers. I'll see her when I get back."

"Okay, okay, but remember this: of all the outlaws I've known, the O'Leary's are the meanest, back-shootin' cowards of the worst kind. That being said, you'd best be careful and never let 'em see your backside."

CHAPTER 10

Four Days Later

WICHITA WAS A BUSTLING TOWN, but following the directions of the train conductor Jake had no trouble finding the Palace Hotel. He was dressed in a dark blue suit, white shirt with a string tie, black boots, and a light gray Stetson hat. Dressed as he was, he had no trouble blending in with the town's inhabitants making their way along the crowded wooden sidewalks. In his right hand he carried a multi-colored carpetbag containing his gun belt and pistol, a change of long-johns, his work boots, and his everyday work clothes. In the left breast pocket of his suit coat was his deputy marshal badge.

After registering at the Palace Hotel, and leaving the carpetbag in his room, he left the hotel and walked to the Plainsman Saloon, recommended by the hotel desk clerk as the most popular saloon in town. The purpose of this visit was the same as his subsequent visits to three other saloons during the afternoon and early evening. At each establishment he pretended to sip a glass of whiskey while standing at the bar listening to the various conversations going on around him. If a conversation happened to include comments regarding the upcoming trial of Tom O'Leary, he managed to find a way to introduce himself and offer to buy his new companions a drink. In each instance it soon became apparent that the men knew only what they had read in the local newspaper.

Later, when he finished eating supper in the hotel's dining room, Jake returned to the registration desk and asked, "If I wanted to visit the worst saloon in town, where would I go?"

"I guess that would have to be the Red Pepper, Sir, down on the south side of town," replied the clerk, but I don't recommend going there," he added with a conspiratorial whisper. "It's a place known for bad whiskey, whores, card sharks, and even a few killings over a game of cards and such."

"Much obliged," said Jake as he turned and walked toward the stairs leading to his room on the second floor.

In his room, Jake changed from his suit and tie to his everyday deputy marshal work clothes, boots and hat. After lipping on his vest, he stuffed his deputy marshal badge deep into a pocket. Determined to not draw attention to himself, he purposely left his gun belt and pistol in the room, hidden away under his mattress.

The Red Pepper was a run-down saloon with a putrid stink of sweat, beer, and stale tobacco. The whores trolling for customers among the gambling tables and wheel games were dressed in soiled costumes and were much too old to be plying their trade. The men at the bar and around the room easily met the unsavory images Jake had hoped to find. He was surprised to see that none of the men were armed, and assumed the local sheriff was taking no chances with anyone interrupting O'Leary's trial.

As he had done earlier in the day, Jake stood at the bar sipping a glass of whiskey while listening to the conversations filtering around him. As a newcomer in the saloon he quickly became a target for the establishment's four whores, who approached him, apparently hoping he would find at least one of them worthy of the two dollars they were asking for their favors. After his dismissal, they each stormed away cussing and demeaning his manhood.

Above the hum of conversations near him, Jake suddenly heard someone say, "Yep, looks like old Tom is finally goin' to meet the hangman. Reckon it's one thing to kill common folks, and they say he's killed a lot of 'em, but he was careless and stupid to kill a sheriff in front of witnesses."

Turning away from the bar, and looking in the direction of the voices, Jake heard another man at a table in a far corner of the room continue the conversation, "Yeah, in all the time I've knowed Tom he's never left a witness alive."

Jake left the area of the bar and began wandering around the room, pretending to watch the various poker games in progress. Eventually he moved near the table where the men were still talking about Tom O'Leary.

"I'd like to break Tom out of jail," said a third man, "but the sheriff's got too many deputies on guard day and night. It'd be pure suicide makin' an attempt."

Pretending he had heard only the last part of the men's conversation, Jake turned to them and said quietly, "Couldn't help overhearin' you gents talkin' 'bout breakin' Tom out. You sure his brother, ain't comin' to do the same?"

Startled, the men looked at each other with obvious uncertainty while Jake held his breath, hoping this Tom O'Leary had a brother.

"You know the O'Leary brothers, mister?" said one of the men with a suspicious tone in his voice.

"Yeah, rode with 'em both one time or other," Jake replied, pulling out one of the empty chairs around the table and sitting down without an invitation. "It's hard to believe Jim would let Tom swing without at least *tryin'* to bust him out."

"I don't know 'bout that," replied one of the men. "The last time they was together, they got to fightin' and nearly killed each other. Tom bit a chunk out of Jim's ear and that ended it."

"Yeah," said Jake. "I remember somebody sayin' somethin' 'bout that. Said it were the right ear."

"Naw, it were his left ear. Jim was so mad he said he'd kill Tom if he ever saw him again. Course it weren't the first time either one of them said that. But it wouldn't surprise me none if Jim were around somewhere lookin' to embarrass the sheriff."

"Well," said Jake standing up, "if you see Jim, tell him I was lookin' for him to return the money I owed him."

"Money you owed him?" repeated the man doing most of the talking. "Oh, sure, sure, I'll tell him. So what's your name should Jim come around?"

"Just tell him Jake. He'll remember me."

He won't remember me, Jake thought as he left the saloon, *but the fish just might swallow the bait and come lookin' for some easy money.*

Now that Jake knew Tom had a brother named Jim, he began to think of how he could find out if they were with Flack's gang when his parents were murdered. As he made his way back to the hotel, he thought, *there just might be a way, providing the sheriff will cooperate.*

Early the following morning, dressed again in his suit and tie, Jake entered the courtroom and took a seat in the back. When the sheriff brought Tom O'Leary into the courtroom through a side door, Jake pulled the brim of his hat down low over his eyes and bent forward slightly. Peeking out from under the brim, he saw that O'Leary was of medium height and build with a ruddy, pock-marked face. His dark-brown hair was wildly disheveled and the ends of his bushy, bandito-styled mustache extended down past the corners of his sneering mouth. He was dressed in faded blue pants and a soiled, long sleeved black shirt with holes worn through at the elbows. Jake was disappointed when he could not recall seeing the man with Flack. After O'Leary was seated at a table with his back to the audience, Jake leaned back in his seat but continued to keep his hat pulled low over his eyes.

The trial lasted two hours, and the jury of six men reached agreement in less than ten minutes. Tom O'Leary was convicted of murder and sentenced to death by hanging. The execution was ordered by the judge to take place at sunrise the following morning.

Later in the day, dressed as he was at the trial, Jake stopped in front of two deputies holding rifles and blocking the front door of the sheriff's office. He was wearing his deputy Marshal badge and his gun.

"I need to talk with Sheriff Hagan," said Jake in an easy manner.

"And who the hell are you?" replied the larger of the two guards as he spat tobacco juice on the wooden walkway between Jake's boots.

"United States Federal Marshal Jake Tanner," Jake replied as he looked down and eyed the brown spittle splattered on his boots, "and if you do that again mister you won't have enough teeth left to spit through."

"That so!" said the deputy with a sneer. "So what's your business with the sheriff, *Mr. United States Federal Marshal?* He's got a hanging tomorrow and ain't got no time for jawin'."

"I think if you give the sheriff my name, he'll see me," said Jake. "Of course, I wouldn't want to be you if you were to ignore my askin' and he heard 'bout it."

Hesitating a moment, as if thinking over the implied threat, the deputy responded in a gruff voice saying, "Wait here! And you better not be playin' me for no fool."

Jake said nothing in response, knowing the sheriff would see him because Marshal Farnsworth had telegraphed the sheriff asking him to help Jake should the need arise.

"Glad to meet you, Marshal Tanner," said Sheriff Hagan as Jake was ushered into his office. "I got Marshal Farnsworth's message. What can I do for you?"

Hearing this, the deputy cleared his throat, shuffled his feet, and said weakly, "Will you need me for anything else, sheriff?"

Smiling, the sheriff replied, "No, Mr. Turnbull. From what I've just heard, you've embarrassed yourself enough for one day."

Red-faced, the deputy turned around and slunk from the office.

"Thanks for seein' me, Sheriff," said Jake. "Fact is, I got two favors to ask and they're both a might unusual."

"Not a problem, Marshal. But I'm a man who believes that favors need to work both ways, and if you're willing to trade favors, should the need arise, I'll do what I can."

"I wouldn't have it any other way, Sheriff."

"Good, now what can I do for you."

"Tom O'Leary." said Jake simply. "I believe Tom and his brother Jim were part of a gang that murdered my folks some years back. And what I've got in mind is tryin' to find out if they were part of it."

"I'd sure like to oblige," said the sheriff, "but even if it was Tom, he's going to hang tomorrow morning, and there ain't nothin' you or me can do about that."

"I understand, Sheriff. That's why I come askin' for favors."

"Okay, suppose you spell it out for me."

It was late evening when Jake entered the sheriff's office through the back door. The sheriff's deputies guarding the rear of the building had been alerted and they made no attempt to challenge him. He was now dressed in dirty, ragged, cowboy attire, and in his right hand he carried a bottle of cheap whiskey.

"You sure you really want to do this?" asked the sheriff.

"Yes," replied Jake without hesitancy. "But first I need a couple of minutes."

Jake turned and walked out of the office through the same back door and into the alley, where he stuck a finger down his throat and heaved up the remains of his evening meal. Making sure a liberal amount of his vomit had soiled the front of his shirt; he took a mouthful of whiskey, swished it around in his mouth, and then spit it out on the ground.

"How do I smell?" Jake asked when he re-entered the sheriff's office.

"Like the worse kind of puking drunk," replied the sheriff while taking a step backwards.

"Then I guess I'm ready."

Reaching down to the top of his desk, the sheriff picked up and pulled on a pair of leather gloves. "Any particular way you want this done?" he asked.

"No, just make it look convincin'."

Standing in front of Jake, the sheriff balled up his right fist and used a round house punch to hit Jake hard on the left side of his face, causing blood to spill from his mouth and down his shirt.

Staggering backward from the blow, Jake recovered and again stood in front of the sheriff saying, "Again, only higher this time, above the eye."

The sheriff complied with Jake's request, and Jake's left eyebrow split open like a ripe melon. Blood poured down the right side of his face.

"Once more," Jake gasped in pain as he again staggered to recover from the blow.

This time the sheriff's left jab hit Jake in the nose hard enough to draw blood but, hopefully, not enough to break it.

"That better be enough 'cause I ain't goin' to hit you again," said the sheriff while pulling off his bloody gloves in disgust. "I've knocked a few rowdy drunks around to quiet 'em down, but I ain't never had a man take a beatin' like yours without cryin' out some. You got pure grit, Marshal."

"Can't say I ain't hurtin'," said Jake while wiping his mouth with the back of his hand. "Appreciate your doin' me this favor."

"Yeah, well, can't say I'll ever ask you to return this particular favor. You ready for me to get my deputies?"

"Ready as I'll ever be."

Opening the back door of the office, the sheriff motioned for Deputy Turnbull and another deputy to come inside. "We're ready," he said. "Toss him in like we discussed, but make sure he don't get hurt more'n he already is."

"Yes sir," Turnbull replied with an impish grin as he and the other deputy grabbed Jake roughly by the arms and began dragging him face down along the floor and through the thick, heavy door leading to the jail cells. When they reached the cell next to Tom O'Leary's cell, they entered and dropped the seemingly unconscious Jake on the floor.

"What the hell is this?" Tom yelled angrily, standing up from the bunk he was sitting on and grasping the bars separating the two cells. "Get that pukin' pile of crap out of here! If I'm gettin' hanged in the morning, I shouldn't have to put up with no stinkin' drunk all night!"

With an ugly grin, Deputy Turnbull reached through the bars of Tom's cell, grabbed him by the throat, and said, "Come mornin', O'Leary, the hangman is gonna put a rope around your scrawny neck and send you to hell, fire and damnation. Now shut the hell up 'fore I come in there and make you wish you'd kept your mouth shut."

Tom said nothing as the deputies locked the door to Jake's cell and walked away laughing. Slowly, he released his grip on the cell bars and sat back down on the hard bed. He couldn't say anything because fear had closed his throat. He had never been so alone and afraid. Just the thought of a black hood over his head and a knotted rope around his neck made him sick to his stomach. With his elbows on his knees and his hands covering his face, he began to cry softly for the first time in his adult life.

"Stop all that damn blubberin'!" Jake hissed as he raised his head only high enough to look around the cell. "Don't give 'em no reason to come back here."

Tom looked up abruptly, obviously shaken and surprised by Jake's sudden sobriety. "What the hell ... and I weren't blubberin', just clearin' my throat."

"Sure sounded like blubberin' to me."

"Well it weren't. And I don't take lightly havin' a stinkin' drunk talk to me that-a-way."

"Okay, then I guess you don't want to get out of here 'fore they hang you in the mornin'."

"What!" said Tom loudly as he stood up and gapped open-mouthed at Jake.

"For the last time, keep your damn voice down and listen to me," said Jake in a harsh whisper. "I ain't drunk. I was just pretending so the sheriff would throw me in here with you. Now be quiet and let me get some rest. I think those deputies busted a rib."

"Who are you?" Tom whispered, a small ray of hope in his voice.

"It don't matter who I am. Just know you'll be out of here in a couple of hours if you cooperate."

"A couple of hours! No shit! But how? How you goin' to do it?"

"Relax, you'll know soon enough."

"Well I'll be damned," said Tom with relief. "I never thought anybody would come."

Groaning in real pain as he turned over on his back, Jake said, "Not even Jim?"

"You know Jim?" asked Tom with surprise.

"Of course, who do you think is payin' me to keep you from gettin' hanged."

"Jim's here in Wichita? He's getting' me out?"

"No, stupid, I'm gettin' you out. Now be quiet."

"So, where's Jim?"

"Don't know."

"What do you mean, you don't know?"

"I mean, I don't know. Jim said I was to get you out and then we'd meet someplace close by that only the two of you would know 'bout. He said I'd get paid when we got there."

"What place? I don't know 'bout no place he'd be."

"Then you'd better think on it real fast 'cause you ain't goin' nowhere 'til I know where I'm gettin' paid."

"I swear," said Tom whining, "I don't know 'bout no such place. Me and Jim didn't always get along all that well."

"Yeah, I heard 'bout you bitin' off part of his left ear in a fight," said Jake with a small laugh.

"Huh! You know 'bout that?"

"Sure, Jim showed me. He's still mad as hell 'bout it, but says blood is blood and I got to get you out. He said he'd do it himself, but if he got caught you'd both be gettin' hanged."

"He knows I'd try gettin' him out if he was goin' to hang," said Tom soberly.

"Yeah, yeah, enough of all this jawin'," said Jake irritably. "Where's this place we're goin' to meet Jim? Come on, Tom, I ain't doin' nothin' 'til I know where Jim will be waitin' for us."

"Okay, okay, I been thinkin' on it. I'm sure it'll be that big rock pile just outside Medicine Lodge, 'bout twenty miles from here. The only other place is El Fortaliza in Mexico, but that's too far off. Now what's your plan for getting' me out of here?"

"One more thing," said Jake. "I told Jim I wouldn't get his brother out 'less I was sure you was really his brother."

"What! Of course I'm his brother. Who else would I be?"

"The sheriff's stooge for one thing," said Jake. "Somebody he's got locked up pretending to be Tom O'Leary while all the time he's got Jim's brother hid away so nobody can break him out of jail. Fact is, I've had a feelin' all along that this sheriff will do 'bout anything to make sure Tom O'Leary gets hanged, including puttin' one of his own deputies in that cell where you're sittin'."

"But I am Tom O'Leary," Tom cried in alarm. "The same man everybody saw in the court room today."

"I weren't in town today," Jake replied. "Figured it might not look good if the sheriff saw a stranger hangin' 'round town."

"But I'm the real Tom O'Leary," Tom repeated. "You've got to believe me."

"I'm a suspicious man by nature, Tom, if that's who you really are, and I never trust anybody on their say so. You got any proof of who you are?"

"Proof! Hell, I ain't got a penny in my pocket, much less any proof of who I am."

"Well, that's 'bout what Jim and me figured, and that's why we come up with a way to prove you're either his brother or the sheriff's stooge."

"Oh yeah, and how you goin' to do that?" said Tom.

"By tellin' me something that only you and Jim would know. Something the sheriff would never know."

"Okay, like what?"

"Well, Jim told me you and him and three others killed a man named Tanner 'bout nine years back. He told me the names of the other three men and said if you was really his brother, you'd know their names. So, if you're Jim's brother, tell me their names."

"What the hell … do you take me for some dumb-ass fool?" said Tom angrily as he jumped to his feet. "There ain't no way I'm goin' to tell you somethin' like that, and I don't think Jim would ever tell anybody 'bout a killin' we done."

"Well, guess that's 'bout it then," said Jake as he rolled onto his side facing away from Tom. "You're either the sheriff's stooge or a dead Tom O'Leary come mornin'."

"No … no wait … wait, there's got to be somethin' else. I … I mean … there's got to be somethin'."

Jake did not respond as he squirmed to find a more comfortable position on the cell floor. He had anticipated Tom's reluctance to trust him so easily. But he also knew that time was on his side, and that Tom would become more and more anxious as the time before his hanging passed swiftly by.

"Come on, mister," Tom tried again. "Maybe Jim told you somethin' else. Like when we was in the Confederate army and deserted 'fore the end of the war 'cause we didn't want to die like dogs. We hadn't eaten for three days, there weren't no clean water 'cept when it rained, and the major said if we didn't advance on the enemy, he'd shoot us himself."

Jake continued to lay unmoving on the floor as Tom talked on and on about his escape from the war. It was only when he paused for a moment and heard Jake's pretence of soft snoring that he became alarmed.

"Hey! Hey you! Wake up!" Tom whispered urgently as he rattled the bars separating the two cells.

"What the hell!" said Jake in a sleepy voice as he rolled over onto his back.

"You've got to get me out of here,"

"Stop all that damn noise," Jake hissed without moving. "If you're okay with the sheriff hangin' you in a couple of hours, the least you can do is let me get some sleep. I've got to be ready to ride out in the mornin'."

"No, no please," sobbed Tom as tears rolled down his cheeks. "I'm sorry, really. You've got get me out of here."

"I don't have to do nothin'," said Jake with a yawn. "I told Jim I'd get you out if I was sure you was his brother. But I guess you ain't, so don't bother me no more."

"No … wait … wait … okay … I'll tell you. It were Roy Flack, Burt Tolman, and William Culver."

"Okay, so why did you kill Tanner?" Jake asked casually as he rolled over to face Tom.

"What! You said all you needed was the names," said Tom, alarmed.

"Yeah, but now I'm curious."

"But that weren't part of the deal," Tom whined pitifully.

"It is if I want it to be," Jake replied. "Either satisfy my curiosity or hang, I don't care either way."

"Damn it, I don't know, I really don't know," replied Tom angrily. "Maybe it had somethin' to do with Tanner bein' in the army with Flack and Tolman."

"Tanner, the man you killed, was in the Confederate army with Flack and Tolman?"

"Can't say for sure, just figured they was from the way they was talkin'."

"Any idea where any of 'em are now?"

"Last I heard, Flack won a saloon in a poker game somewhere in Texas, Amarillo maybe. Ain't never heard nothin' 'bout the others."

Groaning while getting on his knees, Jake said, "Okay, enough jawin', it's time we got out of here."

"How … how you goin' to do it?" Tom asked eagerly.

"Don't worry, it's all been taken care of. I'm goin' to puke up more of my dinner and then start hollerin' that I can't breathe. You start hollerin', too. And when the deputies come runnin' you tell 'em I'm choking and to get me out of here 'fore I die on 'em."

"Then what?"

Reaching into his left boot with his right hand, Jake withdrew a slim, eight-inch knife from a sheath hidden in the lining of his boot, "Once I'm in the sheriff's office I'll take care of the deputies with this knife and then come back and let you out."

"What happens once we're out? We can't just walk away."

"No kidding. Are you're really that stupid?"

"Sorry. I'm just jumpy 'bout getting' out of here, that's all."

"All right, just relax. I've got six horses waiting out back and four men in groups of two who'll lay false trails in different directions from the one we'll take."

"You sure it'll to work?"

"It will if you do your part. So start hollerin'."

Tom's yells for help brought the two deputies running. Muttering and cursing about the stink of vomit surrounding Jake, they yanked him roughly from his cell and dragged him to the sheriff's office. The heavy wooden door separating the office from the row of cells closed with a thud, but after that there was nothing but silence.

"You hear all that?" Jake asked the sheriff.

"Every word, Marshal."

At sunrise the following morning the sheriff led a procession of deputies and a bare headed, bleary eyed Tom O'Leary from the jail to a high scaffold next to the courthouse. A large, noisy crowd in a holiday mood had gathered to witness the hanging. Two deputies tied Tom's hands behind his back and dragged him stumbling and protesting to the top of the scaffold, where the sheriff led him to a place over the trap door. The hangman, arms folded across his chest and hooded to hide his identity, stood close by.

Tom, soaked with sweat and trembling, searched the crowd with desperate eyes for the man who had promised him freedom.

"You got any last words?" asked the sheriff in a harsh voice.

Tom opened his mouth but only sputtered incoherently as a growing pool of urine soiled the trap door.

"Okay preacher," said the sheriff as he motioned to a man with a priest's collar around his neck. "Get on with the prayin'."

The preacher droned on for an overly long time, as the crowd shifted restlessly and young boys shouted cat-calls at the killer.

When the preacher finished his prayer, the sheriff turned to the hangman and said "Do your duty, hangman."

The hangman, dressed in a dark blue suit and hooded to hide his identity, walked from his place by the trap door and stood in front of Tom. From an inside pocket, he slowly pulled out a black bag, placed it on the top of Tom's head, and pulled it down only to his eyes. It was at that point that the hangman lifted his own hood and stared directly into Tom's face. "Remember the man you killed, the one named Tanner?" Jake whispered angrily. "That was my pa, and now the law is goin' to hang you, just like you hanged him."

Tom's eyes opened wide with shock as he recognized the man who, just hours earlier, had promised to set him free, a man now wearing a Deputy United States Marshal's badge.

Jake looked into Tom's anguished face for several seconds before continuing to lower the black hood. He then lowered his own hood, placed the rope with the knotted noose around Tom's neck, jerked the knot tight against the left side of his head, and then whispered in Tom's ear. "With everything you told me I won't have any trouble findin' your brother and seein' him hanged, too."

Walking back to the trap door lever, Jake waited only a moment before activating the trap door. When the rope jerked to a stop, and Tom's life ended, Jake reminded himself that as Tom's hangman he was a representative of the law, and it was the law that hanged Tom O'Leary.

CHAPTER 11

DURING HIS RETURN TRIP TO Dodge City, Jake felt strangely at odds with himself. Before the hanging he thought he would feel satisfaction by looking into Tom's eyes, telling him who he was, and then watching him drop through the trap door to his death. When he saw Tom's lifeless body dangling at the end of the rope, however, he felt no satisfaction, no sense of vengeance fulfilled. Tom O'leary was dead, and the only thing noteworthy about his death was that Jake now knew with certainty that the O'Leary brothers were with Flack, Tolman, and William Culver when his mother and father were brutally murdered.

It was late afternoon when Jake stepped off the train in Dodge City. To late, he decided, to report to the marshal's office. After four days of riding the train and encountering various delays in route, he was just plain tired. Instead, he decided to walk the short distance from the train station to the Owen's home, where he knocked on the front door.

"Emily, Emily, come quick!" called Beth excitedly after she had opened the door. "Jake's home!"

From the floor above, and then down the stairs, Jake heard hurried footsteps that he was sure belonged to Emily. At the bottom of the stairs Emily slowly walked toward Jake, arms outstretched, eagerly seeking his embrace. Surprised, Jake hurried to her as he realized that she was somehow changed. Gone were the sad, vacant eyes and the timid motions of a frightened girl. Instead, she was smiling, wearing a faint blush of make-up, and she was beautiful.

"Emily ... is ... is this really you?" said Jake as he looked admiringly into her eyes. "What happened? I mean, how did you do this?"

Emily, looking past Jake, fixed her eyes on Beth and said, "My friend."

Beth, lowering her eyes, said, "It has taken a while, but I believe she has finally come to know and trust me and my father. I think she is doing much better, don't you?"

"Why yes, yes, of course. It's just that ...."

Jake stopped talking as Emily raised her right hand and gently touched the bruises and cuts on his face. "You ... are hurt."

Jake was dumbfounded. It had been so long since he had heard Emily speak that the sound of her voice was only faintly familiar. Turning, and looking at Beth, he said, "What ... when ...?"

"We've been saving it as a surprise. I hope you're pleased."

"Pleased? Oh Emily, I can hardly believe it. You're talking and no longer afraid."

"Yes ... I am happy ... to have you home ..., Jake."

Later that evening, as Beth and Jake sat quietly on the Owens' front porch swing, Beth said, "Are you as happy as I am, Jake?"

"Happy! How could I not be?" Jake replied, turning toward her with a warm smile. "Seeing Emily like her old self is more than I ever hoped for."

Blushing at Jake's failure to understand that she was happy because she was sitting beside him, Beth was about to say so, when she saw that behind his kind words, he looked troubled. "What is it, Jake?"

she asked squeezing his hand. "I can see that something is troubling you. Please tell me what it is."

Hesitating for several moments, as if searching for the right words, Jake sighed and said, "Well, it's Emily. I mean ... I couldn't be more pleased. But, at the same time ... well ... I can't help worrying."

"Worrying about what?"

"About ... well ... suppose somethin' happens in the future, somethin' that jogs her memory about the past. You know, 'bout seein' our folks killed. Could that cause her to go back to what she was before?"

Not having thought of this possibility, Beth gasped and said, "Oh no, Jake. We can't let her go back. We just can't."

"No, we can't. But that's only part of what's troublin' me."

"But what else could there be?" asked Beth.

"It's complicated."

"Please tell me anyway. I need to know."

Taking his time, Jake told Beth about his trip to Wichita and his confirmation that the O'Leary's were part of the gang that murdered his parents. He also told her he knew where he might find Flack, and that if Flack was now a respected businessman, he might never again commit a crime for which he could be brought to justice.

"Do you remember when we first talked about Emily, about why she acted so afraid and strange?" asked Jake.

"Why yes, of course."

"And do you remember me tellin' you that me and Emily were the only witnesses to our folks bein' killed, and, because she couldn't talk, it would just be my word against Flack and the others if they was ever brought to justice?"

"Yes, I remember."

"Well, that is what's troublin' me. I mean ... now that she can talk, Emily's account of what happened, along with mine, might be enough to convince a judge to hang Flack and the others. In fact, her testifyin' might be the only way to ever make 'em pay for what they done. Yet askin' her to talk about a nightmare she's been tryin'

to forget might be more'n she could stand. It might cause her to …
well … go back to what she was forever. And I can't let that happen,
Beth, I just can't."

"Yes, I see what you mean, said Beth softly. So, what are you
going to do?"

"I don't know, at least not yet. But the one thing I do know is that
I'd rather them killers go free than risk Emily's sanity."

Marshal Farnsworth leaned back in his chair and grinned when
Jake walked into his office an hour after sunrise. He had just read, for
the second time, the telegraph message from Wichita's sheriff. "Sounds
like you had an interestin' time in Wichita," he said with a grin.

Jake stopped mid-stride when he saw a sheet of yellow telegraph
paper lying on the marshal's desk. "Sendin' messages seems to get
faster every day," he replied, taking his usual seat in front of the
marshal's desk.

"Looks like you took quite a beatin'," said the marshal, eyeing
Jake's cuts and bruises. "Hope you got what you were lookin' for."

"Yeah, and a few more things," Jake replied casually.

"And what does that mean?"

"It means O'Leary told me that Flack, Tolman, and my Pa
all served together in the Confederate army, and maybe that has
somethin' to do with why they killed my folks. He also told me where
I might find Flack."

"Well, you're just full of information!" said the marshal with
surprise as he sat up straight in his chair. "But why would them being
together in the army be a reason for killin' your folks? That don't make
no sense at all. And what about Flack?"

"Well, O'Leary said he heard that Flack won a saloon in a poker
game in Amarillo. And while it may not be in our jurisdiction, I figure
it might be worth takin' a look."

"Son, we're United States Federal Marshals, and, as far as I'm
concerned, the whole damn country is in our jurisdiction. Just be

careful and don't spook him, because if it is him, you may want to know where you can find him when the time comes."

"Yes sir. If it's all right with you, I'll leave tomorrow."

Amarillo, Texas, was by far the largest city in the west Texas panhandle. Although still a cow town, it was beginning to show some of the social graces of advancing civilization. There were two first-rate hotels and several of its better saloons were frequented by some of the town's more important gentlemen.

Jake, dressed in his dark blue suit and gray Stetson hat, registered at the Royal Palace Hotel, and went straight to his assigned room. He tipped the old man carrying his carpet bag a silver dollar and told him he'd get two more if he brought Jake a bottle of the hotel's best whiskey within the next five minutes. Four minutes later three waiters knocked on his door with a bottle of whiskey and a platter of fancy pastries. Jake knew he had made the right first impression.

After eating dinner in the hotel's dining room, and leaving a generous tip, he left the hotel, and began frequenting the various saloons along the town's major roadway. At each saloon he ordered a shot of whisky, and then walked among the various games of chance, betting here and there and mostly losing. Dressed as he was, and losing a moderate amount of what seemed to be a plentiful supply of money, it wasn't long before an equally well dressed man approached and introduced himself as the owner of the establishment. The first owner, accompanied by a very large man who Jake assumed was his bodyguard, looked and acted like an effeminate Eastern dandy. The second owner was old and fat with white hair. The appearance of two other saloon owners also failed to resemble what Jake thought Flack might look like. Being only twelve years old when his parents were murdered, Jake was not concerned that Flack might recognize him nine years later. It wasn't until the owner of the fifth saloon suddenly appeared and introduced himself that Jake's interest was aroused.

The man was about fifty-five years old, clean shaven, with reddish-colored hair.

"Good evening, Sir," said the man warmly as he offered his hand. "I'm Daniel Franklin, owner of this fine place of amusement. And you are ...?"

"Jack Waterman," Jake replied casually, as he grasped the man's extended hand and searched his face for any hint of recognition. His gut was telling him that the man could be Flack but he was not sure, having never seen Flack up close and given the effect of nine years of aging.

"Well, I'm certainly glad to meet you, Mr. Waterman. My informants have told me you are new in town and staying at the Royal Palace. Please accept my welcome to Amarillo, and feel free to entertain yourself however you like. Should you wish ...shall we say ... some female companionship, all you need do is ask. We provide this service for only our finest gentlemen."

"Yes, I'm sure you do, Mr. Franklin, but my purpose in visiting Amarillo is of a somewhat different nature."

"Oh, I see, and if you don't mind my asking, sir, just what sort of purpose might that be?"

"I'm afraid I am not at liberty to say just now," Jake replied with a faint smile, "but perhaps we can meet in private tomorrow."

"Now why would I want to do that?" Franklin asked with a confused frown.

"Because I believe it is with you that I have been asked by my employers to discuss a most important matter."

"Me?" replied Franklin with surprise. "I don't understand."

"You will, if you agree to meet with me."

After a moment of thoughtful hesitation, Franklin said, "I do not normally meet with someone without knowing his purpose, Mr. Waterman. But you intrigue me. Shall we say ten o'clock in my office at the rear of this building?"

At precisely ten o'clock the following morning, Jake knocked three times on a door with a sign proclaiming the premises to be that of Mr. Daniel M. Franklin, proprietor of the Prairie Queen Saloon. The door was opened quickly by a large, muscular man busting the seams of a suit at least two sizes too small. A pistol in a shoulder holster was clearly visible under his coat and his coal-black eyes were cold and mean.

"You Waterman?" he demanded in a booming voice that reeked with the stink of whiskey.

"I am," Jake replied calmly.

Stepping back through the doorway, the man turned and pointed to another door on the far side of the room. "He's in there waitin' for ya, and I'll be outside the door in case there's any trouble. You get my drift, Mister?"

"There won't be any trouble," replied Jake with a casual air as he crossed the room.

Ignoring Jake's assurance, the man followed him across the room and stood beside the door as Jake raised his hand and knocked twice. The door opened and Daniel Franklin said in a cheerful voice, "Welcome, Mr. Waterman. Please come in. Can I get you some coffee?"

"No thank you." Jake replied as he entered the room and removed his hat. "I had two cups with my breakfast just a short time ago." Like the day before, Jake was being especially careful to make sure his manners and speech mimicked that of a refined gentleman. He suspected Franklin was doing the same, but for him it seemed to come more natural, perhaps because he'd had more time to practice.

Turning to the large man standing by the door, Franklin said, "That will be all, Jackson. I'll call if I need you."

"Yes, Mr. Franklin," Jackson replied in a respectful tone as he closed the door.

"Well now, that being settled," said Franklin, "please be seated, Mr. Waterman, and we'll get down to business. "And, if it's not too much to ask, just what is it you're selling?"

"Why, I'm not here to sell you anything, Mr. Franklin," Jake replied innocently as he settled himself in an overstuffed leather chair opposite Franklin's expansive mahogany desk. "Rather, my only purpose at this time is to ask if you would like to become a very rich and powerful man?"

"But I'm already a rich and powerful man, Mr. Waterman," Franklin replied as he also sat down.

"Well then, I guess you won't be interested in what I have come to discuss," said Jake as he leaned forward in his chair as if to stand up. "Before I leave, though, I must admit that I'm sorely disappointed, because I was told by some very important men in our govern ... ah ... I beg your pardon, sir, I meant to say ... *our group of business leaders* ..., that you were the very man they have been seeking."

"Now hold on." said Franklin quickly, motioning with both hands for Jake to remain seated. "I didn't say I wasn't interested. Fact is, I'm always interested in profitable opportunities, and unless I'm mistaken, you almost used the word *government*. Now what part of our government would that be, Mr. Waterman?"

"Ah, yes, yes, an unfortunate slip of the tongue I'm afraid," Jake admitted as he sat back in his chair, "but now that I have misspoken, I cannot stress strongly enough that you must ignore my mistake, because not doing so will surely jeopardize the important matter I have come to discuss with you."

"Why yes, of course, Mr. Waterman, I understand completely, and I assure you, sir, that I am a man whose discretion you can trust."

"Thank you, Mr. Franklin. I am most relieved."

"Think nothing of it," said Franklin grandly as he sat back in his chair with a grin. "Now, what exactly is it you want to discuss?"

"A most confidential matter," replied Jake, "a matter so confidential that I can only say at this time that the details will be forthcoming should you be the man we have been looking for. Therefore, I have been instructed by ... my associates ... that I must first verify that you are, in fact, that man. And if you are, we will know with certainty that

you have the background, resources, and daring to undertake this …
ah … delicate enterprise."

"Enterprise?" said Franklin with a frown. "What kind of
enterprise?"

"An enterprise of great importance to our country, and to Texas
I might add, and of such magnitude that the entire population of the
United States will come to know and respect your name," Jake replied
earnestly.

"Well, if it's only verification you want," said Franklin with a
small laugh, "just go out on the street and ask anybody who I am.
Hell, everybody in this part of Texas knows me."

"Yes, I'm sure you are right, sir, but that's not quite the depth of
verification we're looking for. We already know you're a respected
businessman here and elsewhere."

"Then I don't understand," said Franklin. "How can I verify who
I am other than as I have just stated?"

"That is the very heart of our problem," Jake replied. "You see, we
have been told that the man we are seeking has had a previous secret
life and has been hiding his identity for many years."

"A previous life?" said Franklin with astonishment. "Why, I've
never heard of such a thing."

"Are you saying you never served in the Confederate army?" asked
Jake.

"Well … yes, I served in the Confederacy."

"And you served with distinction for the duration of the war?"

"Of course"

"And you did not desert the army before the end of war."

"I most assuredly did not," said Franklin sternly as he sat forward
in his chair, "and I take offense at being asked such a disparaging
question."

"I'm sorry, Mr. Franklin," said Jake. "No offense was intended. It's
just that my associates have insisted on my asking you these particular
questions as part of their verification process."

"And why would they do so? It's an insult to any respectable man."

"Yes, most assuredly," replied Jake. "Suppose, however, that someone has told us that you did desert. What would your response be?"

"That it is a despicable lie," said Franklin angrily, "and anybody who said so is a damn liar."

"Yes, some people can be very unkind about that sort of thing," said Jake calmly. "Please be assured that it is not our intent to bring any such accusation to public notice. In fact, one of the things we fear most is that such an accusation might inadvertently become public. Please know that any ... well ... admission ... regarding your Confederate service, or any other part of our discussion, will never leave this room."

"You're right, Mr. Waterman, an accusation like that will never leave this room because I have no *admission* to make. I have always been an honorable man who served the Confederacy with distinction, and I demand to know who has said otherwise!"

"Does the name Burt Tolman mean anything to you, Mr. Franklin?"

Thoughtful, but without showing any hint of recognition, Franklin said firmly, "No, I don't recall ever hearing that name. Why do you ask?"

"Because he told us that he and the man we are looking for served together in the Confederate army and both deserted just as the war was about to end."

"Well, you have been badly misinformed, Mr. Waterman. I have never heard that name before, and I am outraged that such an accusation has been made against me."

"Yes, yes, I'm sure you are, Mr. Franklin," said Jake, "and I apologize for having mentioned it. Please understand that Mr. Tolman is a highly regarded member of our organization and has been at the forefront in trying to find the man we are seeking -- a man by the name of Roy Flack. Apparently Mr. Tolman has made a mistake in thinking you might be this man, and, again, I apologize. If however, after consideration, you wish to continue our discussion, I will be staying at the Royal Palace Hotel for two more days. In the meantime, should you feel the need to confirm my identity, you might address a telegram to Mr. Tolman in Dodge City. If not, I will know that we have been misinformed and I will continue my search elsewhere. Good day, Mr. Franklin."

The following day, still posing as Waterman, Jake talked with the president of Amarillo's two banks. The purpose of the visits, he said, was to ask about the bank's security measures and confidentiality should a large amount of cash and gold be deposited sometime in the future. He then visited with Amarillo's mayor regarding the city's current political climate and growth potential. Mentioned casually was his interest in the number of large cattle ranches within a hundred miles around the city. Early on the second day Jake rented a horse and buggy and drove out of town. He knew that all of his movements in and around Amarillo would be observed and he was not disappointed. A man as big and clumsy as Jackson made a poor spy. Although still not convinced that Franklin was Flack, Jake's actions during the two days were a desperate attempt to pique Franklin's curiosity enough to make him commit, one way or the other.

Tired and discouraged after a restless night of waiting to hear from Franklin, and not having done so, Jake packed his carpet bag and checked out of the hotel. Defeated, he now knew that, even if Franklin admitted he was Flack, it was useless information unless substantiated by somebody else. And there was nobody who could do that. *I've been on a fool's errand*, he thought angrily to himself.

Jake was seated and looking forlornly out the window, when a blast of steam from the engine obscured the station platform as the train jerked forward. It was at this moment that Jake's thoughts were interrupted by somebody taping him firmly on the shoulder and thrusting a note in front of his face. Surprised, he read the note quickly, and turned around in time to see Jackson hurrying away. Grabbing his carpet bag from the overhead bin, Jake raced to the back of the car and jumped from the train.

"I was surprised to get your note, Mr. Franklin. I thought our business was finished."

"As I said before, Mr. Waterman, I seldom overlook a profitable opportunity. And now that I have confirmed who you are, perhaps we can get down to business. Mr. Tolman was brief in his reply and said that I should take your word as gospel."

"Thank you," said Jake with a broad smile. "Did he say anything about my other activities while in your city?"

"He didn't have to," Franklin replied. "I've had you watched since the day you arrived. I am curious to say the least. First you visited the banks, then the mayor's office, and then you spent a day talking with the owners of the three largest ranches in the territory. Just what are you and your associates after, Mr. Waterman?"

Laughing, Jake said, "I guess I wasn't very careful was I? Actually, I wasn't trying all that hard, because I thought you were not interested in pursuing our discussion."

"Well, let's say that I am. Where do we go from here?"

Taking a small notebook from inside his coat pocket, Jake said, "The fact that you took the opportunity to confirm my identity with Mr. Tolman tells me you know him from a different time. And that, in and of itself, tells me that your real name is Roy Flack. Is that correct?"

Frowning with apparent uneasiness, Franklin said, "I haven't used that name for a long time, and I don't want to use it now. My name is and always will be Daniel Franklin. Is that understood?"

"Absolutely," Jake replied. "That is exactly what we also want. Your true identity must always be kept secret in order for our … enterprise … to be successful."

"Okay, so now what?" said Franklin anxiously.

"You have confirmed my identity by telegraph with Mr. Tolman," said Jake in a serious tone. "Now, for obvious reasons, I must confirm that you are not Daniel Franklin pretending to be Roy Flack in order to learn the purpose of our enterprise and take advantage of this knowledge."

"What! I just admitted who I am," said Franklin, alarmed.

"Yes, and I believe you. But my associates insist on this final confirmation."

"All right, all right, what do you need?"

Turning the page of his notebook, Jake said, "Mr. Tolman told us that nine years ago you and he, and three others, hanged a man and shot his wife. If you are Roy Flack, Tolman said you would know the last name of the man you hanged. Can you tell me that name?"

"What the hell has that got to do with anything?" raged Franklin.

"Nothing at all," Jake replied. "It is just the final validation of your identity. The hanging itself is of no importance to us."

"Yes, yes, all right, the man's name was Tanner. Now what?"

"Now you wait," said Jake. "I will take this information back to our group for further discussion, and, at an appropriate time, you will be given directions to a secret location where all the details of our plan will be explained. In the meantime, you are to remain here and continue your normal activities. Do not attempt to contact Mr. Tolman again as he will not be at the same location. Absolute secrecy is critical and must be guarded at all times. Do you understand?"

"Yes, of course," Franklin replied eagerly. "I understand completely."

"Then it is time to say good-by for now," said Jake as he held out his hand to the man who had murdered his parents. And as Franklin grasped his outstretched hand Jake thought, *and somewhere, somehow, the time will come when either the law hangs you or I kill you myself.*

"What the hell!" said Marshall Farnsworth with astonishment. "Are you saying he admitted he was Flack?"

"Yeah," Jake replied in a tired voice after the long trip back to Dodge City.

"So how'd you do it?"

"It's a long story, and maybe best told after I get a nights' rest. But your idea of having Flack telegraph Tolman in Dodge City for verification of my identity was the final thing needed for Flack's confession."

Laughing softly, the marshal said, "Yeah, and I almost spoiled that. I was out beatin' on Chuck Waverly for beatin' on his wife when the message came in. I'd alerted Mac at the telegraph office to expect a message 'bout Tolman, but he forgot. I just happened to go by there on my way back to the office when he was scratching his head over it."

"Then we got lucky and it worked," said Jake.

"But now what?" asked the marshal. "You know he won't admit who he is in court, and without other evidence, he'll walk away a free man."

"Yeah, I know. But I ain't ready to take him to court just yet," said Jake. "I ain't got it all figured out yet, but I'll know it when the time comes."

"Well, you'd better not take too much time. He just might get skittish and disappear again."

"Oh, I think he'll be around for a while."

"Really, and what makes you think so?"

"Greed," said Jake as he stood to leave.

"Okay, okay, have it your way," said the marshal with a sigh. Then, as if an afterthought, he continued, "Oh, by the way, this telegram arrived while you were gone. I read it in case it was important. Sounds like Mr. Mayfield is worried about you."

Jake sat down again as he took the message from the marshal's outstretched hand and began reading. When he finished, he looked up and said, "Even after all these years Tolman is still pokin' around tryin' to find me. Willard says he had to wait a while 'fore sendin' this message to make sure he left town."

"Don't you think it's about time you settle this, Jake?" asked the marshal.

"If I could find him, I sure as hell would," said Jake irritably. "I'm tired of looking over my shoulder for that bushwhacker."

"Well, maybe this will help," said the marshal as he opened a desk drawer and pulled out what appeared to be a wanted poster.

"A wanted poster?" said Jake with surprise as he took it from the marshal. "Are you sayin' Tolman is wanted by the law?"

"No, Tolman isn't wanted. You are."

"What?" said Jake as he quickly scanned the poster. "Well I'll be damned. He wants to find me so bad he's willin' to pay somebody fifty dollars for me, dead or alive."

Leaving the marshal's office, Jake walked to the livery stable and sat down on a bench to read the poster again. His name was printed in large capital letters above a crude drawing of a man's face. The reward amount was printed below. In small print at the bottom of the poster were the words, 'Printed by J. B. Colby and Sons, Oklahoma City, Oklahoma.

CHAPTER 12

BURT TOLMAN WAS WEARY AND hungry as he rode into the small town of Lawton, Oklahoma. During the previous three weeks he had been hiding in and around the nearby Wichita Mountains, after robbing a bank in Erick, Oklahoma. This latest robbery was only one of a number of banks he had attempted to rob during the past year, and, like the others, had netted him only a few hundred dollars. After those robberies, the local sheriff and a handful of citizens usually made only a half-hearted attempt to apprehend him, giving up after a few days. The sheriff in Erick, however, had been more persistent, and he and his posse had been close on Tolman's heels from the very beginning. It was only after two weeks of hard riding that the sheriff and his posse gave up and returned to Erick. Tolman did not know the posse had given up until five days later, when his own thirst and hunger drove him out of hiding.

When he and his horse finally staggered into Lawton, his first thought was to moisten his parched throat at the first saloon he saw. But when his horse smelled water from a trough in front of a road-side boarding house, he had no choice but to give the animal its head. Sliding wearily from the saddle as the horse drank lustfully, he was about to do the same when he saw a well-rounded woman sitting on the front porch of the boarding house, fanning herself with a Sears

& Roebuck catalog. Suddenly, the thought of a bath, some home-cooked food, and a soft bed became a compelling argument against a saloon.

"Good day to you, ma'am," he said with forced cheerfulness.

"And a good day to you, Sir," she responded as she struggled with her bulk to stand and then walk toward the porch stairs. "Would you be lookin' for a room, sir?"

"Yes, that I am, ma'am," said Tolman grandly, as he tied his horse to the hitching rail near the water trough. "But I'm only a poor, crippled, preacher man who's been travelin' a long way savin' souls, and I'm tired and well-worn down. It would be a blessin' if you could see it in your heart to give one of God's devoted servants a place to rest."

"Oh my, yes, but of course," the woman gushed at the ruggedly handsome stranger. "Please, come and sit in the shade of the porch and I'll get you a glass of cool lemonade. Oh my goodness," she continued, "it will be such an honor to have a servant of the Lord in my humble home. My name is Irene Pettegrew, only recently widowed from my beloved husband, and sorely in need of the Lord's comfort. And what is your name, sir?"

"I am, madam, Reverend Walter P. Lewis, Shepherd of the Good Faith Christian Church of Saint Louis, Missouri," Tolman lied. Then, looking skyward and throwing his arms wide, he cried out in a loud voice, "Lord, I have traveled far and wide throughout this great land in search of sinners and, I regret to say, I have found many. And like you, Lord, I have preached repentance, and those who have heard my pleas have freely offered themselves up for baptism. But now my soul is weary, Lord," he continued as he lowered his arms slowly and bowed his head, "and I seek not sinners but rest from my travels, for even you, Lord, rested on the seventh day." Then, looking up again to the sky, he said in a gentle voice, "Thank you, Lord, for bringing me to this place of rest and this humble woman. Amen."

Within two weeks Reverend Lewis was a respected member of the community, known for his kind spirit and devotion to God. On the fifth Sunday following his arrival, at Pastor Jason Robert's urging, Reverend Lewis gave a rousing sermon at the pastor's Church of The Everlasting Light. Life was good, and so was the bed of the lonely widow Pettegrew. Tolman was tired of chasing Tanner, at least for the time being, and his ready acceptance by Lawton's citizens was a welcome change, not to mention a pleasant respite from the law.

Two Sundays later Pastor Roberts failed to appear at the church door to welcome the congregation to morning services. Concerned, but not overly so, everyone waited patiently inside the church while two church deacons went next door to the Pastor's house in search of him. When they returned, the foremost deacon read to the congregation a scrawled note from Pastor Roberts, saying his mother was gravely ill and he was forced to leave Lawton at daybreak and hurry to her bedside. The note also stated that he did not expect to ever return to Lawton. The congregation was shocked and dismayed, for it was commonly believed that, due to the pastor's own advanced age, his mother would have been long deceased.

Within an hour, Reverend Walter P. Lewis accepted both the leadership of the church and Pastor Roberts' house. Yes, life was good, so good that Tolman had momentarily forgotten about Jake Tanner and the reward poster. But a few days after moving into Pastor Robert's house he did remember, and sent a telegraph message to the sheriff in Oklahoma City asking if anyone had information about Tanner's whereabouts. The sheriff responded a day later that no one had come forth with any information.

"Are you Mr. J. B. Colby?" Jake asked, without formality, to the man behind the print shop counter.

"No sir, that would be my father."

"And where can I find him?"

"Well, Sir, I'm afraid you can't. He died about five years ago. I'm his son; can I help you?"

"You the one that printed this?" asked Jake as he unfolded the poster and laid it on the waist-high counter. He was dressed in his everyday clothes, but not wearing his deputy marshal badge.

"Ah, now let me see," said the man as he adjusted his spectacles. "Why yes, yes, I printed it. Are you Mr. Tanner?"

"It don't matter who I am," said Jake in a firm voice. "The only thing you need to know is that I'm lookin' for the man you printed this poster for, this *Reverend Lewis*. Do you know where he's stayin'?"

"Oh, I believe he left Oklahoma City quite some time ago, sir. He never said where he was going, but he told me to refer all inquiries about Mr. Tanner to the sheriff."

"What'd he look like, this Reverend Lewis?"

"Well, he was rather regular looking, about like any preacher would look in his black suit and white shirt. He wore a black hat too."

"Was there anything unusual about him?"

"Hum, unusual. Oh, yes, there were a couple of things that caught my eye as curious."

"Like what?"

"Well, like I've never seen a preacher wearing a pistol tied to his leg like a gunfighter. And then there was that other thing."

"What other thing?"

"He was, I guess you'd say, somewhat crippled."

"Crippled! What do you mean?"

"His arm and hand, sir. When I tried to hand him the two large stacks of posters he said he couldn't carry them because he had a bad arm. It was then that I noticed his hand was shriveled up. He told me to deliver the posters to the sheriff myself."

"Which hand and arm?"

"Sir?"

"Which hand and arm was crippled?"

"His left, as I recall. He said he'd been bushwhacked some years back and couldn't lift his arm higher'n his shoulder without a great amount of pain."

"Where's the sheriff's office?" asked Jake.

"Sheriff Dobbson at your pleasure, sir," said the man with an easy smile as he eyed Jake's federal marshal badge, "but I hope you ain't bringin' me no trouble 'cause I'm tuckered out from lockin' up drunks all night."

"No, no trouble," said Jake, "but I understand a Reverend Lewis has been askin' about a man named Jake Tanner. Mr. Colby at the printing office said I should talk to you."

"Oh, yeah, you mean the reward poster. Are you this Tanner feller?"

"That's my name," replied Jake, "along with probably more than a few others. Mind if I ask you some questions about this Reverend Lewis?"

"Don't mind at all, but can't say I'll be much help. He was a strange one and not exactly the talkin' type. Can't say I cared much for him."

"What do you mean when you say he was strange?"

"Suspicious like. Can't put my finger on it, but I got the feelin' he weren't all he said he was."

"Mr. Colby said he was crippled, had a bad arm and a shriveled hand. Said he'd been bushwhacked ."

"Told me the same," said the sheriff. "But I have to wonder why somebody would bushwhack a preacher. When I asked him 'bout it, he said he didn't know neither. He wasn't convincin'. All I can say is that, although he was dressed like a preacher, it'd be my guess he weren't. So, why you askin', Marshal?"

"I'm askin' because this man's real name is Burt Tolman, and when I was twelve years old I saw him and four others hang my pa. He was a neighbor I'd seen in town and I shot him with my rabbit gun. Ever since then he's been lookin' to kill me so I couldn't say who done it."

"Well, I'll be damned," said the sheriff. "Any chance your shootin' him made him a cripple?"

"Could be," Jake replied. "I was aimin' at his chest but saw blood flowin' down his left shoulder."

"Yeah, that might explain it, but 'fore you go, Marshal, I got a question for you. When you find this feller, are you plannin' on arrestin' him or killin' him?"

"Guess that's up to him, Sheriff."

"Good answer. So what do you want from me?"

"Well, Tolman told Mr. Colby to pass all questions about the reward money to you, which I figure means you'd be passing 'em on to Tolman."

"Yeah, that's 'bout right. Only thing is, Tolman told me he moves around a lot so he'd telegraph me from time to time askin' if I'd heard anything."

"Then all I'm askin' you to do, Sheriff," said Jake angrily, "is tell him I know who he really is and that I'm lookin' for him, too."

"Can't say I think that's a smart idea," said the sheriff as he sat down behind his desk and leaned back in his chair.

"Why not?" asked Jake with a frown.

"Because it sounds like you're teasin' a rattlesnake, or in this case a sack full of rattlesnakes that might bite you in the butt and put you six feet under."

Smiling at the sheriff's comment, Jake said, "Why am I gettin' the feelin' that you got somethin' else in mind?"

"Just a suggestion, mind you."

"I'm always open to suggestions."

"Good, because I'm thinkin' of a way you can see if this preacher is Tolman and not expose yourself. And if he is Tolman, well ... you'll need to decide what to do 'bout it."

"Sounds good," said Jake, as he sat down in a straight back chair next to the sheriff's desk. "What've you got in mind?"

"Well, 'bout a week or so back I got a telegraph message from the preacher askin' if anybody was claimin' the reward. I sent a message back sayin' no."

"And?"

"And, the message came from Lawton, Oklahoma. So I figure that if you was to go to Lawton, you might see this preacher feller and know if he's your man. If he ain't, well, at least you'll know. But if he is, then you can decide what to do about it."

"I don't aim to kill him outright, if that's what you're thinkin', Sheriff," said Jake.

"Good, I'm glad you're smarter than that," said the sheriff. "So let's say he is Tolman and he doesn't go for his gun. What would you do?"

"I'd scout around and find out what he's doin' in Lawton," Jake replied, "and maybe how long he's plannin' on stayin'. It might be, after all this time, he's decided I ain't worth worryin' about and he's ready to settle down. If that's true, I've got time to find out what he's been up to 'fore he came to Lawton."

"How long has it been since he's seen you up close?"

"I was twelve at the time of the killin'."

"Good, then it's likely he won't recognize you."

"Are you sayin' what I think you're sayin?" said Jake with astonishment.

"Why not?" replied the sheriff. "Gettin' close to him might be the best way to find out what you need to know. Then, later, you can figure out what to do 'bout it."

"And what do you think I should do 'bout it?" Jake asked with respect.

"I think you should make every effort to bring the man to justice," said the sheriff in a fatherly manner. "Find out if he's been involved in another killin', a bank robbery, horse stealin', or cattle rustling, anything that'll get him convicted by a judge, and maybe hanged. Meanwhile, I'll be lookin' at wanted posters and checking with all the sheriffs here 'bouts to see if any of 'em can come up with somethin'. What do you say, Marshal? You willin' to try it my way?"

It was mid-afternoon when Jake rode into Erick, Oklahoma. He had taken his time since leaving Oklahoma City to let his beard grow out and visit the various towns and settlements along the way. Even though reluctant to wear his deputy marshal badge during these visits, he did so knowing it would entitle him to more information than what might otherwise be granted. So it was when he met Sheriff Blackford. Although the sheriff was initially too vexed to entertain questions from an out-of-town lawman, his manner changed quickly when Jake asked if there had been any recent killings or bank robberies by a man with a shriveled left hand.

"Did you say 'shriveled'?" asked the sheriff as he jumped up from behind his desk.

"Yeah," replied Jake, "a man with a shriveled left hand and wearin' a black suit and hat."

"That's him!" shouted the sheriff. "That's the bastard who robbed our bank and nearly cost me my job. The same varmint me and my posse chased all over them mountains southeast of here. We'd have caught him if we hadn't run out of grub. Quick, tell me how you come to know this gent."

"Seems he's been doin' 'bout the same thing all over the southwest," lied Jake, not knowing how much truth he had actually spoken. "I was down this way on other business and thought I'd drop by and see if he'd been seen around these parts."

"Well he sure as hell has," said the sheriff. "Why I'd ... I'd give two months pay just to have that skunk sittin' in my jail. Believe me, I got enough witnesses so old Judge Crank won't have no trouble findin' him guilty."

"Well, if I come across him," said Jake with a smile, "I just might do you and old Judge Crank a favor. But I'd prefer a hangin' to jail time."

"Don't make no difference to me," said the sheriff. "You get him here and I'll see what I can do."

"What'll you have?" asked the bartender in a tired voice. A stifling heat lay heavy over the town of Lawton.

"Whiskey," Jake replied, as he looked around the almost deserted saloon. His deputy marshal badge was out of sight in one of his vest pockets.

The bartender produced an almost empty whiskey bottle and slopped the last of the liquid into a smudged glass.

Turning to face the bartender, Jake said, "That hotel up the street worth stayin'?"

"Depends on how long you're plannin' to stay. If it were me, and I was stayin' more'n a couple of days, I'd get a room at the Widow Pettegrew's boardin' house. It ain't got no bugs and the widow makes the best fixings in town."

"Sounds good," said Jake as he started to lifted the glass to his lips. "Any other folks stayin' there?"

"Ain't many folks come through here in the heat of summer," replied the bartender. "The widow did have a couple of gents and a lady stayin' for awhile, but one of 'em, a preacher, moved out after folks talked him into takin' over the only church in town. Seems the old preacher just up and left town and ain't been seen or heard from since."

"Sounds like you keep a close eye on what goes on 'round here," said Jake with seemingly casual interest.

"Yeah, I found it can pay in surprisin' ways to keep your eyes open and your mouth shut. And givin' a free drink to our local deputy now and then don't hurt neither."

"Far as I know there ain't no law against keepin' up with local gossip," said Jake. "Say, I knew a preacher man once. A tall feller, all fit and proper and such. A fine man with a good heart, and strong as an ox. I remember a time when he lifted the back of a wagon all by himself so I could pull off a broken wheel. Lifted it easy as nothin'."

"Well, that sure ain't this preacher."

"Why do you say that?"

"Because this preacher can't lift hardly nothin'. Got a bad arm, he says, and his hand is all shrunk up somethin' ugly. Keeps it in his pocket most of the time like he's hidin' it from folks. But I've seen it more'n once."

"Yeah, don't sound like the man I know," said Jake. Placing two bits on the bar, he continued, "Well, guess I'll be headin' over to see the widow."

The Widow Pettegrew welcomed Jake with fluttering eyelashes and longing looks befitting a young maiden. Since Tolman became the local preacher, and entitled to Preacher Robert's house, he returned only occasionally to enjoy the widow's cooking but not her bed. Her only other male guest was an old man who spent most of his days dozing on her front porch.

"I do hope you'll be stayin' with us a while, Mister ...."

"Simmons, Ma'am," said Jake with a quick friendly smile without offering encouragement. " I'll be here only a day or so. My business keeps me from stayin' in one place very long."

"And what business would that be?" she asked.

"Horse tradin' ma'am. I've got a contract to fill for a feller up north of here. Should only take a couple of days."

"Well, I'm pleased you're stayin' with us, even if it's only for a few days," said the widow as she gently touched his arm. "My bedroom is just down the hall from yours, and I hope you'll let me know if you need anything. Supper is served at six and best you not be late. Mr. Higgins is a sleepy old man, but he eats like every meal is gonna be his last."

As fate would have it, Tolman showed up at the Widow Pettegrew's dinner table that very evening. After a moment of anxiety, Jake relaxed when Tolman failed to recognize him and asked him to pass the mashed potatoes. Jake ate quickly and excused himself. Later, the same evening, Jake heard Tolman and the Widow Pettegrew talking and giggling in the room next door, and then the bed springs began to squeak.

At sunrise the next day, in order to appear to be a real horse trader, Jake rode out of Lawton. He had no real purpose other than wasting time, so he began wandering the nearby countryside. It was late in the afternoon when he paused to drink from his canteen and saw a shallow indentation in the ground, where it appeared animals had been digging. On the ground around the area, and snagged on nearby bushes, were small strips of black cloth. Thoroughly curious, Jake dismounted and walked to the edge of the claw-marked hole, where he knelt down and used his gloved right hand to brush away the sandy soil. Immediately the torn sleeve of a black coat and the chewed fingers of a human hand became visible.

It took only a few minutes of digging with both hands to uncover a clerical collar around a man's neck, and twisted tightly around the clerical collar was a thin strip of raw-hide with a uniquely carved wooden cross fastened on the end. Knowing without a doubt that he was looking at the body of Lawton's Pastor Roberts, Jake reached into the grave and used his knife to gently cut the carved cross from the strip of raw-hide. Half an hour later, after covering the grave with a stack of heavy rocks, he returned to Lawton and went directly to the telegraph office.

Jake was wearing his deputy marshal badge and standing by his horse a mile outside of Lawton, when a man on horseback rode up in a cloud of dust. The Sunday morning sun had just risen in the eastern sky and showed promise of another hot day.

"Howdy, Sheriff," said Jake as Sheriff Blackford dismounted.

"Howdy yourself, Deputy. It took me awhile to figure out what you was tryin' to say, but then it came to me sudden-like.

Smiling, Jake said, "I don't trust telegraphers. If I'd told you straight out, it would have been all over Lawton in less than an hour."

"That's what I figured," replied the sheriff. "Are you sure about this?"

"Ain't no question in my mind."

"And you're sure he's still in Lawton?"

"Well sir, I'd bet that if you was to peek through the Widow Pettegrew's bedroom window 'bout now, you'd find him and the widow sleepin' real peaceful. I been watchin' the place all night to make sure he didn't leave town."

"Okay," said the sheriff. "Let's go."

"Not so fast, sheriff, there's somethin' else you ought to know. There's been a killin.'"

"What! You didn't say nothin' 'bout a killin' in your message! Are you sayin' he's killed somebody here 'bouts?"

"That's what I'm sayin', and if you'll follow me, I'll show you what I've found."

Tolman was in a good mood when he entered the church to prepare for the morning service. Even though the Widow Pettegrew had forgiven his long absence and welcomed him to her bed, he was looking forward to preaching a sermon on the sins of fornication. He was also looking forward to a full collection plate supplied by fornicators with a guilty conscience. Within a few minutes the first of his congregation began to enter the church, and he went forward with a broad smile to greet them. Soon the church was filled to capacity, and the congregation began singing the first hymn with fervent passion.

It was at this same time that Jake and Sheriff Blackford dismounted in front of the office of Lawton's sheriff. It took only a few minutes for Sheriff Blackford to tell Lawton's Sheriff Butts and his two deputies what Jake had showed him in the shallow grave. He then handed Sheriff Butts a wanted poster for the man who robbed the Erick

Bank of Commerce, a man described as having a shrunken left hand. Within minutes Sheriff Butts and the others rode out of town in the direction of the grave site.

Tolman was in the middle of his sermon and ranting with fervor when the door to the church burst open, and Jake and the others walked in, led by Sheriff Butts.

"What is the meaning of this?" Tolman shouted angrily from behind his high pulpit, his eyes bulging with fury at this intrusion during the height of his condemnation. "This is the house of the Lord, and I demand that you withdraw immediately!"

While Jake and the others stopped just inside the building, Sheriff Butts continued to walk briskly through the crowded congregation and stopped directly in front of Tolman. "Reverend Lewis," he shouted at the top of his voice, "you are under arrest for bank robbery and the murder of Pastor Roberts."

"What! You can't be serious!" shouted Tolman amid loud gasps from the congregation.

"I ain't been more serious in my life," said the sheriff with a sneer.

"But I'm innocent," beseeched Tolman. And as the congregation stood up in confused silence, he looked out at them and continued, "Surely you can't believe such a horrid accusation."

"No, no, it can't be!" cried a loud voice, as murmurs of discord began to fill the room. "Where's the proof he done it!" shouted someone else. "Reverend Lewis would never do such a terrible thing," shouted the strong female voice belonging to the Widow Pettegrew.

Turning slowly and facing the congregation, Sheriff Butt said in a loud, firm voice, "Calm down, folks, and let me say what needs sayin'. First, I just come from seein' Pastor Roberts lyin' in his grave, and it was plain to see that he was strangled with the strip of rawhide he always wore around his neck that was attached to a wooden cross. But when we searched the grave there weren't no wooden cross to be found.

Second, this man's name ain't Lewis, and he ain't no real preacher neither. His name is Burt Tolman and he's wanted all over the southwest for bank robbery. And while this snake was lambastin' you folks, me and my deputies searched the pastor's house and found over two hundred dollars stolen from the Erick Bank of Commerce. *And with the stolen money we also found this!*" roared the sheriff, withdrawing an object from inside his vest and thrusting it high in the air for all to see.

Women fainted and men shouted curses when they recognized Pastor Roberts' intricately carved wooden cross in the sheriff's hand.

Because the murder of Parson Roberts took precedent over bank robbery, Tolman's trial was held in Lawton's only saloon the following day, where the good citizens of Lawton, rightfully outraged, took three minutes to find him guilty. The judge, equally incensed, sentenced him to be hanged at sunrise three days later. The judge said the only reason he didn't sentence him to hang immediately was that the sheriff needed a few days to build a proper scaffold.

Darkness had fallen over the town of Lawton when Jake walked into the sheriff's office the night before Tolman was scheduled to hang. "Mind if I have a few words in private with the prisoner?" Jake asked the deputy on duty at the jail.

Recognizing Jake as the man responsible for apprehending the killer, the deputy responded without hesitation, "Yes sir, Marshal Tanner, no problem."

Removing a ring of keys from a peg in the wall, the deputy used one of the keys to open the thick wooden door that lead to the jail cells beyond. "The sheriff said nobody was allowed inside the cell, but you can talk all you want from out here," said the deputy pointing to an area a few feet back from the bars of Tolman's cell.

"Thanks, Deputy. I won't be long."

"Yes sir, just knock on the door when you're through."

Jake walked to the area indicated by the deputy and stood looking inside the cell.

Tolman was sitting slumped in a corner with his knees drawn up to his chest. His arms were crossed on top of his knees and his forehead was resting on his arms. "What the hell do you want?" he mumbled without looking up. Hearing no response, he raised his head and looked at Jake. "I said, what the hell do you want?"

Jake continued to stare into the cell and said nothing.

"Get out of here!" yelled Tolman angrily as he jumped up, rushed to the front of the cell, and grasped the bars with both hands.

"You don't recognize me, do you?" said Jake.

"Of course I do," Tolman shouted. "You're the one who found the grave."

"Yeah," said Jake. "But look close. You sure you ain't seen me before?"

"No, 'cause if I had I'd sure as hell remember your ugly face. Now get out of here and let me be."

"Well, guess I shouldn't be surprised," said Jake. "It was a long time ago. As I recall, the last thing you said to me was that you were goin' to find me and kill me."

"You're crazy. The only person I ever said that to was a kid who shot me and made me a cripple."

"Well, I guess that would be me," said Jake with a smile.

Releasing the bars of the cell as though they were too hot to touch, Tolman stumbled back into the cell with a horrified look on his face. "You … you're him? You're the one I've been lookin' for all these years?"

"Yeah, better'n nine years or so, by my count," said Jake. "Least ways that's how long I been lookin' for you and them other murderin' cowards."

"I should've killed you when I had the chance," said Tolman with a snarl as he approached the bars of the cell again, "but I waited too long 'fore getting' off a shot."

"Yeah, I figured it were you tryin' to bushwhack me out on the range, but with you gettin' hanged in the mornin' I guess I won't be worryin' 'bout that any more."

"I ain't dead yet," Tolman yelled as he again raced to the front of the cell. "It were you who done this to me, Tanner. And 'cause of you I got crippled, lost my farm, and my wife and kids all run off."

"Well now, that's a real sad story," said Jake. "The truth is, you brought all that on yourself, and now that I've found you, you're goin' to hang for killin' Pastor Roberts and my folks. Who says revenge ain't sweet?"

"But I never thought … say, wait a minute, how did you find me anyway?"

"I was wonderin' when you'd get around to that," said Jake. "Fact is, you made a couple of stupid mistakes."

"Mistakes? What are you talkin' 'bout?"

"Like havin' that poster printed in Oklahoma City. Once I seen that, it weren't much trouble followin' your trail, especially when I found out 'bout you bein' crippled. Then you robbed that bank in Erick, and hid out in those mountains out yonder. But your biggest mistake was sendin' that message from Lawton to Sheriff Dobbson in Oklahoma City. That told me I'd find you under a rock in Lawton or someplace nearby. So imagine my surprise seein' you across the Widow Pettegrew's dinner table my first night in town. And when I heard Pastor Roberts had come up missin', and that you'd taken over his church, I had a feelin' you had somthin' to do with it. So it didn't come as no surprise when I stumbled across Roberts' grave."

"You was lucky, that's all."

"Yeah, but before I go, I'm gonna ask you one question."

"And what makes you think I'll answer?" replied Tolman in a gruff, sarcastic voice.

"Maybe you won't, but I'm going to ask you anyway. Why did you and the others murder my ma and pa? What did they ever do to you to make you kill 'em?"

"Go to hell. I ain't gonna tell you nothin'."

"Ah, now that's a real disappointment. Especially after talkin' with Tom O'Leary 'fore I hanged him."

"You hanged Tom!" gasped Tolman.

"Yeah, and it were a pitiful sight with Tom cryin' and foulin' himself in front of all them folks laughin' and cat callin'. His neck snapped like a twig when I dropped him through the trap door. I'd told him 'forehand I could save him if he told me why you and the others killed my folks, but he said he didn't know nothin'. I didn't believe him, so I hanged him."

"It was the Colonel and them tintypes," shouted Tolman excitedly, apparently thinking Jake might save him, too.

Stunned, Jake said, "What do you mean, *the Colonel*? What Colonel? And what tintypes?"

Grabbing the bars of his cell until his knuckles were white, Tolman said in a harsh whisper, "Colonel Langston. Durin' the war it was your pa's job to take pictures, lots of 'em. But just before the war was over, your pa disappeared and took all the tintypes with him. The Colonel went near crazy, sayin' we had to find him and kill him. Then, when I saw your pa after all them years, I told him he had to give the pictures to the Colonel. He said he didn't have them, so I told Flack and Flack told the Colonel. The Colonel told us to do whatever needed doin' to get 'em back and then kill your pa."

"But why, what was on 'em?"

Believing he now had the key to freedom in his hands, Tolman said with a twisted smile, "All I'm gonna say is that I know why the Colonel wants 'em, and, if you get me out of here, I'll tell you everything."

"You got it all wrong," said Jake. "At this point there ain't no way in hell you're goin' to avoid the hangman. Even if I could get you out, I wouldn't, 'cause then I couldn't see you get hanged. So, since you won't be answerin' any more of my questions, I guess there's no reason you shouldn't know why you're gettin' hanged for murder instead of goin' to the prison for bank robbery."

Tolman, his eyes wide with surprise, choked out, "What! What are you sayin'?"

"I'm talkin' about the cross."

"What cross?"

"The wooden cross on that strip of raw-hide that Pastor Roberts always wore around his neck. The same strip of raw-hide you used to strangle him."

"So, what about it?"

"You mean to say you never thought 'bout how it got in your saddle bags along with the money you stole from the bank?" said Jake.

Suddenly, Tolman's mouth was moving as if trying to form words, but the only sounds coming out were gasps and sputterings. With color draining slowly from his face, he said, "Are you ... sayin' you ... found it and put it ..."

"Yeah," said Jake. "I figured there might not be enough evidence to prove you killed the preacher, so I made sure there was."

"But ... but you can't do that!" whined Tolman in a frightened voice. "You're a lawman."

"Yeah, ain't that the damndest thing," said Jake with amusement as he walked to the heavy wooden door and knocked loudly. As he walked out of the sheriff's office and down the road toward the Widow Pettegrew's boarding house, he could still hear Tolman's muted yelling, "You come back here, Tanner! You hear me! You can't to this! Please, Tanner, don't do this!"

Sunrise in Lawton was a beautiful sight as the gold and orange rays of the sun slowly crept above the horizon. It could be said that every person in Lawton was gathered on the barren field behind the jail as Tolman was escorted to the scaffold by two deputies. His hands were tied behind his back, and he was sobbing and mumbling incoherently. Only two people waited for him on top of the makeshift tower, Sheriff Butts and the hangman. There was no preacher to say a word for the condemned man, and, judging from the foul mood of the crowd watching, that was just fine. Jake, sitting on his horse at the back of the crowd, watched closely. He was not surprised when he felt only a small amount of satisfaction when Sheriff Butts placed the black bag and the knotted rope over Tolman's head. Instead, it was Tolman's screams and pleading for his life the night before that had fulfilled his need for vengeance.

The hangman, after giving the condemned man a few minutes to contemplate his fate, opened the trap door and Tolman fell to his death.

Where are you, Colonel Langston? Jake thought as he turned his horse away from the crowd and rode out of Lawton. *And what do you have to do with all this?*

CHAPTER 13

Two Days Later

IT WAS WELL AFTER DARK when Jake, sitting beside a dying campfire, was alerted by a twig snapping. Now he knew why his horse had been nervous for the past half hour. Trying not to betray his knowing that someone or something was spying on him, he stood up and casually used the coffee in his tin cup to smother the fire. Once the fire was out, he turned away from the fire pit, picked up the rifle he always kept close by, and took up a position behind two large boulders a few feet away. He had left Lawton two days before, intending to visit Sheriff Blackstone in Erick before heading back to Dodge City. He had not told anyone in Lawton where he was going, and when traveling alone in the wilderness, he always took precautions to make sure no one was tracking him. For someone, or something, to approach his camp site after dark was a good reason for caution.

For a few minutes there was no sound except for his horse's snorting and stomping the ground. Then a man with a deep voice called out, "We don't mean you no harm, Mister. We're just hungry."

Concerned about giving away his position, Jake hesitated a moment before turning his head to the right and cupping his left hand beside his mouth. "How many of you are there," he called out in a gruff voice.

"Just me and another," said the same voice.

"What do you want?" Jake called out in the same tone of voice as he again turned his head to the side.

"Like I said, Mister. We're hungry. Our horses run off or got stole while we was sleepin' and we ain't ate nothin' for two days. We sure could use some grub if you got some to spare."

"Come out from where you are and re-light that fire so I can see you," Jake called out.

"Okay, we're doin' it," said the voice. "Don't do no shootin'."

Within a few minutes the fire began to blaze up and Jake could see a large, barrel- chested man and a much smaller figure standing nearby.

"Where you boys from?" Jake asked, leaving the protection of the boulders and walking toward the fire.

"What do you care?" said a voice behind him.

Jake froze, silently cursing himself for being careless.

"You better keep that shooter on your hip holstered," said the voice.

"You said there was two of you," said Jake, as he looked at the two men standing beside the fire.

"Yeah, well, I lie a lot," said the large man with the deep voice. Then, to the man standing behind Jake, he said, "Get his shooters, Ray, and his gunbelt, too."

"Okay, you heard the man," said Ray. "Drop everything and move over to the fire."

Seeming to obey without further comment, Jake dropped the rifle, moved his left hand slowly toward his gunbelt, unbuckled it, and let it begin to slip from his hips. But at the last moment, just as the belt began dropping to the ground, he reached down and tried to grab the butt of his pistol. That was the last thing he knew before his world went black.

It was still dark when Jake woke up to a canteen of water being splashed on his face. He was lying on his back and somewhere, through the ringing in his ears, he could hear men laughing. Sputtering and coughing while trying to move his head from side to side to avoid the water, a wave of nausea and pain splintered his brain.

"Time to wake up, Mister," said a deep voice that sounded as if it were a long way off.

"Let me be the one to kill him, Bear," said another high pitched voice. "I ain't kilt nobody in nearly two months."

"We ain't goin' to kill him just yet, Shorty."

Slowly, Jake began to understand the words being spoken. "What … what do you want?" he asked in a groggy voice.

"Folks tell me you been ridin' 'round askin' lots of questions," said the deep voice. "And 'cause that's been a bother to them same folks, we've be hired to find out what you know and don't know."

"What're you talkin' 'bout?" asked Jake, racked with pain.

"Let me scalp him," said Shorty, gleefully, while pulling a skinning knife from a sheath on his belt. "That'll get him talkin'."

"Put that damn knife away," said Bear with disgust. "You'll get your chance to cut on him when I'm finished. Now then, mister, what do you know about some gent by the name of Langston?"

Jake was dumbfounded. He had heard that name only two days ago, and already someone was threatening to kill him. "Langston?" said Jake with a confused look on his face that he hoped was convincing. "Hell, I ain't never heard of anybody by that name."

"Well, somebody thinks otherwise," replied Bear with a grunt as the toe of his boot smashed into Jake's ribs, "and if it takes all night I aim to get what I come for."

"I swear," gasped Jake with renewed pain, "I ain't never heard of anybody named Langston."

"Damn it, Bear," said Ray with irritation in his voice. "I ain't gonna hang around here all night while you play with this gent. How 'bout we put his bare feet in the fire? I saw that done once and it didn't take no time 'fore the man told everything he knew."

"Yeah, and probably a bunch of lies too," replied Bear. "I'll bet a man bein' tortured like that'll say anything you want him to say to get you to stop, and that ain't what we're bein' paid for. Now you two fools go get our horses while I figure out how to get this gent talkin'."

As Ray and Shorty walked away grumbling, Bear stood next to Jake and said, "I'm gonna get what I come for, Tanner, one way or the other. Now, tell me what you know about Langston?"

"I told you. I don't know any Langston," said Jake as a cough racked his body.

Again Bear's boot slammed into Jake's ribs.

Coughing and rolling onto his side, Jake pulled his knees up to his chest to ward off further blows, and as he did he reached inside his left boot with his right hand and palmed the slim, eight inch knife hidden inside.

"You ain't very smart are you?" said Bear angrily as he leaned over Jake and grasped him by the front of his shirt, his face only inches from Jake's face.

"Ain't never said I was," Jake grunted in response. "But I'm smarter'n you," he continued, plunging the knife deep into Bear's throat.

Blood gushed from the slashing wound, and a gurgling noise was the only sound Bear made, as he rolled onto his back and tried to pull the knife from his throat.

"At least I'm smart enough to search a man's hat and boots," said Jake, staggering to his feet.

Suffering from severe chest pains and a deep gash on the back of his head, Jake stumbled to where Ray had tossed his pistol. As he fell to the ground and grasped the gun, Shorty walked into the light of the campfire with two horses. Seeing Bear rolling around on the ground covered with blood, Shorty drew his gun. Jake, although barely conscious and rocked with pain, was faster and Shorty fell to the ground, fatally wounded. Then, from deep within the shadows outside the fire light, Jake saw the flash of a gun shot and felt a bullet hit him in his left leg. Rolling to his right, Jake fired his pistol three times in the direction of the flash and heard a grunt of pain and a curse from Ray. The next sound he heard was a horse galloping away into the night.

"So, are you ready to tell me what happened?" asked Sheriff Blackford.

Jake was lying in bed in Erick's only hotel. A doctor was standing close by looking worried. Gazing around the room, Jake said, "How'd I get here?"

"Suppose you tell me," said the sheriff. "Two days ago you rode into town leadin' two horses with each of 'em carryin' a dead man tied over the saddle."

Jake didn't think the sheriff needed to know everything, so he said, "Can't rightly say I know a whole lot, Sheriff. I was camped a day's ride from here when two men approached my campfire after dark sayin' they was hungry. I let 'em come in close, and the next thing I know a third one come up behind me and I'm fightin' for my life. I killed the two tied on them horses, but the third one shot me in the leg and got away. Don't remember much else 'til I woke up here."

"What do you think they were after?" asked the sheriff.

"They never said," Jake lied. "But there ain't no doubt they meant to kill me. When can I get out of here?"

"The doc says you've got a bad gash on the back of your head, a couple of busted ribs, and that leg wound. Looks like you'll be stayin' with us a while. You ever seen these men before?"

"No."

"Well, the big one calls himself Bear, but his real name is Mike Flannery. I've got a wanted poster on him for train robbin'. The other one is a cowardly little weasel, who went by the name of Shorty. His real name is Melvin Haws. Story is that Haws liked usin' his skinning knife to cut people. Can you recall anything 'bout the third one?"

"Only that the others called him Ray. I never saw his face. But the really strange thing is that there was somethin' about his voice that made me think I knew him."

"He was probably just some drifter the other two picked up along the way," said the sheriff, "but I'll keep checkin' my wanted posters anyway. In the meantime, just relax and rest up some."

"Ain't got time for that," said Jake as he struggled to climb out of bed.

"Now hold on there, Marshal," said the doctor, laying a firm hand on Jake's chest. "You've got some mighty serious injuries and it's going to be a while before I can let you get up. Sheriff, if this man even tries to get up without my say-so I want you to chain him to this bed."

"You bet Doc," said the sheriff with a broad smile. "It'll be a pleasure."

For the next two weeks, as Jake recovered from his wounds, four thoughts kept running through his mind: *How did Bear know where to find me? How did he know my name? Who sent him and the others to kill me? And who is Colonel Langston?*

It seemed strange to be riding back into Lawton only a few weeks after leaving, long weeks of recovering from his wounds and thinking long and hard about the four questions swirling around in his mind. The only conclusion he came to during all that time, was that the answers to the first three questions were in Lawton. Lawton was the only place where Colonel Langston's name had been spoken, and the only thing that made sense was that someone besides Jake had heard it. Someone had then passed the information to the colonel, and the only quick way to do that was by telegraph.

"Afternoon, Sheriff," Jake said as he walked into Sheriff Butts' office.

"Well I'll be damned," replied the sheriff as he stood up behind his desk. "What brings you back to Lawton so soon?"

"I wish it were for a good reason, Sheriff, but it ain't."

Flopping back down in his chair, frowning, the sheriff said, "The last time you was here, Marshal, you solved a murder and we had a hangin'. Are you here now to solve our latest killin'?"

"Your *latest* killin'?" asked Jake, astonished.

"Well, not long after you left town, our telegraph office caught fire and burned to the ground in less than five minutes. After the fire was out, and we was scratchin' around in the ashes, we found old man Henderson burned to a crisp. At first I thought maybe he'd knocked over his oil lamp and the fire was an accident, but when I looked closer I could see that his head had been bashed in with what most likely was an axe. He was a nice old man, and didn't deserve to go out like that. Since then I've talked with most everybody in town, but nobody heard or saw anything."

"So you've got no idea who might have done it?" said Jake.

"No, and can't figure no reason for doin' it either."

"Did anybody suddenly leave town after the fire?" asked Jake.

"No, can't say I know of ... no ... no wait ... now wait a damn minute. It might be nothin', but I heard that the very next day the bartender at the White Owl Saloon didn't show up for work. And now that I think on it, I ain't seen him since then, neither."

"What's his name?" asked Jake with growing excitement.

"Ray Gibbons."

When Jake rode out of Lawton, he knew with certainty that Ray Gibbons had watched him enter the sheriff's office and then listened to his conversation with Tolman. He had then used the telegraph to send a message to Langston, and, in return, got an order to kill Jake, because he was getting too close to the truth. Old man Henderson was then killed to destroy any link that could lead back to the Colonel. So who is Ray Gibbons, he thought, other than a bartender and a collector of local information for a price? And when Gibbons heard Tolman speak Langston's name, how did he know not only the importance of that information, but how to get a message to Langston? The only plausible answers to the first three questions, was that Gibbon somehow knows Langston and is willing to commit murder and arson to protect Langston's secret.

CHAPTER 14

UPON HIS RETURN TO DODGE City from Lawton, Jake told Marshal Farnsworth about finding Tolman, his conviction for the murder of Pastor Roberts, and watching as Tolman was hanged. The marshal smiled and seemed pleased. Jake did not, however, tell him about planting Pastor Roberts' cross in Tolman's saddle bags. As far as Jake was concerned, the least said about that subject, the better. For reasons even he did not fully understand, he also did not tell the marshal about Tolman's reference to Colonel Langston.

Now, ten months after leaving Lawton, Jake was growing restless because in spite of his quiet search for information regarding Colonel Langston, it failed to materialize. As directed by the marshal, he had, among other things, successfully intervened in a land dispute resulting in an acceptable agreement by both sides, captured a cattle rustler (who had been poaching on several ranches), and threatened three men with jail or worse if they ever mistreated their wives again. Each morning he started his day by looking at all the newly-arrived wanted posters and reading local newspapers, searching for anything that might give him a clue to finding Langston, Jim O'Leary or

William Culver. He also became a frequent visitor to the Owens home, and was astonished when Emily told him she had accepted a part-time clerical position in Dodge City's largest mercantile store. Jake's immediate reaction was that she was not yet well enough to accept such a position. Later, though, amid Emily's tears and at Beth's urging, he relented with the understanding that, if Emily showed any indication of a relapse, the employment would be terminated.

The knock came softly, and Beth rushed from the parlor to the front door, pausing only long enough to look into the hallway mirror and fluff her hair once more. She was wearing her prettiest dress and her long blond hair hung down around her shoulders in ringlets.

"Good evening," said Beth, smiling radiantly as she opened the door.

Jake, standing at the doorstep dressed in his dark blue suit and holding his hat at his waist with both hands, was pleased with the look of surprise on Beth's face. "Guess you've never seen me dressed up like some dandy," he said.

"No ... I ... I don't believe I have," Beth replied. "And I must say, you look very handsome."

"Well, it's the only suit I've got," said Jake as he brushed at imagined dust on his coat sleeve, "but it's just as well 'cause I don't know what I'd do with another one."

Beth, her deep blue eyes twinkling with mischief, said, "One suit is all a man needs if he ever decides to take a lady walking, or maybe even dancing."

"Oh, I ain't never danced," said Jake, his face beginning to flush, "but I sure do like walkin'. Like when you and me was walkin' that time. You know, when I was tellin' you 'bout Emily not bein' my wife."

"Oh yes, I remember very well," said Beth, reaching out to grasp both of Jake's hands in hers, and pulling him gently through the doorway and into the house. "Father is out with some friends and Emily is resting upstairs," she continued, still holding his hands and walking backward toward the parlor. "When I told her you said you wanted to talk with me, we both assumed you meant just me. Is that really what you want?"

"Yes, I can talk with Emily later if need be."

"If need be?" said Beth with a look of concern. "Is something wrong?"

"No ... well ... not really, at least not right now. It's just that ... well ... I want to talk with you about a decision I'm going to have to make, a decision about Emily."

"You know I'll help however I can," said Beth, releasing his hands and turning toward the parlor. "Let's go in here where we can sit and talk."

Among other things, the Owens' ornate parlor included two large, overstuffed, light blue velvet sofas facing each other in front of a large fireplace. Between the sofas was a low, rectangular table with a small vase containing fresh flowers. Beth, obviously comfortable in her own home, quickly took a seat on one of the sofas. Jake, hesitant and unsure of where he should sit, sat down on the sofa opposite her.

Beth smiled as she patted a spot on the sofa next to her and said, "I promise I won't bite if you come and sit beside me."

"Well, I just figured ..."

"You *figured* it wouldn't be proper to come and sit beside me without my permission. Isn't that right?"

"Yeah," Jake replied with embarrassment. "I'm just a cowpoke callin' on a lady in a fine house."

"Why, Jake, I'm surprised at you. I thought by now you would know you are always welcome in my father's house, and that I think you are the finest man I've ever known."

"Well, I don't know why you'd think such a thing. I ain't got much money to speak of, no place to call home, and not much education. About the only thing I own is my horse and saddle."

"Do you really think those things matter to me, Jake? Do you think I can't see beyond those things and see the strong, kind, and caring man you are? Please, come and sit beside me."

Jake was momentarily confused. He knew Beth was grateful to him for saving her life, but she had more than repaid any such debt by taking Emily into her home and caring for her. She had always showed him affection, and seemed pleased to see him, but he had never imagined that she thought of him in the way she had just described. *Could it be,* he thought, *that she has feelings for me?* Gulping down his doubts, he did as she asked.

Turning sideways to face Jake as he sat down, Beth said, "Well now, what is it you want to talk with me about?"

After nervously clearing his throat, Jake also turned to face Beth and said, "Ah ... well ... there are a couple of things that have been on my mind lately. But first, how is Emily? I mean, is she still showin' signs of gettin' better by talkin' and not bein' afraid of her own shadow? Or has workin' at the general store ... well ... caused you any concern that she might be revertin' back to the way she was?"

"Oh, I'm not concerned at all," Beth replied. "Yes, she comes home a little tired, but she obviously enjoys the work, tells me she likes making a little money of her own, and seems very happy. But why are you asking? I thought you could see all this for yourself."

Again Jake hesitated, unsure how Beth would respond to what he wanted to say. Finally, trusting in her concern for Emily, he said, "Do you remember me tellin' you 'bout findin' Flack, the leader of the gang that killed my folks?"

"Yes, of course. You said you found him in Amarillo."

"Yeah, that's right. What I haven't told you, though, is that he has changed his name, owns a saloon, and is well regarded, which means he's no longer an outlaw. Meaning, if he doesn't make any mistakes, like killin' somebody outside the law, I will never be able to bring him to justice."

"Yes, I see what you mean. So what are you going to do?"

"Well, I'm not sure there's anything I can do, at least not right now. But suppose ... just suppose ... that Emily was to get well enough to testify in court. I know we've talked about this before, and at the time we both thought we could never allow such a thing, but that was before Emily started gettin' better. And ..."

"Oh my," interrupted Beth. "Are you now saying that, because you can't bring this man to justice any other way, you're willing to take a chance and ask Emily to live through her nightmare again? How could you, Jake? How could you ask her to do that?"

"No, no, wait," said Jake, holding up his hands in defense. "I'm only sayin' that *if* there came a time when Emily could testify, it just might be the *only* way to bring Flack to justice."

Beth sat quietly, obviously thinking about Jake's quandary. After a moment, she turned to face Jake and said in a soft voice, "I'm sorry I spoke sharply. I know you wouldn't do anything to hurt Emily, but I'm not sure she will ever be well enough to tell anyone what she saw that horrible day, or that she will ever want to."

"I know," Jake replied with a sigh, "and I'm only thinkin' of such a thing if there's no other way and Emily could somehow be able to do it. Even then, even if she could do it, it may not be enough. I mean, suppose we get Flack into court, and then Flack's lawyer finds out about Emily not bein' in her right mind all them years? A smart lawyer probably wouldn't have any trouble convincin' a jury she still ain't in her right mind and is makin' everything up."

"Yes, and that could be a crushing blow for Emily," said Beth. "Oh, Jake, I want so much for you to find a way to end all this, for your sake and for Emily's. But I know you can't until you keep your promise to your father. I understand, I truly do, but please know in your heart that no matter how long it takes, I will wait for you."

"You'll wait for me?" said Jake with a frown of confusion.

"Yes, for you, and for Emily of course. It is my hope that someday Emily will be able to have a life of her own, and then I will be waiting just for you."

Confused, but with a ray of hope in his heart, Jake said, "But … but what about a life of your own? Surely you've seen all the young men in town lookin' at you, and I know there's been more than a few who've come knockin' on your door. Yet I've never seen you out walkin' or dancin' with any of 'em. I've checked most of 'em out and they're all nice fellers with enough money to buy you a fine house and all."

"What do you mean, you've *'checked them all out?'*" said Beth, horrified.

"Well, I ... I never thought ... well ... that you'd mind," said Jake, stumbling over the words. "I just want the best for you, that's all."

"Well, let me tell you this, Mr. Tanner," said Beth, her voice rising. "In the future I'll let you know when I want someone *checked out.*" Then, the harshness in her voice faded and she began to laugh openly in a way that let Jake know she was only teasing.

Breathing a sigh of relief, he said, "Then you're not really angry with me?"

"No, of course not, silly. I'm flattered. But, just so you know, I am not interested in *any* of those young men. There is only one young man I am interested in, and that young man is you, Jake Tanner. And I don't care if you don't have any money, or a fine house, or own only your horse and saddle. And if you don't kiss me this very minute I'll ..."

And so he did, eagerly, with tender softness.

After the kiss, and several moments of embarrassed silence, Beth took Jake's hand in hers and said, "You said there were a couple of things you wanted to talk to me about. What was the other thing?"

Smiling, Jake said, "I wanted to ask you to take a walk with me and teach me how to dance."

Two weeks later Jake was registered at a St. Louis, Missouri, hotel. It was not the most exclusive hotel in St. Louis, but the rooms were clean and the dining room food had proven to be excellent. Jake had arrived by train the day before and had taken custody of a prisoner to be transported to Kansas City for trial. But because he arrived late in the day, and the train to Kansas City was not scheduled to leave for another two days, the St. Louis marshal had agreed to hold his prisoner until train time. With nothing else to do, Jake had taken a room at the hotel.

He was just finishing his evening meal when the hotel's uniformed bell captain entered the dining room and called out softly, "Message for Mr. William Culver, message for Mr. William Culver."

Jake's right hand, holding a fork with a bite-size piece of apple pie balanced on the end, froze in mid-air near his open mouth. Seconds passed as his hand remained frozen while his eyes searched the room to see who would respond to the bell captain's call.

On the far side of the room a man raised his hand without turning around. The bell captain approached the man, delivered the message by leaning down close to the man's ear, and departed. The man was sitting at a table with another man and a woman, both of whom appeared to be in their mid to late thirties. Also seated at the table were two young girls, who looked very much like the woman, and a boy who appeared to be a few years older than the girls. Everyone sitting at the table was well dressed in the latest fashion, and there seemed to be a feeling of warmth and happiness as they smiled and laughed together.

Jake's heart pounded as he contemplated the odds that this man was the same William Culver who took part in the murder of his parents. Lowering his hand slowly and placing the fork near the uneaten portion of apple pie, he could not help staring at the back of the man seated across the room.

The man was heavy-set and dressed in a light gray pinstriped suit. His black hair was neatly trimmed and, even from behind, Jake could see the man wore a full face beard. He was gesturing with his hands as if telling a story while his audience at the table laughed.

After a few minutes a waiter approached the table and presented a bill to the man. It was apparent the meal was over and the group was preparing to depart. Knowing he could not let this opportunity slip by without confirming that this was, or was not, the man he had been seeking all these years, Jake stood and walked across the room where the children at the table were already starting to stand.

"William Culver?" said Jake in a firm, ominous voice that was only loud enough for those in the immediate area to hear.

The man did not move, but all the other faces at the table looked at Jake with startled expressions.

Hesitating for only a moment, and without turning around, the man said with a hint of resignation, "Hello, Jake, I've been waiting for you."

Astonished by the man's reply, Jake said, "You … you've been waiting for me?"

"William, who is this young man?" said the other man as he grasped Culver's arm.

"It's nothing, nothing at all, John, just business. Will you please take Katherine and the children home? I'll be along shortly."

"But we were going to …."

Raising a hand to silence the man, Culver said, "Really, John, it's nothing to be concerned about. This gentleman and I have a business matter to discuss, something that will not wait for a better time."

"Are you sure?" said John with an anxious expression on his face. "He's wearing a pistol and a Federal Marshal's badge."

"Yes, yes, I'm sure. I'll be fine."

Jake remained standing behind Culver in continued astonishment as the man and woman began to escort the three children from the room, their glances in Jake's direction reflecting their uncertainty. John paused as he passed Culver and placed a hand on his shoulder. Leaning over, he looked into Jake's eyes with suspicion and whispered loud enough in Culver's ear for Jake to hear, "I'll wait up for you at home."

"Yes, of course," Culver replied with an attempt at joviality. "We'll have a nice glass of brandy together."

With quick, searching glances at Jake, the man and woman followed the children toward the dining room exit. Jake noticed the hint of fear in the man's eyes and tried to soften the sternness of his face with a tight lipped smile.

"Have they gone?" Culver asked evenly, continuing to face forward.

Turning his head to confirm their departure, Jake said, "Yes."

"Then please come and sit down," Culver said while gesturing to the chair opposite his.

Hesitating only a moment to collect himself, Jake walked around the table and sat down. Looking across the table at the man, Jake had the feeling that he knew him, not by sight, but by some other means. "You called me by my first name without even lookin' at me," said Jake harshly. "Have we met before?"

Leaning back in his chair, Culver looked at Jake in an appraising manner and said in a softer voice, "That badge on you're chest says you're a United States Federal Marshal."

Continuing to look Culver in the eye, Jake responded in a hard controlled voice, "Yeah, that's what it says. But you didn't answer my question."

"Are you going to arrest me?"

"Depends."

"Depends on what?"

"Depends on if you're the William Culver I'm lookin' for."

The man continued to look at Jake without apparent concern. "You don't recognize me, do you, Jake?"

"No. Should I?"

"No, I guess not. But, then again, I'm not the same man I was when you knew me."

"You keep calling me by my name and inferrin' that I should know you," said Jake, "but I can tell you straight out that I've never met anybody face to face named William Culver.

"Yes you have."

"No, I have not," hissed Jake as he leaned forward menacingly with narrow, angry eyes. "Because the William Culver I'm lookin' for is a murderer."

"Yes, I know."

"What! Just who the hell are you, mister?" said Jake, losing patience with the man.

"My name is William Culver, co-owner of the St. Louis Cattle Brokerage House, along with my brother whom you just met. I was known to you, Jake … as Billy, the gunfighter, who taught you how to shoot."

Jake gasped in audible astonishment, his eyes showing his surprise. "What the hell, where you …."

"Yeah," said Billy, leaning forward, his arms on the table. "I was with the others when they came to your family's farm, but I swear I didn't know they were going to kill anybody. I was just a dumb kid looking for excitement, and since then I've wished every day of my life that I'd never been part of it. But I was, and I can't change that."

Jake was stunned. It had never crossed his mind that the man whose life he saved many years ago was the same man he had sworn to kill. The same man who became his friend. Angry, Jake said through clenched teeth, "But you were still there; you were part of it!"

"Yes, you're right. I was there, and I was part of it. But after I met you, and saw the hurt in your heart and the hate in your eyes, I gave up that life and I've never looked back. You actually saved my life twice, Jake -- the first time by patching up my wounds, and the second time by healing my soul. Ever since then I've tried to live my life in a way that might, in some small way, make up for the loss I caused you and the families of other men I've killed. In fact, I asked my brother to name his son Billy as a constant reminder of what I once was and never want to be again."

Jake stared dumbfounded at Culver. Minutes passed as his mind tried to process the most improbable of circumstances. Finally, his anger cooling, he looked down at the top of the table and shook his head wearily from side to side. "I ... I don't know what to say. I've waited most of my life to find you and the others and make you pay for murdering my family. Now I find that a man I thought was my friend lied to me."

"No, I never did," said Billy. "You told me about your family being killed, and I never let on that I knew anything about it. When you told me about your promise to your father, well ... I decided to teach you how to use a gun because I knew you were going to need it to survive. I left that gun for you knowing that someday you might use it to kill me."

"Damn it, Billy, I ...."

"Yeah, I know. I've made a problem for you. But ...."

"No, wait! Hold on a minute," said Jake, sitting up straight with a startled expression on his face. "If you're the real William Culver, where's your red birthmark."

"What birthmark?"

"The birthmark I saw on the left side of your face when you were tendin' the horses. I saw it clear as day. But I didn't see it when I found you half dead, and I don't see it now."

"Oh, yeah, that. Well, what you saw wasn't a birthmark. What you saw was the beating Flack and the others gave me when I tried to stop them from hanging your father. By then they were so riled up, because they couldn't find what they were looking for, that I thought they were going to kill me. Sometimes I wish they had. Then, when they killed your mother ... well, I knew I was through with them, but getting away from that kind of life was harder than I thought. I discovered by accident, in a gunfight I didn't start, that I was a natural with a fast draw and one thing led to another. Then you came along."

Once again Jake was shaken by this new revelation, and in a strange way saddened that he had hated this man for so long for something he had tried to stop. "I ... I didn't know. I guess I owe you an apology, I mean, for tryin' to stop 'em."

"You don't owe me anything, Jake. It's like I said before, you saved my life and at the same time gave me a new one. You've seen my brother and his wife and children. Together we own a prosperous business and I'm trusted and respected by my associates. Next month I'm going to marry a wonderful woman and start a family of my own. What more could a man ask for in this life?"

"I can't think of a thing," Jake sighed.

Both men were quiet for a while as they contemplated all that had occurred during this unexpected meeting.

"Have you ever found out what they were looking for?" Billy asked.

"Not really. There's been talk about some tintypes and a Colonel Langston, but not much else."

"What about the others? Have you found any of them?"

Jake hesitated, mulling over his answer. He responded simply by saying, "Tom O'Leary was convicted of killin' a sheriff and the law hanged him. Tolman murdered a preacher and took over his church. I found the preacher's body and made sure Tolman was also hanged. I'm lookin' to do the same for Jim O'Leary and Flack."

Nodding his head in affirmation, Billy said sadly, "I can understand your needing to do that, Jake, and I can't blame you. But now the question is, what are you going to do about me?"

Looking Billy straight in the eyes, Jake said without hesitation, "Nothing. But in return I want you to do something for me."

"Anything, Jake, just ask."

"Okay, what I want is this. Should the time ever come when I get Flack or O'Leary in a court of law for killin' my folks, you'll come forward and testify."

Billy looked at Jake a long time before saying, "That's asking a lot, Jake. Something I don't think I can do."

"Why not? You just said you'd do anything."

"Because my life as a gunfighter would become public, and that would ruin my family's business, our reputation in the community, and everything I've tried to do to redeem myself. I know that sounds selfish, but I must think of what is best for my family. I can't do it, Jake. I'm sorry."

"It ain't like its goin' to happen tomorrow," said Jake with more than a bit of anger, "and it may never happen at all. All I'm askin' you to do now is think about it, because in the end your testifyin' in court might be the only way to bring these killers to justice. Just think about it."

"I can't do it, Jake. I'm sorry, but I just can't."

CHAPTER 15

September 1878

TWO AND A HALF MONTHS after Jake's return from St. Louis, Marshal Farnsworth was called to Washington D. C. to testify before Congress regarding his overall reduction of lawlessness in the mid-western states. It was while the marshal was gone that Jake read a newspaper article concerning a bank robbery in San Antonio, Texas. According to the article, the bank was held up by three men who killed two bank tellers and escaped with over eight thousand dollars. As the men rode out of town, spraying bullets to discourage anyone from trying to stop them, they also killed a woman and the child in her arms. The article ended by saying that one of the bank robbers was identified as Jim O'Leary, and that a one-thousand-dollar reward was being offered for him and five hundred dollars for each of the other two men, dead or alive. Knowing the Mexican border was close at hand, Jake remembered Tom O'Leary telling him about a Mexican bandit who harbored American outlaws at a place called El Fortaliza.

Jake was especially careful as he supervised the unloading of his two horses from the train in San Antonio. After caring for the animals during their long train ride, now was not the time to become negligent and allow them to be injured. Considering the distance from Dodge City to the Mexican border and beyond, Jake had decided to expedite his arrival in San Antonio by traveling by train and using his own horses instead of buying horses of an unknown quality at his destination. His primary concern was that O'Leary might have already left El Fortaleza, or that he had never been there in the first place.

At sunrise the following day, Jake left San Antonio and rode southwest in the direction of Del Rico, a small Texas settlement along the Rio Grande River and the Mexican boarder. From San Antonio's sheriff, he learned that the distance from San Antonio to Del Rico was about a hundred and fifty miles, along a trail that included a number of other small settlements. The sheriff did not know how far it was from Del Rico to El Fortaliza, but had heard it was a hard three days ride over hot, barren, and sparsely-populated country. He also said that he had heard stories about El Fortaliza and a Mexican bandit named Bustamente, and that no lawman who had gone there had ever returned. Seeing that his words of caution had not slackened Jake's determination, the sheriff gave him three sets of hand and leg irons and wished him luck.

The days from San Antonio to Del Rico passed slowly. Although he was anxious to cross the Rio Grande into Mexico, Jake knew it was foolish to push the horses faster than prudence dictated. As the miles passed, he continued to search his mind for the key that would open the door to El Fortaliza and the capture of O'Leary. Idea after idea was evaluated and eventually rejected, primarily due to a lack of knowledge about El Fortaliza and the number of outlaws hiding there. The only idea that seemed to have merit involved a trade in American dollars. This scheme, however, generated its own set of questions, like how many dollars, how he would get the money, how much O'Leary was paying the bandits, and whether the bandits would accept a higher amount to hand O'Leary over. And if the bandits did accept a higher amount, how could the money be exchanged without the bandits trying to kill him and just steal the money? Jake knew it was stupid to carry a large number of American dollars into the bandit's hideout. Yet, if a trade agreement was made, the bandits would need their own assurances that they would be paid. It was only after mulling over these questions many times that answers finally started to revealed themselves.

Jake had no difficulty sending a message to Dodge City from the Del Rico's telegraph office. As expected, it took less than a day to receive an answer. After a meeting with the owner of Del Rico's bank and the town's sheriff, Jake crossed the Rio Grande into Mexico. He knew his plan was risky and that O'Leary would probably not give up without a fight.

From the Rio Grande southward, Jake camped each night without a fire and slept on the ground a short distance away from his two tethered horses. While he trusted his horse's sense of smell and danger to provide an alert system, he did not want the horses to give away his position in the event of an ambush. During the day he moved steadily but cautiously, avoiding contact with local inhabitants who might report his presence to other bandits in the area. Several times he skirted small villages at a distance and used his spyglass to scout the barren, open land ahead.

Each day a brilliant, unrelenting sun rose and fell in a cloudless, blue sky. During the heat of the day the extreme temperature sucked the moisture from his body and blistered his lips. As expected, he found only traces of stagnant, polluted water in the dried-up creeks he crossed. The only drinkable water was that which he carried, and he horded it like a miser with his gold. He was especially careful to avoid skyline ridges and the crests of mountains, where his silhouette could be seen easily. To avoid leaving a trail, he kept to hard, rocky ground whenever possible.

On the fourth day, rounding a small hill, Jake saw in the distance a structure located along the shore line of a slow-flowing stream, struggling to survive in a dry river bed. Dismounting, he hid the horses in a grove of mesquite trees and climbed to the top of the hill, where he lay on his belly and took out his spyglass. Through the glass he saw a square, fort-like structure surrounding a village of adobe buildings with dusty, rose-colored tile roofs. Jake now understood why the village was called El Fortaliza, the Spanish words for 'The Fortress.' Guarding the entrance to the fort were two men, each wearing an assortment of ragged, cowboy-type clothing, sombreros, and carrying rifles.

In the center of the village was a plaza and a decorative well, from which an old woman and a child were bringing up buckets of water. Facing the plaza and the entrance to the fort was a church with a cross mounted on top of its rounded bell tower. About two hundred yards from the fort, and on the same side of the steam as the fortress, were three hills of various heights, all sparsely covered with sagebrush.

The following day, two hours before sunrise, Jake rode to the back side of the highest hill near the fort and climbed to the top. There, lying on his stomach amid the sagebrush, he peered again through his spyglass. At this height, he could see almost everything that went on within the walled structure. Soon, after the sun started its climb into the clear morning sky, the men guarding the entrance to the fort were relieved by two other men. At the same time, a movement at the rear of the fort caught his attention. Looking closely, he observed two more guards being relieved at a gated rear entrance that he had not noticed before.

As the village began to awaken, Jake saw a white man stagger drunkenly from a cantina on the far side of the plaza. He was barefoot, bare chested, and wore only a pair of faded blue pants. Upon reaching the well, he pulled up a bucket of water, lifted it high over his head, and turned it upside down, drenching himself from head to toe. After shaking his head vigorously from side to side, spraying the air with shimmering water droplets, he looked back toward the cantina as two more white men staggered out, cursing and laughing.

Moments later, a young woman crawled out from the cantina on her hands and knees while dragging a pistol in the dust. Seeing the man standing near the well, she stood up with wavering difficulty and took several staggering steps toward him. Shading her eyes from the bright sun with her left hand, she screamed something at the man in Spanish and tried to pull back the hammer to fire the weapon. The man, seeing the pistol pointed in his direction, ran to the woman, twisted the pistol from her hand, and drove his fist into her belly. As the girl doubled over and gasped for air, he savagely smashed the pistol down on the back of her head, dropping her face-down on the ground where she lay motionless. Cocking the pistol, the man stood over the girl and aimed it at the back of her bloody head.

At the same instant a shot rang out, and the man staggered backward with a look of bewilderment as blood spurted from a hole in his chest. Falling slowly to his knees, the man gamely attempted to fire the pistol in the direction of his assailant, but before he could another bullet slammed into his chest. The last bullet tumbled him over backward and onto the flat of his back, where he laid completely still.

Startled, Jake continued watching as a bareheaded man wearing knee-high black boots, black pants, and a puffy white shirt came into view from a building opposite the cantina. With a silent flicking motion of his still smoking pistol toward the cantina, the other two men retreated quickly inside. Holstering his pistol, the man hurried to the side of the young girl lying in the dirt. Dropping to his knees, he gently rolled her over on her back and spoke to her, as if pleading for her to awaken. Receiving no reply, he lifted her up in his arms and carried her limp body across the plaza and into a building, from which he had apparently come.

Slowly the people of the village resumed their normal activities, ignoring the body lying near the fountain. A few hours later two men wearing tattered white shirts and pants, sandals, and sombreros, came and lifted the dead man up by his arms and legs and tossed him face-down over the back of a donkey. The men and the donkey then left the village through the rear entrance and walked out of sight behind one of the low hills about a half mile away. A short time later, when the men and the donkey re-entered the village through the rear entrance, the donkey's back was now bare. Considering the short time the men were gone, Jake assumed the dead man was simply dumped on the open desert for scavengers.

During the following two days, Jake continued watching the village, but only occasionally saw the other two white men he had seen the day of the shooting. The guards at the front and rear entrances to the village were changed about every four hours, and Jake counted a total of twelve different bandits, including the man who had saved the life of the young girl. Because this man never stood guard duty, Jake assumed he was the bandit leader, Pedro Bustamente. Each night Jake retreated to the grove of mesquite trees to eat and sleep without a fire. Although he yearned for a steaming cup of coffee, and was tired of eating cold beef jerky and rock-hard biscuits, he knew better than to risk building a fire. While the fire itself could be hidden from view, the smell of smoke from a mesquite fire could be detected down-wind miles away.

At mid-afternoon on the third day, Jake left his hiding place and began riding a wide circular route around the fort. Soon after crossing the dry river bed, and its shallow stream a half mile east of the fort, he found the body of the man Bustamente killed. The coyotes had left little meat on the fast-whitening bones, and only the man's face, left lying face down on the sandy ground, had so far escaped ravishment. After digging a hole and burying the man's remains, he placed as many rocks as he could find over the grave and continued onward until he completed the circle south of the fort. He was now in a position to cross the river bed only slightly ahead of the front entrance of the fort. At this point he turned north and again crossed the stream. His purpose in taking this circular route was to add to his knowledge about the fort and cause confusion about his own camp's whereabouts. Exiting the stream, he rode onward until he stopped on the open plain about a hundred yards from of the fort's front entrance.

The guards at the fort's entrance saw him immediately and appeared to call out to someone inside the village. While he waited to see the bandit's response to his appearance, Jake took out his tobacco makings, rolled a cigarette with slightly trembling fingers, and touched a burning match to the end of the paper. He also removed his deputy marshal badge from a vest pocket and pinned it on the lapel of his vest. He knew that within the next few minutes his plan would either succeed or he would be dead.

Moments later, two men spurred their horses to a gallop as they rode out to meet him. Stopping in a cloud of dust only a few yards away, one of the men challenged him in broken English, saying "What you want, damn gringo?"

"I'm United States Federal Marshal Jake Tanner and I've come to talk with Senor Bustamente," said Jake as he flipped the remains of his cigarette on the ground in front of the bandits. He knew he could not appear to be intimidated by these men.

"He no talk with stinking gringo. I kill you now," said the man with a sneer as he reached for his gun.

Without hesitation Jake drew his pistol and shot the man in the throat. As he watched the man fall from his now snorting and bucking horse, Jake pointed his pistol at the other man, who was trying to control his own startled mount. With frightened eyes the man turned his horse and raced back to the fort. Soon a man Jake assumed to be Bustamente rode out from the fort's entrance. He did not hurry his horse, a shiny black stallion, and gave the appearance of being unconcerned with Jake's arrival. He was dressed as before, except he now wore a black sombrero trimmed with silver trinkets. Jake was relived to see that the man was too proud to be thought a coward and had come alone.

Like the men before him, Bustamente stopped his horse a few yards from Jake and sat quietly in his saddle while staring at the dead bandit lying on the ground. The dead man's horse stood nearby pawing the ground.

Shifting his eyes from the dead man to Jake, the bandit said, "Why did you kill this man, Marshal Tanner?"

To Jake's surprise the bandit appeared to be about his own age and spoke very good English. He was clean shaven, well groomed, and stared unafraid at Jake with eyes like lumps of coal. Jake was also surprised the bandit knew his name.

After a moment's hesitation, Jake said, "You speak English well, Senor Bustamente, and you are not an old man as I was told."

"Si," said the bandit. "I learned your language as a child from Spanish missionaries, and the old man you speak of was my father, Pedro. He was captured by the Mexican Army and hanged two years ago. My name is Carlos. And you, Marshal Tanner, have not said why you killed this man."

"He said he was going to kill me and started to draw his pistol," answered Jake with simplicity. "As you can see, his pistol is on the ground near his hand."

"Si, I was told you are very fast. He was foolish, yes?"

"Very foolish," replied Jake, nodding his head in agreement. "I've come a long way to talk with you, Senor, and then I am greeted by a man who tries to kill me. What else could I do?"

"Si, you were right to kill him. He was the stupid bastard of a whore. I should have killed him myself a long time ago."

"I don't want to kill any more of your men," said Jake.

"That is most wise," said Bustamente, nodding and smiling, "but I have many men, and losing a few makes no difference."

"I reckon you could be right," replied Jake. "But by my count there are now only eleven of you."

"Hum," said the bandit. "You have been watching us."

"Of course. Do you not watch both your friends and enemies to determine their strengths and weaknesses?"

"Si ... that is the way of a wise man. But wise or not, Marshal Tanner, you are either a very brave or a very stupid man. Do you think that you can come here and kill all of us? And for what purpose?"

"For the American outlaws you're protecting."

"I am protecting no American outlaws," said the bandit easily with outspread arms and a grin that betrayed his words. "Why would you think such a thing?"

"Because I've seen them through my spyglass," said Jake, relieved that the men he saw were Americans. "I saw you kill one of them."

With sudden, smoldering anger in his eyes, the bandit sat upright abruptly and said, "You mean the gringo pig that slipped into my house while we slept, stole my grand-daughter, and raped her. Yes I killed him, and I'll kill the rest of them if they so much as get in my way."

"You were right to kill him," said Jake approvingly. "Did he kill the girl?"

"She is near death!" the bandit continued heatedly. "Her mother cries and wails. I think she will die soon."

"Most unfortunate," said Jake.

"Si, and I have only myself to blame. I gave your outlaws three old whores but they wanted young women. I have no young whores; they have all run off to Mexico City where they can make more money."

"Ah ... yes, the problem of being a bandit leader, I suppose," said Jake with false sympathy.

Oh, no, *Marshal*, I am not a bandit like my father, killing and stealing from gringos and Mexican peasants. I only provide a place for outlaws to hide and rest. They have much money to pay for my protection."

"Do you have many outlaws staying in your village?"

"No, only two now. Why, are these men important to you?"

Breathing easier now that he knew the village was not infested with outlaws, Jake asked, "Was the one you killed named O'Leary?"

"No. His name was Banyon."

"Is O'Leary one of the other two outlaws?"

"Si. He is the one with the beard and almost always wears a red shirt and brown vest. Carruth is the other one, a skinny, unwashed pig who boasts about all the men he's killed. But, again, why do you ask?"

"O'Leary and the others robbed a bank in San Antonio and killed four people, includin' a woman and the child in her arms. I'm here to take 'em back to Texas to hang."

"You, alone, are here to take them from me?" said the bandit with a small laugh.

"Yes."

"But you can't expect me to just let you have them," said Bustamante as his laughter changed to indignation. "They have paid for my protection."

"Yes, and how much did they pay you?" asked Jake, taking the first step in his plan.

"The price for my protection for one month is two hundred American dollars for each gringo."

"And you already have their money?"

"Si, of course."

Jake paused for a moment while pretending to be in deep thought. "Only two hundred dollars?" he finally said. "That hardly seems worth the trouble they've brought to your village. How would you like to have a thousand more American dollars?"

"A thousand more!" exclaimed Bustamente with a shrewd look in his eyes. "Do you have a thousand American dollars in your saddle bags, Marshal?"

"Do you think I'd really do something that stupid said Jake with a small laugh.

"No, no, of course not," replied Bustamente smiling. "I was only making a joke. Come ...come to my village and we will talk about your thousand American dollars."

"Thanks, but I prefer to talk here," Jake replied."

"Talk here? Ah yes, it is good that you are a cautious man, Marshal. Well then, yes, we talk here. And what is it I must do to earn your thousand American dollars?"

"Give me the two American outlaws."

"And now you are making a joke, yes?"

"No, no joke," said Jake with a serious face.

"That is impossible," sighed Bustamente. "If I'm foolish enough to give these men to you, even for a thousand American dollars, then other outlaws will not come and pay for my protection. The land here is no good, and the river gets dryer each year. Without American outlaws, my people must leave this place or die."

"No, I think you're wrong, Senor Bustamente. Think about it this way. American outlaws always need a place like El Fortaliza to hide and feel safe, but if other outlaws know that you sold these men to me for a thousand dollars, how much more do you think they'll pay. Perhaps instead of two hundred dollars you can demand … say … five hundred dollars … or maybe even a thousand American dollars. The men you are now protecting stole much more than a thousand dollars from the bank in San Antonio, yet each one paid you only two hundred dollars. I think your protection comes very cheap and you can do much better."

"Si," said Bustamente with a thoughtful expression about his eyes. I see some wisdom in what you're saying. But … you must understand that I have taken money from these men and therefore have a duty to protect them."

"And what does your duty say I must do to convince you otherwise?"

For several minutes Bustamente sat quietly in his saddle while contemplating Jake's question. Then, with a smile on his lips, he said, "I think you must come and take them by force, if you can."

"Yes, and when I come for them, what will you and your men be doing?"

"We will be protecting them, of course, but often we hear very little of what goes on in the village, especially at night when we are sleeping."

"Ah … I see," said Jake. "You, too, are a wise man that sees the good that comes from takin' money from outlaws and then selling them to someone who will pay you even more."

"Yes, a very profitable concept I must agree. But now ... about the one-thousand American dollars. Since you say you do not have the money in your saddle bags, how will I be paid if you are successful in capturing or killing these men?"

Smiling, Jake said, "You will have your money when we reach the Rio Grande at Del Rico."

"We!" said Bustamente with an incredulous look on his face. "What do you mean, 'we'?"

"I mean you and three of your men will come with me and my prisoners to the Rio Grande, where you will wait on the Mexican side of the river with my prisoners. I will cross the Rio Grande, get the money, and return with three men of my own and pay you."

Laughing, Bustamente said, "Do I really look that stupid, Marshal?" Then, turning serious, he continued, "To Texans I am a bandit with a price on my head, and being so close to the border would make it easy for you and your men to capture or kill me for the reward. I think this is a trick -- our talk is over."

"No, wait," said Jake as Bustamente started to turn his horse around. "I assure you, this is not a trick, but if you have a better plan, tell me."

Slowly turning his horse back toward Jake, Bustamente hesitated for several minutes before saying in a cautious tone, "If it were just me and you, the American outlaws, and the money in the middle of the Rio Grande, with our men on each side of the river watching with rifles for a trick, perhaps a trade could be made."

"I think your plan is a good one that I am willing to accept," said Jake.

"Good, good, then it is done. But I must warn you, Marshal, when you come to take these men from me, you must not alert my guards until after you have killed or captured them. If you are successful, my guards will not interfere with you. But if you are not, my guards will shoot to kill and throw your body to the coyotes, just like Banyon. Agreed?"

"Agreed," said Jake.

"Just one more thing," said Bustamente. "O'Leary and Carruth know you killed one of my men. They will want to know who you are and why you are here. What should I tell them?"

"Tell them I've come to take them back to San Antonio to hang."

"So … you wish to make them … afraid, yes?"

"No, I want them to laugh and think they can kill me. I want them to be waiting for me when I come for them."

"And when will that be?"

"Who can say?" Jake replied with a shrug of his shoulders. "Maybe today or tomorrow, or perhaps in four days, maybe a week or two. Tell them that when I'm ready, I will come."

"Ah, I'm glad I'm not your enemy, Marshal. You have a clever mind to go along with your fast gun. Now I must return to my village, but I will be watching to see how you try to capture these men, especially when they know you are coming for them."

For the next three days Jake watched everything that went on within the fort that he could see from his hill-top hideout. Each day before dawn, he saw Carruth remove a chair from inside the cantina and sit all day in the shade near the door of the building. He was dressed in cowboy attire that included a black vest over a dingy white shirt. On his head was a flat-brimmed black hat. It was only during the early light of dawn on the forth day that he saw O'Leary carrying a rifle and sneaking into the village church through a rear door. A few minutes later he was not surprised when O'Leary climbed through a hatch on the flat roof and crawled on his belly to a short wall along the edge of the roof facing the cantina. Carefully sliding the barrel of the rifle through one of the small drainage openings, he adjusted his prone position in order to point the rifle at the cantina where Carruth was sitting. Each day thereafter the outlaws repeated the setting of their ambush. After nightfall both men returned to the cantina.

As the days passed, Jake could see the men squirming in the blistering heat and becoming more lax as the waiting continued. Jake, however, was cool and comfortable under a small shade structure he had constructed and camouflaged with uprooted sagebrush.

Each day, watching the outlaws set their trap, Jake also looked for weaknesses in the fort's construction that might allow him unseen access. It didn't take long for him to see that about two feet below the top of the high walls surrounding the village were numerous holes about one foot in diameter. And located about five feet below the holes on the inside of the walls, were shooting platforms where defenders could stand and shoot without exposing themselves.

Four hours before dawn on the twelfth day, as the moon began to sink below the horizon, Jake hurried to the base of the wall, twirled his rope high over his head, and heaved it up and over the wall. It wasn't until his fourth throw that the rope snagged on what he hoped was part of a shooting platform. After testing the rope with his full weight, he scaled the wall, slipped over the top on his belly, and dropped silently to the shooting platform. Hearing no evidence of discovery, he climbed down a nearby ladder to the ground.

Moving silently over the soft earth inside the perimeter of the fort, he approached the rear gate. The opening from one side of the gate to the other was about twenty-five feet of open ground. Peering into the darkness, Jake waited for the guards to repeat a pattern of behavior that he had observed from his hiding place night after night, the occasional lighting of two cigarettes from a single match. Because when that happened he knew the guards would experience night blindness long enough for him to move unobserved from one side of the gate to the other.

Minutes dragged by as Jake waited nervously to hear the faint scraping sound of a match being lit. Time was running out, and if the men didn't light a match soon, he would have to leave the fort the same way he came in and try again another night. Suddenly, a flickering flame erupted, revealing the faces of the guards as they lit their cigarettes. Seconds later, when the flame died, Jake hurried across the open space and continued moving through the village until he was behind the church. Entering the church through the same back door used by O'Leary, he climbed the spiral staircase leading to the hatch through the roof. Crouching over to avoid being silhouetted as he stepped through the hatch and onto the roof, Jake closed the hatch softly and knelt behind its hinged edge to wait.

The sun was just minutes from peeking over the horizon when O'Leary lifted the hatch and started to climb through, only to be hit on the back of the head and falling unconscious half-in and half-out of the opening. With little effort Jake pulled O'Leary's limp body up and onto the roof, hog-tied his hands and feet together behind his back with strips of rawhide, and gagged him with his own neckerchief. Then, with O'Leary's rifle and hat in hand, he crawled on his belly to the edge of the roof, poked the barrel of the rifle through the opening, and pointed it in the direction of the cantina. To complete his deception, he placed O'Leary's hat over the stock of the rifle in such a way as to make it appear O'Leary was sighting down the barrel of the rifle.

To avoid being seen by Carruth as he sat in front of the cantina, Jake crawled back to the hatch, climbed down the stairs, and left the church through the back door. Because the church was located between him and the cantina, he had no trouble moving around behind several other adobe buildings until he was behind the cantina.

Pausing for a moment to catch his breath, he looked among the various stones lying on the ground around him until he found the one he wanted and picked it up. Hefting the round, fist-sized stone to feel its weight, he crept along the side of the cantina until he reached the front and peeked around the corner. Like all the days before, Carruth was sitting on a chair in front of the building like bait on a hook. Stepping back from the corner and away from the building, Jake tossed the stone high over the cantina and toward the fort's entrance. The stone landed with a loud thump as dust billowed into the air. Startled, Carruth jumped to his feet and took several steps toward the front gate while reaching for his pistol.

With the outlaw's back to him, Jake drew his pistol, stepped around the corner of the building, and yelled in a loud, firm voice, "Hold it right there, Carruth."

Carruth froze like a statue, and a full half minute passed until he said in an easy voice, "That you, Marshal?"

"That's right," replied Jake in an equally calm voice.

"You ain't goin' to shoot me in the back are you?"

"I ain't like you, Carruth. Now real easy like, raise your right hand high over your head and unbuckle your gunbelt with your left hand."

"Sure, Marshal, anything you say."

As Carruth's gunbelt fell to the ground, Jake said, "Now kick it away, raise your left hand over your head, and turn around slow."

Slowly, Carruth did as he was told and turned around. "You enjoyin' yourself, Marshal?" he said with a half-smile.

"Ain't nothin' to enjoy," Jake replied. "At least not 'til we get to San Antonio and I see you hanged."

With a broad smile on his face, Carruth glanced up at the roof of the church and said, "Yeah, I bet you'd enjoy that, Marshal. But it ain't goin' to happen 'cause you're 'bout to die."

"Carruth," said Jake with a smile of his own, "you're almost as dumb as you look. The only thing I'm 'bout to die from is laughing at you two jackasses tryin' set up a really stupid ambush."

The look of confidence faded from Carruth's face as he again looked up at the roof of the church and shouted, "Damn it, O'Leary, shoot the bastard."

With a quick look at the church himself, and then back at Carruth, Jake said, "If you're lookin' for O'Leary to do your killin', you'd best know he's got a lump on his head and is a might tied up."

"Come on, O'Leary!" Carruth shouted again in a panicked voice as he staggered backward a step. "Kill him."

"It's just me and you, Carruth. You can live a few more days or die right here. What'll it be?"

With a look of desperation, and obviously trying to bluff, Carruth lowered his hands to his sides and said in a bold, seething voice, "You see my shooter layin' there, Marshal? It's got fourteen notches on it, one for every man I've killed. There ain't no man alive faster on the draw than me."

"And how many of them notches is for the men you shot in the back and the women and children you killed?" asked Jake.

"You shut your filthy mouth, Marshal, or I'll shut it for you!" screamed Carruth.

"Yeah, yeah, yeah, you're a real killer," said Jake as he walked up to Carruth, holstered his pistol, and smashed him full in the face with his right fist.

Carruth fell backward on the ground as blood gushed from his nose. "You bastard," he wailed, "you busted my nose."

"Yeah, and if you think that hurts," said Jake with disgust, "you're gonna feel a whole lot worse when you're standin' over the hangman's trap door with a black bag over your head and a rope around your neck. Now get up and stop that belly-wallowin' 'cause I ain't got time to stand here jawin' with some blow-hard coward."

Carruth, still trying to stem the flow of blood from his nose, struggled to stand up as a loud hand-clapping sound came from across the plaza.

"Bravo, Marshal Tanner," said Bustamente as he walked toward the two men. "I have waited many days for you to appear, and even I thought you had given up trying to find a way inside my walls.

"I reckon these two geniuses thought I'd just ride into their little trap and wait to get shot," said Jake. "Ain't no accountin' for stupidity."

"And that goes for me as well," said Bustamente.

"What?" asked Jake with a quizzed look on his face.

"You evidently found a weakness in my walls that an enemy could find just as easily. Come, eat and drink with me and tell me how you evaded my guards."

By mid-morning Jake had Carruth and a still groggy O'Leary bound with hand irons and mounted on their horses. He had also removed the bridles from the outlaw's horses and tethered them together in a single line by a length of rope. Banyon's saddled but riderless horse was the last in the long line.

Unlike his brother, Jim O'Leary was almost as tall as Jake and most women would likely consider him handsome, were it not for the brooding meanness in his dark brown eyes. Although his clothes were not tattered and filthy like Carruth's, the smell surrounding his person gave evidence of his abhorrence to bathing. With his dusty, sweat-stained hat placed carefully over his gashed and bleeding head, O'Leary sat slumped in his saddle like a beaten dog.

Bustamente and three of his men joined Jake and his string of horses as they departed the village through the fort's front entrance. Once outside the fort, Bustamente turned north toward the Rio Grande while Jake continued straight ahead.

"Where you going, Marshal?" called Bustamente as he turned toward Jake and spurred his horse to catch up.

"Can't leave without my pack horse and Banyon," said Jake as he continued forward toward a grove of mesquite trees in the distance near the base of a hill.

"Banyon?" said Bustamente, frowning. "But the coyotes have already had their fill of him."

"Yeah, they took a bite or two for sure," replied Jake. "But there's enough left to take back to Texas, providing you can stand the smell."

"Marshal, you continue to surprise me."

"Oh ... why's that?"

"Your persistence, for one thing. I've never known anyone to steal a dead man from scavengers just so he could take it back to Texas, stink and all. Why would you do such a thing?"

"So folks in San Antonio will know they ain't goin' to be bothered any more by him and these other two jackals," replied Jake. "Not to mention the reward money bein' offered for all three of 'em."

"You Americans are loco," said Bustamente with humor, "but if you can stand the stink of a rotting body in the hot sun, then me and my men will do the same."

"Oh, it ain't Banyon's body that's stinkin'," said Jake. "Just part of his head and some bones the coyotes didn't run off with 'fore I buried him for a while."

Bustamente was only partially right. During the days that followed, Bustamente's men refused to come any closer than a quarter mile upwind from the decaying smell. Whenever possible, even Jake and Bustamente tried to do the same. O'Leary and Carruth complained constantly about the smell, but were ignored.

When camp was made the first night, Jake took one pair of hand irons and the length of chain between them from a saddle bag and grudgingly led Banyon's horse downwind to a stand of mesquite trees. Selecting a tall tree with a thick trunk, he used the rope from Banyon's saddle to tie the sack-blanket containing Banyon's remains high among the tree's branches. Satisfied that the sack was not within reach of the scavengers he'd seen during the day, he wrapped the chain around the tree and locked the hand irons together, forming a locked loop around the base of the tree.

Later, after serving O'Leary and Carruth a meal of cold beans and warm water, Jake and Bustamente's three men led the two outlaws to the tree where Jake had tied Banyon's sack-blanket. After much protesting about the smell, the men were forced to sit on the ground under the tree while Jake removed one of each man's leg iron and locked it to the chain wrapped around the base of the tree.

"What the hell are you doin', Tanner?" said O'Leary with a worried look. "That stinkin' smell is gonna draw every varmint from here to the border."

"You're right," Jake replied. "And that's why I'm leavin' you baby killers here to keep 'em away."

"You're out of your mind," screamed Carruth. "They'll come in packs and tear us apart in seconds."

"Yeah, they might do that," said Jake, as he turned and walked to another tree where he retrieved two stout, six-foot-long tree limbs he had cut and trimmed earlier. "So you boys better make good use of these."

That night, and each night thereafter, Jake and the others could periodically hear screaming curses and the thump of sticks striking intruders who protested with yelps and barks. Meanwhile, Jake and Bustamente shared the same campfire and enjoyed the same meal of warm beans, jerky, corn tortillas, and coffee. Cautious and reserved at first, as each man sought to appraise the character and caliber of the other, they soon felt secure enough to communicate comfortably.

"You're a hard man, Marshal," said Bustamente on their second night, after Jake returned to the campfire with Bustamente's three men.

"Cold-blooded killers deserve every cruelty that can be heaped on 'em," declared Jake defensively.

"I'm not judging you, Marshal, but it appears you have a hate for these men that's beyond that of an ordinary lawman. Do you have a personal grudge against these outlaws."

"More'n a grudge," said Jake in a calmer voice. "But only for O'Leary. I don't give a damn 'bout Carruth."

"You want to tell me why?"

"Sometime, maybe."

"Then perhaps you can tell me why you decided to capture these men alive rather than just killing them."

"Because neither one of 'em gave me a reason to make that choice," replied Jake. "My job as a federal marshal is to bring 'em 'fore a judge and let the law decide if they're gonna live or die."

In late afternoon of the fourth day, Jake and the others stopped and made camp a quarter mile from the Mexican side of the Rio Grande River. The following morning Jake rode across the river into the town of Del Rico, where he went first to the sheriff's office and then to the town's bank. Within a half hour he met the sheriff and his two deputies at the edge of the Rio Grande. Signaling Bustamente on the opposite shore, Jake rode into the wide, shallow river alone and stopped in mid-stream. Bustamente and the three horses carrying O'Leary, Carruth, and Banyon's remains waded out through the muddy water and stopped a few feet in front of Jake.

"Is the money in those saddle bags on your shoulder?" Bustamente asked.

"As we agreed," Jake replied as he stripped the bags off his shoulder with his right hand and held them out to Bustamente.

Bustamente, seeing that Jake was holding out the saddle bags with his right hand, said with a smile, "If you had offered me the money with your left hand I would have been tempted to kill you, Marshal."

"I thought you might think that," said Jake, "so which hand will you use to give me the rope holding my prisoners' horses?"

"Ah … we … you and I … are amigos after all this time, yes?" said Bustamente as he handed the end of the rope to Jake using his right hand while taking the saddle bags with his left hand.

"Yeah, reckon we are," replied Jake.

"And there is no need for me to see if the money is in these bags is there?"

"You're welcome to look, Carlos. I have given you my word."

Looking deep into Jake's eyes, Bustamente replied solemnly, "One does not doubt the word of an amigo, Jake. I have no reason to look in the bags."

"Perhaps we'll meet again, my friend," said Jake.

"I also wish it to be so, Marshal." And without another word, Bustamente turned his horse and splashed through the water to the far shore. Upon reaching dry ground he turned to face Jake, raised his open right hand in salute, and then raced off into the desert in a cloud of billowing brown dust.

CHAPTER 16

"THAT SEEMED TO GO WELL," said Del Rico's sheriff as Jake's horse and the others climbed up the gentle slope of the Rio Grande on the Texas side of the border.

"Couldn't agree more, Sheriff," said Jake, with a half-smile as the sheriff turned his horse around and rode beside Jake toward the center of the town. "Any objection if I use your jail for my prisoners?"

"Consider it yours. How long you plan on bein' in town?"

"Figure I'll stay the night and head out by sun up. You got anybody 'round that takes pictures?"

"Ben Thornberry is the owner of our weekly paper, and he has a camera," said the sheriff. "Why do you ... oh my God! What the hell is that awful smell?"

"Oh, that's Banyon," Jake replied. "Bustamente killed him for violatin' a young girl and then left him out on the desert for the coyotes. I figure that if I could get a picture of him, or what's left of him 'fore he's buried, that'll satisfy the folks in San Antonio 'bout payin' the reward. That and I won't have to smell his stink no more. Tell Mr. Thornberry I'll pay for the picture."

"I don't think you need to concern yourself about payin'," said the sheriff. "I'm sure Ben will be more'n willin' to take a picture for his newspaper. I'll see to it myself."

"Much obliged, Sheriff. You got an undertaker who can bury Banyon?"

"Yep, old man Harris builds the box and puts 'em under, providin' he's sober. The town pays him fifty cents for each one he puts down."

"Banyon don't deserve no box," said Jake with disgust. "Just have Harris dig a hole, toss in what's left of him, and cover him up. And no marker neither."

"Seems a bit harsh, Marshal, but I guess you got your reasons."

"If you'd seen what he did to that young girl, you'd feel the same way, Sheriff."

"Yeah, reckon I might. What do you want me to do with his horse and tack?"

"I don't think his saddle will be worth anything, stinkin' the way it does. And it'll be a while 'fore his horse smells right. Best you bury the saddle along with Banyon and give the horse to some poor folks who could use it."

"Okay," replied the sheriff, "whatever you want."

"Appreciate your help, Sheriff. I'll be headin' out at first light, but I'll only be takin' O'Leary. Me and him got some business to take care of, and I'd be obliged if you'd keep Carruth in your jail 'til I come back. I'll pay for his keep while I'm gone."

"Ain't no problem, Marshal, and there ain't no need to pay. Not after what you've done."

After a long hot bath and a change of clothes, Jake left his hotel room and started down the building's interior staircase to the saloon below. As he came into view of the saloon's many patrons, all conversations ceased, the piano player on the small stage stopped playing, and all heads turned in his direction. Jake continued down the stairs with indifference until he reached the last step, when conversations started to grow and the piano player was again pounding the yellowed ivory keys.

"What'll you have?" asked the barkeeper as Jake approached the hotel's bar.

"Coffee, hot and strong."

"Yes sir, Marshal Tanner. I've been boiling a pot for the last half hour or so. Ought to be ready 'bout now."

As the barkeeper poured the thick, black, steaming liquid into a tin cup, Jake could only wonder what stories had already started making their rounds through the small town. The fact that the barkeeper already knew him by name and sight indicated his reputation was already well formed.

"Hello, Marshal," said a cheerful male voice at his elbow. "Mind if I join you?"

"Depends on who's asking?" said Jake, turning to look at the man.

"Name's Ben Thornberry, editor of the Weekly Gazette. I have the pictures you wanted, but oh what a horrible stink."

"Oh, yeah, thanks," said Jake, as he took three pictures from the man and laid them side by side on top of the bar. "I only asked for one but appreciate your generosity."

In the pictures Banyon's head and other remains had been placed on the ground in a shape resembling what might have been a human being. The only identifiable part was what little remained of Banyon's face.

"Would you mind if I used one of these pictures in my gazette?" Thornberry asked.

"Nope, might make a few other murderin' scum think about the consequences before robbin' and killin' good folks."

"Yes, yes, I quite agree," replied Thornberry with enthusiasm. "And I would be most appreciative if you would tell me how you managed to kill one murderous outlaw and capture the other two all by yourself. I'm sure my readers will want to know."

"They were stupid," said Jake as he raised the coffee cup to his mouth.

"Stupid!" replied Thornberry, obviously astonished by Jake's response. "Is that all?"

"Yes," replied Jake angrily as he slammed the cup down on the bar and turned to look at Thornberry with exasperation. "Stupid for robbin' and killin' innocent folks, stupid to think no one could stop 'em, and stupid for bein' either dead or 'bout to be dead for all their efforts."

Cowered by Jake's fierce outburst, but stubbornly persistent, Thornberry stepped back from the bar and stammered, "But ... but how did you do it? Surely you must know that my readers will want to know all the details. You're a hero, Marshal, and I can guarantee that if you tell me your story, you will be known across the entire country as *'The Avenging Lawman.'* A clever title, don't you think?"

Jake gave Thornberry a single, disgusted look, picked up the two remaining pictures, and walked away without comment.

Sunrise was only minutes away when O'Leary, locked in hand irons, was helped on his horse and the chain connecting his leg irons run under the horse's belly. O'Leary's loud protests at not being able to dismount by himself were ignored.

The ride out of Del Rico was uneventful until mid-morning, when Jake reined in his horse and dismounted near a large outcropping of rugged boulders. O'Leary's horse, tied to the back of Jake's saddle by a short length of rope, came to a stop a few feet away. Ignoring O'Leary, Jake gathered twigs and branches from a nearby dead mesquite tree and started a fire in an already blackened fire pit. It was the same fire pit he had used the morning before entering Del Rico on his way to the Mexican border. Once the fire was burning steadily, he reached under the canvas tarp covering his supplies on the back of his pack horse and withdrew a blackened coffee pot, a cloth bag containing coffee grounds, an iron skillet, a small side of salted bacon, and a canteen of water. After dropping a small handful of coffee grounds in the pot and adding water, he placed the pot at the edge of the fire to heat. Then, removing his knife from a scabbard on his hip, he used a flat rock warming near the fire to slice strips of bacon and place them in the iron skillet.

"Ain't you goin' to invite me for breakfast?" asked O'Leary in a high, teasing voice, as he continued to sit chained to his horse.

Jake said nothing in response and made no movement toward allowing O'Leary to dismount. Soon the coffee was brought to a boil and the bacon sizzled and popped in the skillet, each part of the morning meal, sending out its own rich aroma to the crisp morning air. Jake's own stomach growled noisily and his mouth watered with anticipation. From his own reaction to the strong, delicious odors, he knew O'Leary was experiencing an even stronger reaction, not having had anything to eat since crossing the Rio Grande the day before. Jake had been adamant with the sheriff about denying O'Leary any food while in his jail. He did tell the sheriff, however, that O'Leary could have as much water and coffee as he wanted.

"Hey ... Tanner!" yelled O'Leary loudly, concerned after his teasing failed to get a response. "Unchain me and let me get down; I've got to take care of personal business."

Jake continued to ignore O'Leary and concentrate on his cooking, using his knife to flip over the bacon strips now frying crisply in their own fat. Standing up, he walked back to the pack horse and removed a sack of flour, a large metal spoon, and two brown biscuits that looked hard as rocks. He knew O'Leary was watching him closely, expecting to be released from his constraints to enjoy the meal.

Returning to the fire, Jake sat down cross-legged on the ground, removed the bacon from the pan with his knife, and laid the sizzling strips back on the flat rock warmed by the fire. He then plopped a large spoonful of flour into the pan, added a little water from the canteen, and used the spoon to stir the mixture into the hot bacon grease. When the combination was thoroughly mixed he cut the biscuits in half with the knife, placed the four halves in the pan upside down, and used the spoon to ladle the thick gravy over the biscuits until they were soft. Pouring himself a cup of steaming coffee, Jake used his fingers to eat the crisp bacon strips and the spoon to eat the biscuits and gravy right from the pan.

"Damn it, Tanner!" yelled O'Leary. "Get me down! I ain't had nothin' to eat since we left Mexico, and I'm hungry enough to eat the ears off my horse."

Jake turned slowly to look at O'Leary and said in a cheerful, friendly voice, "Mighty fine breakfast I'm havin'. Yes sir, mighty fine."

"You ornery bastard!" shouted O'Leary. "Get your butt over here and let me down. I ain't goin' to stand for you denyin' me food and a personal need."

"I'd be pleased to do that," replied Jake pleasantly as he continued eating, "but first, you've got to tell me where you hid the money from the bank you robbed in San Antonio."

"What!" cried O'Leary. "What the hell are you talkin' 'bout? Bustamente took all the money and then sold us out. There ain't no money. Now get me down 'fore I wet myself."

"You're a bad liar, O'Leary. You got more'n eight thousand dollars from that bank and paid Bustamente only four hundred for the two of you. By my figurin' that leaves more'n seven thousand dollars hid somewhere."

"That's horse turds!" shouted O'Leary. "I'm tellin' you there ain't no money. Whoever told you we got eight thousand dollars was a liar. I swear, it weren't anywhere near that."

"If you say so," said Jake as he chewed on the last strip of bacon and washed it down with a mouthful of coffee.

"Okay, so get me down."

"Nope."

"What! I told you there ain't no damn money! I swore it and I'll swear it again on my poor ma's grave. Now let me get down."

"Nope."

"Don't keep sayin' that!" screamed O'Leary.

"Well, well, look at that," said Jake with casual indifference. "I've eaten everything. Ain't even a bite left for you, O'Leary. Guess you could have some coffee though. You want a nice cup of coffee?"

"No, no," wailed O'Leary. "I don't want no damn cup of coffee."

"Well, guess we best be goin' then."

"What do you mean, goin'? I've got to take a piss!"

"Go ahead, ain't nobody stoppin' you."

As Jake started scrubbing the pan and spoon with handfuls of nearby sandy soil he looked over at O'Leary and saw the man's face turn red with anger. Turning back to his task, he soon heard the sound of water splattering gently on the ground under O'Leary's horse. Smiling to himself, Jake was sure a fair amount of O'Leary's urine had fouled his pants and then found its way into his boots, making for an uncomfortable day of stinking britches, soggy feet, and an empty belly.

Dousing the fire with the remaining coffee, Jake replaced the coffee pot and other items beneath the canvas tarp and retied the pack. Mounting his horse, he gently spurred the animal and turned it southward, back toward Mexico.

"Where the hell you goin'?" said an angry O'Leary through clenched teeth.

"To get the money," said Jake in a calm, deliberate voice.

"You dumb bastard, I told you there weren't no money."

"Well, if there ain't no money, what do you care where we're goin'?" said Jake. "Seems like you'd be happy goin' anywhere except San Antonio, where you're sure to get hanged for bank robbery and murder."

"Shut up, damn you! We ain't to San Antonio yet. I'm warning you, Tanner, you better sleep with one eye open 'cause if I get the chance I'll kill you with my bare hands, cut you in little pieces, and feed you to the buzzards."

Without looking back at O'Leary, Jake laughed loud and long, knowing his laughter would aggravate the outlaw even more.

An hour later they crossed the Rio Grande into Mexico. And although O'Leary continued making disparaging remarks about Jake's heritage, they failed to elicit a response, and he finally reverted to a sullen silence. Jake felt as if he could feel O'Leary's hate-filled eyes digging into his back like a Bowie knife, but that was exactly what he wanted. He wanted O'Leary to hate him as much as he hated O'Leary. It would make squeezing the location of the money from him that much more satisfying.

As they proceeded southward, Jake stopped three times and each time used a short handled axe to cut down a mesquite tree measuring about six inches in diameter at the base. Once the tree was down, he removed all the small branches and trimmed its length to about twelve feet. He then tied each pole to the pack horse to be dragged along the ground. Each time he performed this task O'Leary asked him what he was doing, but Jake refused to even acknowledge his question.

By mid-afternoon they came to a series of dry, criss-crossing arroyos on a flat rocky plain. Carefully maneuvering his horse over the slippery surface, Jake led his and the other two horses through a series of twists and turns until he stopped near a jagged, oblong opening in the earth about five feet in diameter. Dismounting, Jake picked up a rock and tossed it into the opening. The rock struck the side of the opening opposite from where Jake was standing and then tumbled from side to side as it descended into the depths, making a soft thud sound as it hit the bottom of the shaft. The only other noise coming from the shaft was a loud buzzing sound made by disturbed rattlesnakes. It was a snake pit Jake had discovered on his way to El Fortaliza.

"Come on, Tanner," said O'Leary with an uneasy quiver in his voice. "Stop messin' with them snakes. I hate them bastards more'n you."

"Naw, … I'm thinkin' we'll stay a spell," said Jake as he walked back to the pack horse and began to untie the three posts.

"Stay! What the hell for? If you keep disturbin' them rattlers they'll come out of there mad as hell."

"Yeah, they sure might. Not a pleasant thought, huh?"

"Hell no, so let's get out of here. That rattlin' makes me mighty uneasy."

Ignoring O'Leary, Jake dragged the three posts to the edge of the hole, and again using the short handled axe, he dug three equally spaced holes around the pit. He then removed from his saddle bags two items he had purchased in Del Rico the day before: a ten-foot length of half-inch hemp rope and a wooden pulley about the size of his open hand. Using the hemp rope, he tied the three posts and the wooden pulley all together at one end and then threaded half the length of his lariat through the pulley. Grunting and sweating as he worked, Jake stood the three posts up and then spread them apart to form a three-legged tripod. He then walked the tripod over to the snake pit by moving one leg at a time and placed each leg in a hole he had dug around the edge of the pit. Both ends of the lariat now hung down into the pit from the pulley tied in the center of the tripod.

"You goin' fishin' for rattlers," mocked O'Leary, laughing as he watched Jake struggle with placing the last post in a hole.

"Guess you could say that," said Jake. "Now all I got to do is find me some bait. You got any bait, O'Leary?"

"Now what kind of fool question is that? Course I ain't got no bait. I don't even know what kind of bait you use for snake fishin'."

"Well now, that's a bad thing. Here I'm all set for snake fishin' and I ain't got no bait, except for you, of course."

"What!" said O'Leary in a startled, terrified voice. "You're crazy as hell if you think I'm goin' down in that hole."

"Yeah, I been called crazy a lot lately," said Jake, "but I'm sure in the mood for some tasty snake come dinner time. Why, I once heard an old cowboy say that when a rattler strikes, and sets his fangs deep in a feller, and you pull that feller up out of the snake pit real fast, the snake comes right up with him. Then all you got to do is grab the snake by the tail, crack it like a whip, and its head will plum snap off. I heard it said that a roasted rattler tastes better'n prairie chicken."

"You are crazy!" shouted O'Leary.

"Yeah," said Jake while looking cross-eyed at O'Leary with a scowl. "Course them who call me crazy don't live long. I just hate it when folks say I'm crazy."

"I didn't mean you was crazy, crazy," O'Leary apologized hurriedly. "You just need to get out of the sun for awhile, that's all."

"Where's the money?" said Jake as he abruptly turned serious.

"Money? Hell, Tanner, I told you there ain't no money. Why do you keep askin' me that?"

"Because all that money ain't goin' to do you no good after you're dead. It'll just lie around somewhere and rot away. Now, where'd you hide the money?"

"I swear, I ain't got no money hidden no where."

"Okay," sighed Jake as he approached the right side of O'Leary's horse and used a key to unlock the leg iron on O'Leary's right leg. As the leg iron and chain dropped down under the horse, Jake savagely pushed O'Leary from the saddle, toppling him onto the ground in a stunned heap. Moving swiftly, Jake again locked the lose leg iron around O'Leary's right leg, dragged him to the edge of the pit, pulled one end of the lariat out of the pit and tied it securely to the chain between O'Leary's leg irons, and left him on his back with his legs dangling in the pit. The unmistakable buzzing of the rattlesnakes started again.

"What the hell are you doing!" shouted O'Leary.

"Where's the money?" repeated Jake with hardness in his voice as he leaned over and stared into the eyes of the bewildered outlaw.

"I swear to God, Tanner, there ain't no money," said a panicked O'Leary as he grunted and tried to pull his legs up out of the pit. "We gave it all to Bustamente."

Without another word, Jake removed O'Leary's neckerchief from around his neck and tied the outlaw's still chained hands to the belt around his waist. He then removed his own neckerchief and bound it tightly over O'Leary's eyes. As O'Leary struggled and cursed, small rocks and dirt around the hole fell into the pit and the buzzing became even louder. With O'Leary cursing and still trying to lift his legs out of the pit, Jake led his horse around to the other side of the tripod, pulled the other end of the lariat out of the pit, and used a slip knot to tie the end of the rope to his saddle horn.

"Where's the money, O'Leary?" Jake shouted.

"There ain't no damn money," cried a terrified O'Leary, sobbing as he struggled to keep his feet up and out of the pit.

Slowly, Jake urged the horse forward until the lariat was taut and O'Leary's legs were raised horizontal over the edge of the pit.

"Where's the money, O'Leary?"

Hearing no response, Jake prodded the horse forward again until O'Leary, screaming, was pulled off the side of the pit and held dangling upside down over the pit of deadly vipers.

"Where's the money?" shouted Jake.

O'Leary, screaming hysterically, grasped his belt with his chained hands and tried to pull his head and chest up and out of the pit. Jake could hear the loud, persistent buzzing of the rattlesnakes from over twenty feet away. Still the outlaw refused to answer.

Cautiously, Jake backed the horse toward the pit until half of O'Leary's body disappeared below the rim of the hole, stopping the horse when he figured O'Leary's head was about ten feet from the bottom of the pit. O'Leary's terrified screams echoed out of the pit with a muffled, hollow sound.

Dropping the reins of the horse to the ground, an action the horse had been taught to recognize as a signal to remain standing where it was, Jake walked back to the edge of the pit and looked down. O'Leary's body was frozen rigid, and his voice started to crack and become hoarse from constant screams of terror.

Picking up a rock the size of a silver dollar, Jake threw it hard at O'Leary; hitting him sharply on his right arm. Apparently believing he had been bitten by one of the snakes, O'Leary screamed even louder and began squirming and shaking uncontrollably.

"Where's the money?" Jake yelled down into the pit.

"I'll tell you, I'll tell you!" O'Leary screamed at the top of his voice. "Just get me out of here. I've been snake bit."

"Tell me where it is and I'll pull you up."

"Damn it, Tanner, I'm begging you. Please, please, get me out of here."

Jake threw another rock and hit O'Leary on his left thigh.

"I'm bit again," O'Leary screamed.

"Tell me where you hid the money."

"We buried it in an old Mexican army fort near La Gloria," sobbed O'Leary.

"Where exactly is it buried?"

"In a cellar under the fort where they kept gun powder for their cannons. Please, Tanner, get me out of here. I'll do whatever you want."

"I'll get you out," said Jake, "but if you're lyin' to me, we're comin' right back here for some more snake fishin'."

"I ain't lyin'. Oh God, I swear I ain't lying."

"Yeah, just like you swore there weren't no money."

Jake returned to his horse and encouraged the animal forward until O'Leary's head was above the rim of the pit. Dropping the reins of the horse to the ground once more, he walked back to the pit, leaned against one of the tripod posts with one outstretched hand, and grabbed O'Leary by his belt with his other hand.

"Back up, Sandy," he called to his horse. As the horse backed slowly toward the pit, Jake pulled O'Leary to one side away from the opening and dropped him on the ground.

O'Leary immediately pulled his body into a fetal position and sobbed and shook uncontrollably. "Quick," he cried out in panic, "cut me where they bit me."

"You ain't bit," said Jake with disgust as he tore off O'Leary's blindfold.

"Yes … yes I am. I got bit twice. Please … please, Tanner, cut me so the poison can bleed out. I once seen a man get snake bit. His leg got all swollen up and turned green and he died screamin' his head off less'n two days later."

"I said you wasn't bit. You just think you was."

"I ain't bit?" said the outlaw, sobbing as he slowly emerged from his curled position and rolled up his sleeve to search for the tell-tell signs of fang marks. "But I heard them snakes rattlin' all around me, and felt 'em bite my arm and leg."

"Yeah, and you'll hear'em and feel'em again if you've lied to me," threatened Jake. "Next time I'll drop you to the bottom so them snake can have their fill of you."

The money was exactly where O'Leary said it would be, buried two feet down under the dirt floor of the cellar. During their ride from the snake pit to the abandoned army fort, and then to the Rio Grande and Del Rico, O'Leary was a changed man. Gone was the killer bravado, replaced by a broken man whose dreams at night were haunted by the terrors of the snake pit.

As Jake, O'Leary, and Carruth rode into San Antonio, a rowdy crowd gathered and followed them as they rode through the town to the sheriff's office. By the time Jake turned the horses toward the sheriff's hitching post, the crowd had grown to several hundred, chanting angrily over and over, "Hang 'em now, hang 'em now."

Jake dismounted as the sheriff walked out of his office and stood, hands on hips, under the covered porch of the jail. The sheriff had heard the noisy crowd coming down the deeply-rutted road and timed his appearance on the porch to coincide with Jake's arrival. He had learned the day before from one of his deputies, who happened to come across Jake on the road to San Antonio, that Jake's prisoners were about to become his responsibility.

"Have to admit I never thought I'd see you alive," said the sheriff.

"I figured as much," said Jake. What he really thought was that the sheriff was embarrassed that Jake, rather than himself, had brought the killers to justice.

Nodding to his deputies standing nearby, the sheriff said, "Get those murderin' cowards off them horses and lock 'em up."

"I'll get 'em off," said Jake, "but I want those hand and leg irons left on 'til they're hanged good and proper."

"No need to tell me my job, Marshal," replied the sheriff in a testy voice. "What about the other one. Did he get away?"

"No. Not 'less you consider bein' dead getting' away."

"You killed him?"

"Nope. Bustamente killed him."

"What for?"

"For violatin' a young girl. I brought the stink and what little the coyotes hadn't eaten across the Rio Grande. The sheriff in Del Rico said he'd see him buried."

The sheriff appeared to be at a loss for words for a moment. Finally he said, "I was wrong about you, Marshal. You're about as hard a man as I've ever seen."

After a bath, a change of clothes, and a hot meal in the Grand Hotel dining room, Jake left the hotel carrying the beat-up saddle bags containing the money from the bank robbery.

When he entered the bank a few minutes later, he strolled over to one of the tellers, plopped the saddle bags on the counter, and said quietly, "I'd be obliged if you'd inform the owner of this bank that I need to speak with him."

"And who should I say you are, sir?" replied the man with an air of disdain as he looked down his nose at the dusty bags.

"Deputy Marshal Tanner," Jake replied without taking offense at the man's curt manner.

"Oh, yes sir, right away, Marshal Tanner. Sorry I didn't recognize you, sir. You look a might different from this morning." Without waiting for a response from Jake, the teller scurried away toward an office at the rear of the bank. Within seconds, a tall, obese man hurried out from the office, followed by the beaming teller.

"Marshal Tanner," said the man, smiling and holding out his right hand toward Jake. "I'm Carl Harrington, and I can't tell you how grateful we are for you bringing in those killers."

By this time all of the bank's tellers and the half dozen or so bank customers, previously waiting for service, were crowding around looking awe-struck at Jake.

"Thanks," said Jake, modesty, shaking hands with the bank owner. "I just come by to return what's left of the money they stole from you folks."

"Really!" exclaimed Harrington with obvious astonishment as the crowd of customers gasped in surprise. "Why, I … I just don't know what to say."

Pushing the saddlebags toward the man, Jake said, "I'd appreciate you countin' out what's in here so there won't be no misunderstandin'. Your sheriff said they took about eight thousand dollars from you folks, and the bandit leader who was givin' 'em protection said he was paid six hundred dollars. By my figures, that means there should be about seventy-four hundred dollars in these bags."

"Why, yes … yes of course, I'll count it out right here," said Harrington. As he spoke, the crowd grew even larger as word of the returned money spread rapidly to people outside the bank.

Removing the bills gingerly from inside the saddle bags, Harrington stacked the money on the counter with slightly trembling hands. After separating the bills by denomination, he started counting silently to himself. As his count of the money approached seventy-two hundred dollars, he began to count out-loud until the total amount counted was seven thousand, four hundred, and ninety-three dollars.

"Why … that's … that's exactly how much was taken after six hundred dollars is added to it," said Harrington in shocked amazement. "It's all here; every dollar is here, except the six hundred. My God, it's hard to believe," he continued as he looked at Jake with respect and admiration. "How can we ever thank you?"

"Well," replied Jake, "I was told there was a thousand dollar reward for O'Leary and five hundred dollars for each of them other two, dead or alive."

"Yes, that's right," said Harrington proudly. "The State of Texas has authorized me to pay the reward money to anyone who could prove they earned it. By bringing in O'Leary and one of the others, you've certainly earned your fifteen hundred dollars."

Reaching into his vest, Jake removed the picture of Banyon's remains lying on the street in Del Rico. "Guess you better make that two thousand dollars, Mr. Harrington."

"My Lord," said Harrington. "You killed the third one?"

"No," said Jake as he pointed to the picture. "His name was Banyon and he was killed by the bandit leader. I brought what was left of him across the border and got him buried in Del Rico."

The crowd gasped, and then exploded with loud conversations between the onlookers.

"Then ... then I'll arrange for you to be paid two thousand dollars," said Harrington.

"No, just fifteen hundred," said Jake. "Like I said, I didn't kill Banyon.

"But what about the five hundred dollar reward for Banyon? He's dead, no matter who killed him, and somebody should get the reward money."

"You're right," said Jake, "So I want you to divide it evenly among the families of those folks who got killed in your bank and out on the street."

"Oh my, yes ... yes, of course. That is a *very* good idea, and a *most* generous one, Marshal. I'll have the money ready by the end of the day."

"Thanks," said Jake, "but no need to hurry on my account. I won't be leavin' 'til after the hangin'."

Saying nothing more, Jake turned and walked out of the bank as the crowd of people, stunned into silence, opened a pathway for him. No sooner had he left the bank than the crowd recovered its voice, and Jake could hear the cheering and shouting as he entered the sheriff's office a block away.

"Sounds like some excitement down at the bank," said the sheriff. "Guess I better go have a look-see."

"I just came from there," said Jake. "Ain't nothin' to worry 'bout, just some kind of celebration goin' on."

"Well, if you say so. Folks will tell me about it sooner or later. What can I do for you, Marshal?"

"I'd like to see O'Leary, if it ain't too much trouble."

"No trouble at all. Go on back. The door leadin' to the cells is open."

There were eight small cells in the jail behind the sheriff's office, four on each side of a central aisle. Of the eight cells, one contained a drunk, snoring loudly, while lying in his own vomit on the cell's filthy floor. Carruth was in a cell opposite the man and O'Leary was in the last cell on the right. Both were still shackled in hand and leg irons and empty tin plates lay on the floor near the front of the cells. O'Leary was lying on a straw-filled mattress on the floor, his face against the back wall of the cell.

"I see you got fed," said Jake while looking into O'Leary's cell.

"And I guess you got your reward money," replied O'Leary, not bothering to change his position on the mattress.

"Yeah, but that ain't why I tracked you all the way down to Mexico and put you in that snake pit."

"No? Well if it weren't for the money, why *did* you?" asked O'Leary as he sat up and turned to look at Jake with hate in his eyes. "What the hell did I ever do to you?"

"*What did you do to me?*" Jake replied with a savage snarl. "I'll tell you what you did. You horse-whipped my pa 'til there weren't hardly any skin left on his back, and then you and them other sons-of-bitches hanged him and killed my ma."

"What?" said O'Leary while struggling to his feet. "Whoever told you that is a damn liar."

"No, you're the liar!" shouted Jake in a rage. "I saw you. And don't tell me you don't know Flack and Tolman and Culver. You and your brother was with 'em when you came to my folks place lookin' for some tintypes. And when you couldn't find 'em you murdered my folks."

For a long moment O'Leary stood stupefied in shocked silence, his eyes glazing over, remembering days long past. Exhaling slowly as his shoulders slumped, he said softly, "Well I'll be damned. You're his kid, the one who shot Tolman."

"Yeah, I'm his kid," said Jake bitterly, "and now you're goin' to hang just like your brother, Tom."

"Tom's dead?" O'Leary asked as his head jerked up and a muffled sob escaped his lips.

"Yeah, he killed a sheriff and I hanged him. I can't say he died well."

"Ahhh ... damn ... damn it to hell," said O'Leary in a distraught voice. "Tom's dead and gone and ... and it's all my fault. I got tired of our pa beatin' on us whenever he came home drunk, which was most nights, so one night I met him at the door with an iron fry pan and bashed in his head. We didn't wait 'round to see if I'd killed him, just grabbed his pistol and run off with the clothes on our backs. Tom weren't a bad brother, Tanner, least ways 'til we started robbin' banks to get by. But after he killed his first man at fifteen, it seemed like he was always looking for the next one. I tried makin' him stop, but it always endin' up with us fightin'. I just couldn't get him to see eye to eye most times. And now he's dead, dead and gone."

As Jake listened to O'Leary's mournful lament, he was surprised when he felt a softening in his anger. Not for the O'Leary brother's part in the murder of his parents, but for the harsh brutality that sometimes made young men become killers.

"I'm sorry 'bout your folks," O'Leary continued. "They seemed like good people."

"What would *you* know 'bout my folks bein' good people?" said Jake as his anger flared once more. "You and the others killed my ma and tortured and hanged my pa when you couldn't find what you was lookin' for."

"Yeah, but that weren't none of my idea and I didn't like it. Flack was in a rage and said if we didn't keep whippin' him 'til he talked, he'd kill us, too."

Jake was surprised by O'Leary's willingness to talk about the death of his parents and the events leading up to their death. "Okay," he said with a softness in his voice that surprised even him. "Tell me everything about that day. What happened?"

"You really want to know?"

"Damn it, O'Leary, I've been waitin' half my life to find out why my folks was killed. And so far you and Culver are the only ones that seem the least bit sorry 'bout it."

"Yeah, well … me and Tom never killed anybody or seen anybody killed 'til that day. We was mostly bank robbers who took up with Flack when he told us he was on to somethin' big."

"Big like what?"

"He never said. But we was down to our last nickel, so I figured we had nothin' to lose by joinin' up."

"Okay, okay, so what happened?"

"Well, your pa was out workin' near the barn when he seen us ridin' in from a ways off. We was comin' hard, and I figure your pa must have recognized Flack or Tolman 'cause he ran for the house like a scared rabbit. I know it weren't me or Tom he was scared of 'cause he'd never seen us 'fore. Anyway, your pa made it to the house 'fore we got there, and the next thing I saw was a rifle pointin' out through a window. Flack shouted for your pa to come out, sayin' he only wanted to talk, but your pa refused. Then Flack said if he didn't come out, he'd burn down the house and kill every livin' thing around.

A minute or so later your pa came out and asked what he wanted. Flack said, "You know what I want, so go get 'em." Your pa said he didn't know what Flack was talkin' 'bout and started to go back into the house. Flack drawed his shooter and put a bullet next to your father's head and into the front door of the house, stoppin' him dead in his tracks. After that we tied your pa to a tree behind the barn and whipped him, tryin' to get him to talk.

When that didn't work, Flack had us stand him up on a wagon, throw a rope over a limb of the same tree, and then put a noose around your pa's neck. Me and Tolman would haul him off the ground a couple of feet and hold him 'til we heard him choking. Then we'd let him down and Flack would ask him again and again where they were; whatever that meant.

After a couple of times doin' this, your pa said he'd gave 'em to somebody and if him or your ma was killed they'd never find 'em. Flack was like a crazy man. Culver tried to calm him down but Flack knocked him down and kicked him over and over 'til me and Tom stepped in and made him quit. All of a sudden, Flack grabbed hold of the rope and pulled your pa high up over the wagon, holdin' him kickin' and danglin' 'til he was dead.

"I don't think Flack meant to kill him, at least 'til he got what he come for. Once your pa was dead, Flack said we had to kill your ma 'cause she'd say who done it. Me and Tom said we weren't goin' to kill no woman, so Flack shot her when she come out of the house with that shotgun. I don't know what your pa was hidin', Tanner, but I think he thought that, whatever it was, it was the only thing that would keep him and your ma alive. He tried with everything he had to make it work."

Jake was perplexed. He had come to the jail to vent his hatred at O'Leary and demoralize him with thoughts of his impending death. He thought he would enjoy telling him about hanging his brother and describing how Tom trembled and soiled himself while waiting to die. But as O'Leary told the story Jake had waited so long to hear, his anger against the man cooled. Clearly the O'Leary brothers could never be forgiven for the part they played in the violent death of his parents, but perhaps circumstances, rather than premeditation, were partly to blame for their involvement.

It wasn't much of a trial, and the jury returned a guilty verdict without even adjourning to discuss the merits of the case. O'Leary and Carruth were marched without ceremony from the court room to the scaffold behind the courthouse, where Carruth fell to his knees when the sheriff tried to put the black bag over his head. It took two deputies to stand him up long enough for the sheriff to put the noose around his neck and hold him in place until the trap door was opened. O'Leary presented no problems for the sheriff and went to his death without uttering a sound. As Jim O'Leary's body jerked to a violent stop under the trap door, Jake turned and walked toward the hotel without looking back.

CHAPTER 17

DURING A STOP IN AUSTIN, Texas, while on his return trip to Dodge City, Jake sent a telegraph message to Flack in Amarillo. The message was brief, saying only that the necessary proceedings were falling into place and that he would soon receive a visitor. Jake thought that having the message originate in the capital city of Austin would give authenticity to his contrived story of Flack's impending wealth and power. Such a message would also serve to keep Flack firmly on the hook, line and sinker that Jake had cast over the waters of greed and corruption.

"Mornin' Jake," said Marshal Farnsworth as Jake walked into the marshal's office. "Come on in and sit a spell. I think you're goin' to like what I'm about to tell you."

"Glad to see you so cheery, Marshal. If I were to make a guess, I'd have to say you're goin' to tell me 'bout your trip to our nation's capital."

"Since when did you become a mind reader?" said the marshal with a smile, "but the truth is, you're right. After meeting with Mr. Holt, an Under Secretary to the United States Attorney General, I was invited to the White House to meet with the President. And here's the best part, within the next two months the President is going to nominate me to serve as the Attorney General's Deputy Chief Law Enforcement Officer. Then, when Congress approves the nomination, which I'm told they will, I'll be given broad authority over all law enforcement agencies within the entire United States."

Jake was speechless as he watched a beaming smile of pleasure spread across the marshal's face as he spoke. "Well, then, I … I guess that means you'll be leavin' us," he managed to say in spite of his disappointment. He and the marshal had always worked well together, and Jake considered him a father figure of sorts, especially when he helped Jake seek out and find the men who killed his parents.

"Not for a while yet," replied the marshal, "at least not until you're ready to take over for me."

"What?" said Jake with astonishment. "You can't be serious?"

"I'm perfectly serious, and while it's true I've got other deputies with more experience, there ain't one of 'em I'd trust to do the job better than you. So, like it or not, I'm nominatin' you to take over this job.

"I … I don't know what to say," said Jake. "It ain't that I'm ungrateful for your confidence, but I've never figured on bein' a lawman any longer than was needed to find my folk's killers."

"I don't need your answer right now, Jake. Just think about it."

"Yes sir, I will."

"Now," said the marshal, "tell me about Mexico."

For the next hour Jake told Marshal Farnsworth about finding the outlaws in El Fortaliza, Banyon's death, the capture of O'Leary and Carruth, their return to San Antonio with the bank money, and Jim O'Leary's hanging. He also told the marshal he needed a thousand dollars of the reward money to repay Beth's father for the thousand dollars he borrowed to buy O'Leary and the others from Bustamente. He didn't really know why, but decided that his conversation with Jim O'Leary about what happened on the day his parents were murdered was too private to share.

The marshal was clearly impressed. "Now I know I've nominated the right man for this job," said the marshal with genuine admiration. "And puttin' O'Leary in that snake pit so he'd tell you where the money was ... well, that was downright brilliant."

"Thanks," replied Jake. "It also evens the score for him whippin' my pa near to death. But I've got to admit that after he told me where to find the money, I was tempted to let the snakes have him."

"You do have a nasty side," laughed the marshal, "and the thousand dollars you need to repay Mr. Owens is all yours, plus the five hundred for Carruth. You've sure as hell earned it. Now, back to other business, have you heard anything about Flack?

"Yeah," Jake replied, taking on a serious tone. "And I've got a few ideas about him that I'd like to discuss with you, if you've got the time."

"Other'n thinkin' 'bout my new job, I've got all the time in the world. Tell me what you got."

"Yes sir. The problem is, I don't know how much longer I can keep Flack feedin' on his own greed. So I've been thinkin' how I might go 'bout bringin' him to trial."

"You don't say," said the marshal with surprise. "Are you sure you got enough evidence to convince a jury? It's been a long time since your folks were killed, and you told me that Flack is a respected member of Amarillo's social set. That bein' so, it'll be mighty hard findin' an impartial jury in that town."

"Yes, and that's why I'm goin' to have his arrest warrant come from Austin. I know that sounds far-fetched, but when I stopped in Austin on my way back to Dodge City I talked with a lawyer about such a thing. He said that if I can get him enough evidence he'll take it to the state's attorney general and get a warrant to bring Flack to Austin for trial."

"That sounds like a lot of if's," said the marshal with concern. "You said you were the only witness, so where are you goin' to get enough evidence to get an arrest warrant, much less a conviction?"

"You already know some of it, Marshal, but there's some you don't. I just didn't feel it necessary to bother you with all the bits and pieces I've come across 'til I had enough evidence to see if you agree it's time to act."

"Okay, go on."

"It's like you said, up 'til now I was the only witness, but now there are two more. I've also got three witnesses who heard Tom O'Leary say that it was him, his brother Jim, Tolman, and Flack who murdered my folks."

"Really!" said the marshal with surprise. "And who are these witnesses?"

"Sorry, Marshal, but I can't tell you just yet. I promised 'em that I wouldn't reveal their names to anyone 'til I was sure we had a good chance for a conviction. They're afraid their lives would be in danger if their names were to get out."

"Yeah, I see what you mean. Anything else?"

"Yes. Have you ever heard of a man called Colonel Langston?"

"No, can't say I have," replied the marshal with a thoughtful expression. "But I do know that the title of colonel is usually a military one, and a title that carries a lot of power and importance. I was part of a New York union regiment during the war and I made sure to steered clear of officers and sergeants. They have a bad habit of volunteering you for latrine duty or other things that could get you killed. That being said, why is this Colonel Langston important to you?"

"Because I think Colonel Langston is the key to everything.

"What do you mean by 'everything'? And what makes you think he's the key?"

"Because the night before Tolman was to be hanged he told me that my pa's job during the war was to take tintype pictures of Colonel Langston and the war, lots of 'em. But just as the war was ending my pa disappeared and took all the pictures with him. Tolman said the colonel went crazy and told him and Flack that they had to find the tintypes and kill my pa."

"Well, I'll be damned," said the marshal. "That's the first thing you've told me about your folks being killed that makes any sense. Are you sure he wasn't joshing you?"

"No sir, because when I told Tolman I could have saved Tom O'Leary from hanging if he could tell me why my folks were killed, I think Tolman was scared enough to believe that I could save him, too. After that, it all came spillin' out about Colonel Langston and the tintypes."

"Tintypes!" said the marshal angrily. "How could a bunch of damn pictures be important enough to kill people?"

"I've asked myself that question, Marshal, and when I asked Tolman if he knew what was on 'em he said he did, but he'd tell me only if I'd save him from hangin'. He held on to that belief until he ended up hangin' just like Tom."

The marshal seemed deep in thought as he leaned back in his chair. For several minutes Jake could only hear the sound of flies buzzing against the glass outside the office window. "So it is your thinking that it's what's on the tintypes that's at the bottom of all this," said the marshal while slowly sitting forward in his chair.

"Yes sir. I'm convinced that this Colonel Langston, whoever he is, is the man behind the murder of my folks."

"I think you're right," said the marshal.

"Do you think I've got enough evidence to get an arrest warrant for Flack?" Jake asked.

The marshal frowned and hesitated for a moment before speaking, "Well, I'd say that *if* you can get your witnesses to court, and *if* you find the tintypes, then I think you've got a pretty good case. But actually getting a conviction is goin' to be a lot harder, because you've first got to prove this Franklin feller is Flack. If you can't do that, it might sour everything and he'll go free. Now, until that time comes, what are you planning to do?"

"Just keep doin' my job," said Jake. "I don't want to stir nothin' up, like talkin' with the witnesses, 'til I'm ready to get the warrant. But like I said before, I don't think I can wait much longer. Flack could figure out that somethin' ain't right and disappear forever."

Two days later Marshal Farnsworth called Jake into his office and said, "Take a seat, Jake. I've been thinkin' 'bout our conversation and I think you're right. If you're ever goin' to get Flack convicted for killin' your folks, you've got to do it before he gets nervous and decides to run. So here's my thinkin'. Get all your witnesses lined up, have them write down what they saw or heard, have them sign their names and get their signatures witnessed by somebody other than you, and then go see that lawyer in Austin. The sooner we can get Flack locked up, the better. From what you're tellin' me, I think you've got a good chance for a conviction, providin' all your witnesses are still willin' to talk and you can *somehow* find those tintypes."

Jake had never been more nervous than when he knocked on the door of the Owens home that same evening. Ever since leaving the marshal's office earlier in the day, he had rehearsed over and over in his mind what he was going to say to Emily. But no matter how gently he put the words together, he pictured Emily running to her room in terror, and he really couldn't blame her. What he was going to ask her to do was cruel and inhuman, and his only hope was that time had healed her shattered mind.

"Well hello, stranger," said Beth, with a beaming smile when she opened the door. "I was hoping you would come by this evening. Emily and I have a surprise for you."

"That's the best news I've had all day." said Jake, trying to cover up his concerns. "What is it?"

"You'll have to ask Emily."

"Okay, but then I have something I want to ask you, something about when this is all over."

"When what is all over?" asked Beth with a fearful frown.

"When ... when I'm finished bein' a deputy marshal."

"You're thinking of quitting!" squealed Beth with a little jump of excitement. "I can't believe it. You'll never know how much I've ... well, wished you didn't have to ... you know."

"Well, I can't stop just yet."

"Oh, yes … I mean no, of course not, and I don't want to sound like I'm rushing you. But have you thought about what you'll do after you … resign?"

"I haven't got that all figured out yet, but I'm workin' on it. I've heard there's free homestead land up Colorado way that is supposed to be good cattle country. I'm thinkin' 'bout takin' a ride up there sometime soon and see it for myself."

"Really! Oh, that sounds so exciting. I wish I could go. I've never been to Colorado, but I've heard people say it's beautiful."

"Yeah, me too," said Jake wistfully. "But right now I need to talk with you and Emily. It's very important."

"Yes, yes, of course" said Beth. "You go sit in the parlor and I'll get her."

A few minutes later Beth and Emily entered the parlor and Jake stood to greet them.

Emily, when she saw Jake, laughed like a little girl and hurried to bury herself in his arms. "Oh, I've missed you so much," she said, looking happily into his eyes.

"I've missed you too," said Jake, as he held her face gently in his hands. "You will never know how much."

"Tell him about your surprise, Emily," said Beth.

"Yes, yes, and you simply won't believe it," said Emily excitedly.

"Then I guess you'd better hurry up and tell me."

Emily laughed gaily, enjoying the moment. Then she gushed, "Mr. Thompson has offered me a full-time job at the mercantile store. Isn't that grand? And … and … a very nice young man who comes into the store almost every day has invited me to a dance next Saturday night. Isn't that the most wonderful thing?"

Jake was stunned. He had never seen Emily so happy. And when he looked at Beth, standing in the parlor doorway, he saw tears of happiness rolling down her cheeks. It was now obvious to Jake that a complete transformation had taken place in Emily, a transformation that he could never bring himself to threaten.

"Emily, Emily," he said softly as tears of his own welled up in his eyes. "I'm so proud of you. So very proud. And a young man too!" With his own excitement building, he continued, "What's his name? Do I know him? Come on, you must sit down and tell me everything."

With glowing eyes and eager words, she did.

Later, when Beth asked Jake what he wanted to talk with her and Emily about, he shrugged his shoulders and said it wasn't important. It wasn't important because he now knew that he could never ask Emily to testify about what happened that terrible day, even if it meant Flack would go free.

After dinner Beth and Jake took their usual places on the front porch swing. Noting a sudden change in Beth's demeanor, Jake said, "Seems like you've got somethin' on your mind. Are you goin' to share it?"

Smiling shyly, Beth said, "I'd like to, but I'm afraid if I ask you a question, I won't like the answer."

"Only one way to find out," replied Jake, encouraging her.

Fidgeting, and with obvious reluctance, Beth said, "Well ... earlier you said that when this is all over you wanted to ask me something."

"Yeah, that's what I said."

"Well, is that *all* you're going to say?"

"What do you want me to say?" said Jake, teasing.

Now impatient, Beth said with a hint of anger, "I want you to tell me what you are going to ask me when this is all over!"

Jake looked down and studied the toes of his boots. Was it fair, he thought, to ask her the question when there was so much more to do to bring Flack to justice? And there was still the issue of Langston's assassin, Ray Gibbons, who might try again to kill him. But a man could also get killed falling off his horse. And Flack, well, that was something that would have to take care of itself.

Looking into Beth's eyes, Jake said, "How'd you like to see Colorado with me?"

Beth's chin quivered slightly as she said, "Are ... are you saying what I think you're saying?"

"Yeah, well ... I don't think it would be right 'less we was married."

"Oh, Jake," gasped Beth as her hands flew to cover her mouth and tears began to roll down her cheeks.

"I ain't heard your answer yet," said Jake. "And I ain't about to ask your father if I can marry you 'less I first know you're willin'."

"Yes, yes, yes, a thousand times yes," squealed Beth as she threw her arms around Jake's neck and began smothering his face with kisses.

A few hours later, after the excitement had died down, Beth, her father, and Jake sat talking quietly in the parlor. Emily had excused herself to help clear the table and wash the dinner dishes. Although having earlier given his approval of Beth and Jake's marriage, Beth's father was concerned about how Jake would feel and what he would do if Flack's trial turned out badly.

"Are you sure you can get a conviction?" he ask. What he wasn't saying was his fear of reprisals should Flack be found not guilty.

"I'd be more sure if I could find those tintypes," Jake replied just as Emily entered the parlor.

"Tintypes," said Emily in a small voice.

"It's nothing," said Jake as he jumped up and encircled Emily in his arms. "Really, it's nothing for you to be concerned about."

Emily stood frozen as everyone in the room looked at her. Gradually, as Jake comforted her with soft, tender whispering in her ear, her face softened and she spoke as if in a dream. "I remember papa telling me about tintypes. He said they were important and to hide them."

Jake was stunned. "He told you about them?" he asked gently.

"Yes, hide them and tell no one."

"And did you hide them?" Jake asked, trying desperately to keep the excitement out of his voice.

"Yes, I hid them in the cave where we used to play. And mama and papa were crying and I couldn't help them and ..."

As Emily collapsed, Jake caught her in his arms.

"Hurry," said Beth as she turned and raced toward the front door of the house. "Take her upstairs and I'll get Doctor Wickins."

An hour later the doctor entered the parlor and said, "I think she'll be fine. She's sleeping now and I don't think there will be any permanent damage. Just be gentle with her and try not to upset her until we have a chance to see how she recovers."

Two days later, after the doctor assured Jake that Emily had made a complete recovery, Jake told Beth he was leaving town and to keep silent about what he might be doing.

CHAPTER 18

SWALLOWING HARD TO STIFLE THE memory of his parent's bodies laying just a few hundred feet away from where he stood, Jake gently brushed aside the dense foliage hiding the cave's entrance. The cave wasn't very large, and, when he stooped to looked inside, it seemed even smaller than when he and Emily played there together. With growing excitement, Jake dropped to his hands and knees and began to creep inside, followed by Sheriff Brags, who, after many years of service, was still the local sheriff from Jake's childhood. Standing just outside the cave was the current land owner, a farmer named Josh Lancaster.

"Ain't much room to hide anything in here," said the sheriff, trying to adjust his eyes to the darkened interior, "and there ain't enough loose dirt to bury anything."

"Yeah," Jake replied, moving slightly ahead of the sheriff, grunting as he rolled onto his back. "I figure that if my sister was to hide somethin', it would have to be where only somebody small could reach it. And if I'm right … damn … ain't no way I can reach it."

"Reach what?" said the sheriff.

"A place I used to hide things from my sister, at least 'til she found 'em."

"Are you sayin' you can't reach it?"

"Ain't no way," replied Jake. "We need somebody small, like a child."

"Hold on," said the sheriff. "Lancaster has a couple of youngsters. I'll have him get one of 'em."

"Okay, but make sure they bring a stick about two feet long."

"What's that for?" said the sheriff.

"To check for rattlers."

Ten minutes later Jake was crouched just inside the cave's entrance as Mr. Lancaster's twelve-old-son, Jason, crawled toward the back of the cave.

"What am I lookin' for, Mr. Tanner?" he asked as he reached the end of the cave.

"Turn over on your back, Jason," Jake urged.

"Okay," the boy answered a moment later. "Now what?"

"Do you see that small opening right above you?" asked Jake.

"Just barely," the boy answered. "There ain't much light in here."

"You're doing fine, Jason. Okay, now scoot yourself a few feet back toward the entrance of the cave, so your head ain't under the opening."

"Okay, I've moved back a ways," said the boy. "Now what?"

"Now be very careful, Jason, and take that stick you got, put it slowly into that opening, and poke it around a little bit. But do it slow, very slow."

"Okay, I'm doin' it."

"Do you hear anything, like maybe a rattler inside?" asked Jake.

"No sir, no rattlin'. But I hear the stick bangin' on somethin'. Sounds like maybe a tin can."

"Okay. Good. Now move that stick around really hard inside there and listen to see if you hear any rattlers."

"Nope, don't hear nothin', Mr. Tanner."

"That's very good, Jason. Now put your hand up through the openin' and reach inside. Tell me if you feel that tin can you heard."

"Yeah, okay, I'm doin' it and … yeah I feel somethin', feels like a box of some kind."

"Can you pull it out?" asked Jake with growing excitement.

"I think so. I'm pullin' hard, but it seems stuck. No … wait …"

"What is it?" ask Jake.

"I've got it!" said boy with a happy shout as he turned over on his stomach and began scrambling backward out of the cave.

Seconds later Jake held in his hands a metal box that he recognized as having belonged to his father. It was about the size of a large family bible and was crusted with rust and dirt. Holding his breath with anticipation, he pried open the metal lid with a prolonged squeak, looked inside, and found a large number of tintypes. Slowly, with trembling hands, he began to examine the pictures one by one. At first each picture looked pretty much like the others, until one picture took his breath away and caused his heart to skip a beat. Dropping the picture like a red hot coal, his excitement turned to shock and disbelief.

"Where's the marshal?" Jake asked the deputy who was leaning back in the marshal's chair with his feet up on the desk.

"Gone back to Washington. Somethin' 'bout havin' to see a Mr. Holt. I suspect it has somethin' to do with his new job. I gotta tell ya, Jake, he was more'n a bit put-out when you weren't around when he left. Told me I was in charge 'til you got back."

"Well, you might as well get used to that chair, Charlie, 'cause you'll be getting' it back soon enough."

"What! Why's that?" demanded Charlie, clearly surprised, as his feet came off the desk.

"Because I'm leavin' for Texas tomorrow, and once I'm gone, you'll be in charge again."

"Damn it all, Jake. It seems like every time I'm in charge there's either a killin' or some sort of trouble goin' on. I hate bein' in charge."

Immediately after his arrival in Austin, Jake took his carpet bag in hand and walked to the office of the Texas Attorney General's prosecuting attorney.

"So what do you think, Mr. Blackstone?" Jake asked eagerly, as he sat on the edge of his chair in front of the attorney's desk. "Do we have enough evidence for a conviction?"

"I think we have enough for an arrest warrant," replied Mr. Blackstone, "but I'm not sure if I should issue it."

"Why not?" Jake asked, concerned.

"I'm going to be honest with you, Deputy Tanner. The problem as I see it is threefold. First, and foremost, we have to prove that Amarillo saloon owner Daniel Franklin is indeed Roy Flack. With your testimony as our only evidence in that regard ... well ... the outcome is uncertain. Unless we can come up with some other substantiating evidence, the judge might throw out our case without even considering the murder charge. Second, even if we were to somehow convince the judge and jury that Franklin is Roy Flack, your testimony regarding Tom O'Leary and Tolman's confessions are questionable since neither one is available to confirm or deny your claim."

"The Wichita Sheriff and his two deputies heard O'Leary say the same thing I'm sayin'. Ain't that good enough?"

"It certainly helps, yes. It's just too bad we don't also have a confirming witness for Mr. Tolman's confession."

Discouraged by Mr. Blackstone's assessment, Jake said with a sigh, "You said our problem was threefold. What's the third thing?"

"Motive. In questioning you as a witness I will introduce the tintypes as a motive, but without actually having them in my hand, and being able to demonstrate, implicitly, that they were the motive for the murders ... well, our case could be lost on that point alone."

"I don't think so, Mr. Blackstone," said Jake as he pulled the dirt and rust encrusted metal box from his carpet bag on the floor. "I think I have somethin' here that will change your mind."

During the next four hours Jake and Mr. Blackstone reviewed and discussed the contents of the metal box found in the cave. By the end of that time they had mapped out a complete trial strategy, with the exception of proving Daniel Franklin was Roy Flack. That final piece of the puzzle was still missing.

"Although we still have some evidence problems to overcome," said Mr. Blackstone, "I'm going to issue a warrant to have Mr. Franklin arrested and brought to Austin for trial."

Nine days later Captain Glen Morris of the Texas Rangers reported to Mr. Blackstone that Daniel Franklin was now housed in the Austin jail.

CHAPTER 19

GOOD MORNING, SIR," SAID MARSHAL Farnsworth, as he entered the Washington DC office of Mr. James Holt, Under Secretary for the United States Attorney General.

"Good morning to you," replied Mr. Holt. "Please, come in. We have much to discuss."

For the following hour Marshal Farnsworth listened intently as Mr. Holt described how the attorney general envisioned the marshal's role as his deputy chief of law enforcement. As the conversation continued, Marshal Farnsworth became more and more convinced that this opportunity was going to make him a person of real importance in the President's administration.

"Now then," said Mr. Holt, when it was apparent he had finished the formal part of their conversation, "it has come to my attention that there is an important trial coming up in Austin, Texas, that involves one of your deputies."

Smiling broadly, the marshal replied, "Yes sir. I just received the news myself. A man by the name of Daniel Franklin has been accused of being Roy Flack, a well known outlaw and murderer."

"Yes, yes, I've heard all about it, like almost everybody else in Washington, but here is the problem: This man, Daniel Franklin, is reportedly, and I repeat, reportedly, a close personal friend of the

Attorney General, Mr. Sampson, and a large contributor to our political party. If, heaven forbid, it is proven that Daniel Franklin is a notorious murderer ... well ... I'm sure you can see for yourself the possible repercussions. The attorney general, as I'm sure you're aware, has been mentioned as a possible presidential candidate in the next election, and the newspapers would have an absolute field day if such a connection were to be made."

"Yes, of course," said the marshal, "and I assure you that I had no idea that this trial might cause some ... embarrassment for the attorney general and his presidential aspirations. Please inform the attorney general that I will do everything in my power to protect his privacy."

"Excellent, excellent, I can see that you fully understand our predicament, Marshal. And as your deputy's immediate superior, I believe you have an excellent opportunity to impress the attorney general by ... shall we say ... silencing any such purported '*friendship*' between the attorney general and Mr. Flack that might surface during the trial."

"I understand perfectly," said the marshal. "I'll leave for Austin immediately and do everything I can to make sure this ... complication is handled properly."

"Thank you for your understanding, Marshal," said Mr. Holt, smiling as he stood up and extended his hand. "The attorney general has told me himself that he has the greatest confidence in you and is sure everything will go smoothly with you in charge."

Three days later Marshal Farnsworth met with Jake in Austin and told him about the attorney general's concern relative to his friendship with Franklin. "Therefore, I'm sure you can understand the attorney general's interest in the content and outcome of this trial," said the marshal, placing a fatherly hand on Jake's shoulder. "And because I can't be seen as interfering in any way, I'm countin' on you to pass the attorney general's concern along to Mr. Blackstone. Make him understand that under no circumstances should he allow the trial to drift into an area where this purported friendship might become public. Do you understand?"

"Yes sir, I understand, but I don't think Mr. Blackstone will have any control over what Flack's defense attorney might say or do."

"Yes, of course. I want you to know that I'll be keeping a low profile in the back of the court room, and if things aren't goin' well, just look in my direction for instructions."

The next evening, as Jake and Mr. Blackstone were leaving the attorney's office, the sound of a gunshot split the air and a glass window behind them shattered. Jake immediately threw his weight against Mr. Blackstone and both men landed in a heap on the sidewalk.

"Stay down," whispered Jake as he rolled off Mr. Blackstone, drew his pistol, and looked to see where the shot had come from. Another gunshot rang out and a bullet splintered a porch railing close to where the two men were lying. This time Jake saw the flash from the assassin's weapon and fired his pistol twice into a dark space between two buildings across the street. A fraction of a second later there was another gunshot, but this time the flash appeared to be angled down toward the ground.

A large crowd quickly gathered nearby. Jake motioned for them to stay back and then jumped up and ran across the street to a corner of one of the buildings next to the alley. With his back to the building he turned his head and peered around the corner, where in the darkness he saw a man laying face down on the ground. Moving with caution, he entered the alley, kicked away the pistol near the man's hand, and knelt down beside him. Placing his hand on the man's back, Jake felt a shallow rise and fall and knew the man was still breathing.

Mr. Blackstone, cautious as he stepped part way into the alley, asked, "Is he dead?"

"Not yet," Jake replied, "but it won't be long. Come over here and let's find out who he is."

As Jake and Mr. Blackstone knelt down and rolled the man over on his back, the man groaned and a tremor racked his body.

"Do you know him?" asked Mr. Blackstone.

"Yeah," Jake replied with a sigh. "His name is Ray Gibbons. He and a couple of others tried to kill me sometime back."

"But why?" asked Mr. Blackstone.

"Because somebody thought I was gettin' too close."

"Too close to what?"

"Let's see if he can tell us," said Jake.

"Ray," said Jake as he leaned close to Gibbon's face. "Who sent you?"

Gibbons did not respond.

"I said, who sent you?" Jake repeated while using his right hand to give Gibbons a sharp slap on the left side of his face.

Gibbon's glazed eyes opened slowly and tried to focus on Jake.

"Damn it, Gibbons, who sent you to kill me?"

"The ... the general," said Gibbons, with a sharp cough that caused foamy blood to pour from his mouth.

"The general! Don't you mean the colonel?"

"No ... the general, ... he thinks ... you know 'bout ...."

"He thinks I know 'bout what?" said Jake angrily as he again slapped Gibbons face. "Come on Gibbons, who in the hell is this general you're talkin' about?"

Jake never got an answer, because Gibbons was dead.

The following morning, as Jake took a seat in Mr. Blackstone's office, he said to the attorney, "Do you think Gibbons was confused when he said he was sent by 'the general' instead of the colonel? And if not, who is this general and why does he also want me dead?"

"I think he knew exactly what he was saying, Jake, although I'm at a loss as to how Gibbons and a general might fit in with Flack's murder trial, or even if they do somehow fit in. In fact, all this could just be an attempt to divert attention away from the trial for some other purpose, a purpose I can't imagine. However, I have a friend who might be able to help us."

The trial commenced the following day with Judge Henry W. Tucker banging his gavel on a wooden block and calling the court to order. The courthouse was one of the oldest buildings in Austin and was ornately decorated. The judge sat behind a large desk situated on a platform overlooking the entire courtroom. On the left side of his desk, but at a slightly lower level, was the empty witness chair. To the judge's far left, and at the same level as the witness chair, was the jury box where six men sat in stiff attention. In front of the judge's platform on the main floor were two tables, each with two chairs facing the judge. Mr. Blackstone and his assistant were seated at one table, and Daniel Franklin and his attorney, Mr. Jensen, were seated at the other table. Behind the attorneys' tables was a low banister separating the attorneys and the defendant from the public gallery, an area filled with about fifty people sitting in chairs. At least another thirty people were sitting on benches on a balcony above the main floor.

When Franklin first entered the courtroom he was smiling and waving to a large number of supporters, but when he saw Jake sitting in the front row of the gallery his smile turned to a look of confusion. This was the first time he and Jake had come face to face since their clandestine meeting in Amarillo. After sitting down at the defendant's table, he and Mr. Jensen had a hurried and animated conversation, along with alternating looks at Jake as they spoke.

"Mr. Blackstone," said the judge in a loud voice. "Are you ready to proceed?"

"I am, Your Honor,"

"Mr. Jensen, are you ready to proceed?"

"I am, Your Honor."

"Very well," said the judge. "The jury has been selected, sworn in, and instructed by me regarding this case and the charge of multiple murders. However, before we proceed, let it be known that I will not tolerate any profanity, spitting on the floor, or theatrics demeaning to the court's good order and discipline. Am I understood, gentlemen?"

After receiving a verbal acknowledgement from each of the attorneys the judge said, "I will now read the charge against the defendant, Mr. Daniel Franklin."

"Your Honor," said Mr. Jensen sourly, rising to his feet. "This trial is an outrage and is being pursued solely to disgrace the good name of …"

"Sit down, Mr. Jensen," thundered the judge, banging his gavel. "You will have ample opportunity to address this court at the proper time."

After a moment to calm himself, the judge read the charge against Franklin in a monotone voice that likely masked his animosity against Mr. Jensen's disruption of his courtroom. After the reading of the charge, each attorney was allowed to address the jury with a brief summary of arguments for and against the charge.

"Mr. Blackstone," said the judge in a voice that was designed to demonstrate his authority throughout the trial, "you may call your first witness."

"Thank you, Your Honor. I call Mr. Jake Tanner, son of the two deceased persons for which Mr. Franklin is now on trial for murder."

Flack was absolutely shocked. His initial reaction to seeing Jake in the courtroom had been one of concern that the power and wealth offered by Jake, posing as Mr. Waterman, was being threatened by the trial. Now, knowing he had been deceived into admitting both his identity and the murder for which he was now on trial, his emotions were in a state of pure panic. As Jake stood and approached the witness chair, Flack and his attorney engaged in a whispered discussion, during which Flack's fear bordered on hysteria.

"Mr. Tanner," said Mr. Blackstone, after Jake was sworn in and seated in the witness chair. "please tell this court what you observed on the day your parents were murdered in cold blood."

"Objection, Your Honor," cried Mr. Jensen as he jumped to his feet. "There is not yet any proof that anyone was murdered, much less in cold blood."

"There *might be* after you sit down, Mr. Jensen," said the judge sarcastically. Then, to Jake, he said in a much softer voice, "Please tell us what you saw, Mr. Tanner."

For the next half hour Jake described in detail what he saw and experienced on the day his parents' were murdered.

"When you returned home from rabbit hunting, you saw that five men had killed your mother and father," summarized Mr. Blackstone. "Is that correct?"

"No sir," said Jake. "There was five of 'em there, but only four of 'em did the killin'."

"What happened to the fifth man?"

"While the others did the killlin', the fifth man was tendin' their horses. I didn't see him hurt anybody."

"And at that time, did you recognize any of these men?"

"Yes sir. One of 'em was a neighbor named Burt Tolman. I'd seen him a couple of weeks earlier in town arguin' with my pa."

"Do you know what they were arguing about."

"No, sir."

"And after you saw that Mr. Tolman and the other three men had killed your parents, you shot him."

"Yes, but I only wounded him. Then the four of 'em started shooting at me, so I ran and hid in the woods. They were afraid to come into the woods and get me because I still had my rifle."

"At that time did you recognize any of the other men?"

"No sir.

"Mr. Tanner, do you recognize any of those men in this courtroom today?"

"Yes sir. That man sittin' over there," said Jake pointing at Flack. "He was the leader of the gang, and I saw him and the other three men murder my folks."

The courtroom erupted with loud exclamations and cat calls as the judge pounded his gavel for order. "This courtroom will come to order," yelled the judge above the bedlam, "or I'll order the courtroom cleared."

The courtroom quieted with only an undercurrent of murmuring.

"Do you have any other questions for this witness, Mr. Blackstone?" asked the judge.

"Not at this time, Your Honor. But I reserve the right to call him again should the need arise."

"So noted," said the judge. "Mr. Jensen, do you have any questions for this witness?"

"Yes I do, You Honor," replied Mr. Jensen. "I certainly do."

"Proceed," said the judge.

Mr. Jensen walked to the front of the courtroom and stood directly in front of Jake, a smile of confidence on his face as he turned his head and winked at the jury.

"Mr. Tanner, for the purpose of informing the jury, isn't it true that you are currently a deputy United States federal marshal?"

"Yes."

"And as a deputy United States federal marshal, you are sworn to uphold the law and never tell a lie. Isn't that true?"

"Yes."

"Fine, now that we have that out of the way, I have a few questions. First, how far away were you from where the supposed murders took place?"

"About a hundred yards or less," replied Jake.

"And you testified that you were hiding behind and peeking over a large rock on a hillside overlooking your family's house. Is that correct?"

"Yes.

"So, let me see if I have this right. You were hiding behind and peeking over a large rock at four men over a hundred yards away.

And with the exception of one man, who you say you recognized as a neighbor, you had never seen any of these men before. Is that about right?"

"That's 'bout right," said Jake.

"And you were twelve years old and scared. I know I'd be."

"Yes, I was scared."

"And with all that," said Mr. Jensen, "you sit here today, many years later, and say with certainty that you recognize my client as one of the five men who killed your parents."

"No, sir, he is one of the four men who murdered my parents."

"Why?"

"What do you mean, why?"

"Why are you so sure?"

"Because I saw him. He had a reddish colored beard and I heard his voice. I also heard and saw him close up when he tried to talk me into comin' out of the woods after I shot Tolman."

"Is my client, Mr. Franklin, wearing a red beard today, Mr. Tanner?"

"No."

"And other than today, and supposedly the day in question, have you ever seen the defendant, Mr. Franklin, before?"

Jake hesitated, knowing what was coming. "Yes, I saw him in Amarillo."

"Really," said Mr. Jensen, as though surprised at Jake's answer. "Would you tell the court how you came to see Mr. Franklin in Amarillo."

Jake knew he had to tell the truth. So he explained how Tom O'Leary, one of the men with Flack at the time of the murder, told him where to find Flack. He also recounted his attempt to trap Flack into admitting who he was, and then concocting a story to keep Flack in one place until he could bring him to trial.

"So, isn't it true, Mr. Tanner, that you have had a long, smoldering vendetta against the men who killed your parents, and have now, somehow, selected my client, Mr. Franklin, as your prime suspect?"

"No, that is not true," shouted Jake a little louder than he intended. "He admitted to me that he is Roy Flack."

"I see, and were there any witnesses to this, so called, 'admission'?" asked Mr. Jensen equally loud.

"No."

"No," repeated Mr. Jensen in a sad, quiet voice. "And where are all these other men you talk about, Mr. Tanner: Tom O'Leary, his brother Jim O'Leary, and Burt Tolman? All of whom you say participated in murdering your parents. Tell us, Mr. Tanner, why are they not here to testify either for or against my client?"

Again Jake hesitated. "Because they're all dead," he said softly, knowing by the looks on the faces of the jury that he was losing them.

Mr. Jensen, smiling for everyone to see, turned to the jury and said, "They're all dead, gentlemen of the jury. You heard it yourselves. One has to wonder if Mr. Tanner killed them as part of his vendetta."

"Objection, Your Honor," said Mr. Blackstone. "Mr. Tanner is not on trial here and I speak with first hand knowledge when I tell the jury that Mr. Tanner's only connection with the deaths of these men was to apprehend them for their various crimes as a duly authorized federal marshal. It was a judge and jury, much like this one, that condemned each these outlaws to death."

"Sustained," said the judge with a sharp edge in his voice. "I'm warning you, Mr. Jensen, be very careful or I'll find you in contempt of this court."

"Yes, yes. I apologize, Your Honor," said Mr. Jensen with an impatient wave of his hand. "Now, as I was saying, gentlemen of the jury, you also heard Mr. Tanner, a deputy United States federal marshal, say in his own words that he attempted to trap my client into admitting he was this, so called, murdering outlaw, Roy Flack. Now he brings this ridiculous accusation into this courtroom and expects you, the members of this jury, to believe him on his word alone. Why, just yesterday, in front of Mr. Blackstone and other witnesses, Mr. Tanner murdered a man on our very own streets." Then, turning quickly back to face the judge, he continued with a sneer, "I'm through with this witness, Your Honor, and I believe the jury should be too."

The courtroom erupted into bedlam, with shouts, whistles and applauding that drowned out the judge banging his gavel with all his might. It took several minutes before the crowd began to quiet and the judge restored order.

"Mr. Blackstone," said the judge sharply. "I've heard of this incident. Do you wish to address this court regarding Mr. Jensen's assertion?"

"Yes, Your Honor," replied Mr. Blackstone angrily, as he stood up and faced Mr. Jensen. "I would like it to be noted that I object most strongly to Mr. Jensen's assertion that my client *murdered* anyone. The fact of the matter is that Mr. Tanner and I were first fired upon by a man who, for unknown reasons, had previously tried to kill Mr. Tanner. In my opinion, and the opinion of those who were there, Mr. Tanner reacted properly in defending himself and me by shooting and killing this assassin."

"Yes, I quite agree," said the judge as he looked at the jury. "Gentlemen of the jury, you will disregard Mr. Jensen's assertion that Mr. Tanner did anything other than defend himself and Mr. Blackstone from serious harm and perhaps even death. As for you, Mr. Jensen, after this trial I will hold you in contempt, throw you jail, and fine you a considerable sum for trying to mislead this jury." Then, turning to look at Jake, the judge then said, "You are excused, Mr. Tanner."

As Jake left the witness stand, the judge looked back at Mr. Blackstone and said, "Do you have any other evidence or witnesses who can provide additional testimony to support Mr. Tanner's contention that Mr. Franklin is, in fact, Mr. Flack?"

"No, Your Honor."

"I see," said the judge.

"Your Honor!" shouted Mr. Jensen as he jumped to his feet once more. "It is obvious that the prosecution has failed to provide any real evidence to support its contention that Mr. Franklin had anything to do with the death of Mr. Tanner's parents. Therefore, I call for a dismissal of all charges."

Once again the crowded courtroom burst into loud cheering and exclamations.

"Sit down, Mr. Jensen," said the judge in a tired voice as he banged his gavel without enthusiasm. After a few minutes the cheering gradually subsided and the judge said, "Mr. Blackstone, in light of what I have heard, I have no choice but to agree with Mr. Jensen. Therefore, I must …."

"If it may please the court, Your Honor," said a loud voice from the rear of the courtroom. "I believe I have information that will support Mr. Tanner's accusations."

"I object, Your Honor!" yelled Mr. Jensen as he turned and stared at a tall, well-dressed man, making his way through the crowd at the rear of the room. "Mr. Blackstone has already affirmed that he has no other witnesses."

CHAPTER 20

AS THE MAN APPROACHED THE low banister amid a growing rumble of anger and discontent from much of the crowd, both Flack and Jake entered into hurried conferences with their respective attorneys.

"Sir," said the judge as he again used his gavel to no avail. "please state your name and business before this court."

As the crowded courtroom quickly became quiet, the man said, "My name is William Culver, Your Honor, and I'm here to testify on behalf of Mr. Tanner."

"I most strongly protest and object to this … this outrage!" shouted Mr. Jensen as Flack, white faced, flopped down in his chair with apparent dejection.

"On what grounds, Mr. Jensen?" replied the Judge with a hint of a smile.

"On the grounds of … well … ah … failure of the prosecution to disclose its complete witness list, thus depriving the defense a proper chance to prepare."

"I see," said the judge. "Mr. Blackstone, have you ever seen this gentleman, Mr. Culver, before?"

"No, Your Honor."

"So you've never spoken with Mr. Culver concerning this trial."

"No, Your Honor."

"Then your objection is overruled, Mr. Jensen," growled the judge. "Mr. Culver, are you willing to testify in these proceedings of your own free will?"

"I am, Your Honor."

"Then take the witness stand and be sworn in."

As William Culver took the witness stand, the courtroom was completely silent.

Jake and Mr. Blackstone were still talking in hushed voices when the judge called out, "Mr. Blackstone, you have a witness waiting to testify. I suggest you get on with it."

"Yes, Your Honor," replied Mr. Blackstone, shuffling papers on top of the table while trying to gain time to organized his thoughts. "Yes, yes, here it is, I believe," he continued as he picked up a sheet of paper and walked to the witness stand. "Mr. Culver, I understand that this is not the first meeting between you and Mr. Tanner. Is that correct?"

"Yes sir. Mr. Tanner and I met many years ago when most people called me Billy."

"And under what circumstances did you and Mr. Tanner first meet?"

"Well, we didn't actually meet, Mr. Blackstone, at least not in a formal way. You see, at that time I was part of Mr. Flack's gang of outlaws that murdered Mr. Tanner's parents."

A loud gasp filled the crowded court room, and the judge had to rap his gavel only once to obtain silence.

"You were the fifth man, weren't you Mr. Culver?"

"Yes, I was tending the horses while the others did the killing. I tried to stop them, but I was just a kid at the time."

"Mr. Tanner has testified that the leader of the gang, a man by the name of Roy Flack, nearly beat you to death for trying to stop the murder. Is that right, Mr. Culver?"

"Yes sir."

"Can you tell this court the names of all the other men in the gang, Mr. Culver?"

"Yes sir. There was Roy Flack, Burt Tolman, Jim O'Leary and Tom O'Leary."

"Can you tell us exactly what happened that day and why?"

"Yes sir. I overheard Mr. Flack tell the others that there was something they had to find. He said it was important, but did not say what it was or why they needed to find it. When Mr. Tanner's father said he didn't have it, Flack and the others tied him to a tree, and Tolman and Jim O'Leary started whipping him near to death. That's when I tried to stop them and Flack and Tolman beat me near unconscious. Then, when Mr. Tanner's father couldn't, or wouldn't talk, Flack told Mr. Tanner's father that he'd either tell him where *they* were, or they would hang him. I think in the beginning they were just trying to scare him, but after a while, when Mr. Tanner's father finally said he gave it to somebody else, Flack lost his temper, grabbed the rope, and hanged Mr. Tanner's father all by himself. After Mr. Tanner was dead, Flack said they couldn't leave any witnesses, so when Mrs. Tanner came running out of the house with a shotgun, Mr. Flack shot her dead."

"Do you see the man you call Mr. Flack in the court room today?" asked Mr. Blackstone.

"Yes sir. He's the man sitting over there by his attorney, Mr. Jensen."

Once again the court room exploded amid exclamations of disbelief. Slowly the judge restored order.

"I understand Mr. Flack wore a beard at the time. Is that correct?" asked Mr. Blackstone.

"Yes, a reddish-colored beard."

"Are you saying that after all these years, and the fact that the man you say is Mr. Flack is now clean shaven, you can still recognize him?"

"Yes Sir. I rode with Flack for several years and I've seen him clean-shaven many times before. There is no doubt in my mind that Mr. Franklin is Roy Flack, the same man who murdered Mr. Tanner's parents."

The courtroom was strangely quiet until Judge Tucker said, "Do you have any more questions for this witness, Mr. Blackstone?"

"No, Your Honor."

"Do you have any questions for this witness, Mr. Jensen?"

"Yes I do, Your Honor. Mr. Culver, for the record, where and what is your place of employment, and why did you wait so long to come forward as a witness for the prosecution?"

"Objection, Your Honor," said Mr. Blackstone. "Mr. Culver is not on trial and Mr. Jensen's questions are not relevant to these proceedings."

"I submit that my questions are relevant, Your Honor. This witness is unknown to the defense, and the answers to my questions are needed by the defense to establish his credibility in testifying in these proceedings."

"You objection is over-ruled, Mr. Blackstone. The witness will answer Mr. Jensen's questions."

"Do I need to repeat my questions, Mr. Culver?"

"No sir. I am co-owner of a cattle brokerage company in St. Louis, and I waited to testify for Mr. Tanner until I was sure my testimony was needed to identify the defendant as Roy Flack."

"You said you were with the defendant when Mr. Tanner's parents were killed, but did not participate in the murder. That being said, have you ever met Mr. Tanner face to face before today, and if so under what circumstances?"

"Yes, I have met Mr. Tanner face to face before today. In fact, we have met twice before today. The first time was when Mr. Tanner happened to find me near death on a west Texas desert when he was a range rider for a large cattle ranch. I had been critically wounded in a gun fight and was near death. Without knowing who I was, he nursed me back to health. Later, when he told me about the murders, I was afraid to tell him who I was.

"The next time we met was when he again found me, this time in St. Louis. He was trying to gather enough evidence to bring Mr. Flack to trial and asked me, because I was not part of the murders, to identify Mr. Flack and testify against him in court. I told Mr. Tanner that testifying would damage my cattle brokerage business and my reputation in the St. Louis community. I then told Mr. Tanner I would not testify. Later, when I read about this trial, I had to come and see for myself if my testimony would be needed to prove that Mr. Franklin is in fact Roy Flack. I owe my life to Mr. Tanner, and I can no longer refuse to do as he asked."

"So you're a gunfighter, Mr. Culver?"

"Objection, Your Honor," shouted Mr. Blackstone angrily. "Asking Mr. Culver to answer such a question is a transparent attempt by the defense to intimidate the witness and demean his reputation and character."

"I quite agree, Mr. Blackstone," said Judge Tucker with seething anger. "Mr. Jensen, I will see you in my office when this trial is completed. Mr. Culver, you may step down."

After taking a few moments to calm dawn, Judge Tucker said, "Mr. Blackstone, do you have another witness to call?"

"Yes, Your Honor. I now wish to recall Mr. Tanner to the stand."

When Jake was seated in the witness box, Mr. Blackstone said, "Please tell the court about your conversations with Mr. Burt Tolman as he was about to be hanged for his various other crimes."

"I object, Your Honor," said Mr. Jensen in a soft voice without standing. "I fail to see the relevance of this line of questioning."

"Ah yes, I thought you would," said Judge Tucker as he looked at Mr. Blackstone. "You will show Mr. Jensen the relevance of your line of questioning, won't you Mr. Blackstone?"

"Of course, Your Honor."

"Then you may respond, Mr. Tanner."

"Yes sir. When I asked Tolman why my folks were killed, he said they were looking for pictures, tintype pictures. He also told me that he and Flack and my pa were all Confederate soldiers during the war, and it was my pa's job to take pictures. When the war was finally over, he said my pa disappeared with all the tintypes. Then, some years later, when Tolman happened to come across my pa in town, he told my pa he had to give the pictures to a man named Colonel Langston. When my pa refused, Tolman said he told Flack and Flack told

Colonel Langston. Colonel Langston then told Flack to do whatever he had to do to find the tintypes. Tolman refused to tell me who the colonel was, other than his name, unless I helped him escape from getting hanged, and there wasn't any way I could do that."

"Were there any witnesses to these confessions besides yourself, Mr. Tanner?"

"Yes sir. The man who tried to kill Mr. Blackstone and myself last night was a man named Ray Gibbons. I believe Mr. Gibbons has been somehow involved with Flack and Colonel Langston, and that he overheard Tolman's confession. I believe this because last night was not the first time Gibbons has tried to kill me to keep this jury from hearing the truth. As for Tom O'Leary, there are three witnesses who are willing to testify that they heard O'Leary's confession."

"And who are these witnesses?"

"The sheriff of Wichita, Kansas, and two of his deputies."

Turning from Jake to the judge, Mr. Blackstone said, "That is all I have for this witness at this time, Your Honor. But I reserve the right to call him again, if necessary."

"Yes, of course. Mr. Jensen, do you have any questions for this witness?"

"Ah ... well ... not at this time, Your Honor."

"Very well. Mr. Blackstone, you may call your next witness."

Mr. Blackstone called the Wichita Sheriff and his two deputies, all of whom confirmed Jake's testimony regarding Tom O'Leary's confession. Again, Mr. Jensen had no questions for the witnesses.

"Mr. Blackstone," asked the judge, "do you have another witness?"

"I do, Your Honor. I call Mr. David Anderson to the stand."

After Mr. Anderson was sworn and seated in the witness chair, Mr. Blackstone said, "Mr. Anderson, it is my understanding that you are a professor of history at Yale University and a recognized expert on the Civil War. Is that correct?"

"I have been acclaimed as such, yes."

"Objection, Your Honor," said Mr. Jensen in a tired voice. "What does an acknowledged expert on the Civil War have to do with this trial?"

"Oh, I think Mr. Blackstone is once again going to tell us," said the judge. "Isn't that correct, Mr. Blackstone?"

"That is correct, Your Honor. Now then, Mr. Anderson, in order to narrow down the area of interest to this trial, will you please tell the jury something about the unusual nature of the Civil War with regard to the State of Missouri?"

"Yes, of course. As almost everybody knows, Missouri was one of two Border States between the Union and the Confederacy that had a major problem throughout the war. The problem was that it was a divided state, having both a pro-Southern and a pro-Northern government. Thus many of the battles fought in Missouri were guerrilla engagements, turning much of Missouri into a battleground."

"Thank you, Mr. Anderson. Now, with regard to your research of the war regarding Missouri, did you happen to come across a military engagement near the town of Middleton?"

"Oh my, yes. It was a very sad thing. From my research, I found that as the end of the war neared, a train carrying a large amount of Union gold was scheduled to stop for water at Middleton. But somehow, a rogue Confederate armed force found out about the gold shipment and set up an ambush. As a result, not only were all the Union soldiers accompanying the gold shipment killed, but every man, woman and child living in Middleton was also killed ... murdered really. In addition, a large number of men wearing ragtag Confederate uniforms were also found among the dead. It has since become known as the Middleton Massacre."

"Have the men who committed this massacre ever been found and punished, Mr. Anderson?"

"No sir, no one has ever been charged."

"I see," said Mr. Blackstone. "And what about the gold?"

"Oh, no one knows. Over two hundred and eighty thousand dollars in Union gold just disappeared."

"Thank you, Mr. Anderson. Before I dismiss you, I have just two final questions. First, do you recall Mr. Jensen's accusation that Mr. Tanner murdered a man on our very streets yesterday?"

"Yes, I heard the accusation, a man by the name of Ray Gibbons."

"Yes, his name was Gibbons, and in your research of the Middleton Massacre, Mr. Anderson, did you ever come across a man by the name of Ray Gibbons?"

"Why yes, now that you mention it. A man by that name was a Union Army paymaster, the same paymaster who scheduled the gold shipment to go through Middleton, a man who was later accused of passing that information to the rebels and thus becoming a participant in the massacre itself. He, like the others, was never brought to trial due to a lack of evidence."

"Thank you," said Mr. Blackstone. "Your Honor, I have no further questions for this witness, but, for the record, I would like to inform the court that the assassin Mr. Tanner was forced to kill yesterday has since been proven to be Ray Gibbons, the Union Army paymaster who scheduled the gold shipment to pass through Middleton. The same man, who, I believe, cooperated with Colonel Langston in perpetuating the Middleton Massacre and the theft of over two hundred and eighty thousand dollars in Union gold."

"Thank you for so informing the court, Mr. Blackstone," said the judge. "Mr. Jensen, do you have any questions for this witness?"

"I don't even know what he's talking about, Your Honor, or what this has to do with this trial. No, I have no questions for this witness."

"Very well," intoned the judge. "You may call your next witness, Mr. Blackstone."

"Thank you, your Honor. I call Sheriff Brags to the stand."

"I object, Your Honor," said Mr. Jensen, as he looked through various papers laying on the table in front of him.

"Your Honor," said Mr. Blackstone, "I think if Mr. Jenson will look at my list of witnesses he will see Sheriff Brags' name."

"Well, Mr. Jensen, do you still have an objection?" asked Judge Tucker.

"Ah … ah … yes … I mean no, your Honor. Sheriff Brags' name is on Mr. Blackstone's list of witnesses and I therefore withdraw my objection."

"I'm so pleased," said the judge. "Sheriff Brags, you may now take the stand and be sworn in."

After the sheriff was seated in the witness chair, Mr. Blackstone said, "Sheriff Brags, please tell the court how you came to know Mr. Tanner."

"I met Mr. Tanner when he was a young boy, and then again after his mother and father were brutally murdered."

"And did you conduct an investigation into this murder?"

"Yes, I did, but Burt Tolman, who I knew lived a few miles outside of town, and who Mr. Tanner said was part of the gang who murdered his parents, was never found. His farm was abandoned, and he and his family were never seen again."

"Thank you. Now please tell the court when you next saw Mr. Tanner and explain the circumstances surrounding this meeting."

"Yes sir. I next saw Mr. Tanner about two weeks ago. He came into my office and asked if I would accompany him to the farm owned by his family before his parents were murdered. He said that he thought we would find evidence at the farm that would provide a motive for the murders."

"And what, if anything, did you find?"

"In a small hillside cave near the farm, we found a rust-coated box about the size of a family bible."

"Were there any other witnesses to this discovery, Sheriff Brags?"

"Yes, the owner of the farm, Mr. Josh Landcaster, and his twelve –year-old son, Jason."

"Thank you. Did this box or its contents provide the motive Mr. Tanner was seeking?"

"I don't know, but Mr. Tanner seemed to think so. All I saw inside the box were some tintype pictures.

"Did you look at any of the pictures?"

I only saw the picture that was lying on top of the others when the box was first opened."

"And what did you see?"

"What appeared to be a lot of dead people."

Your Honor," said Mr. Blackstone, "I have no further questions for this witness at his time, but reserve the right to call him again if needed."

"So ordered," replied Judge Tucker. "Mr. Jensen, do you have any questions for this witness."

"No, Your Honor."

"Mr. Blackstone," said the judge, "Do you have another witness?"

"Yes, Your Honor. I wish to call Mr. Flack to the stand."

"The jury has yet to decide if Mr. Franklin is Mr. Flack," said the judge. "So until it does, Mr. Blackstone, we will continue to refer to the defendant as Mr. Franklin."

"Yes, Your Honor. Will Mr. Franklin please take the stand and be sworn?"

"Objection, Your Honor," said Mr. Jensen in a quiet voice as he stood up. "Mr. Franklin is the defendant in this trial and is therefore not required to be a witness for the prosecution."

"Quite true, Mr. Jensen. Your objection is sustained." "Mr. Blackstone, do you have another … ?"

"Your Honor, if … if it may it please the court," interrupted Mr. Jensen in a soft, respectful voice, "after consulting with my client, the defense asks for a recess to meet in private with you, the defendant, and Mr. Blackstone."

"Very well," replied the judge as he banged his gavel and stood up to leave the room."

When the judge, the attorneys, and Flack returned to the courtroom fifteen minutes later, the room buzzed with muffled comments and questions.

"Mr. Jensen," said the judge, "I understand your defendant now wishes to plead guilty to the crime with which he is charged. Is that correct?"

Amid gasps and shouts from the gallery Mr. Jensen said, "He does, Your Honor, on the condition that his life will be spared."

"And what is he offering in return?"

"He will testify truthfully for the prosecution, Your Honor."

"Is that acceptable to the prosecution, Mr. Blackstone?"

After looking at Jake, and seeing him nod in concurrence, Mr. Blackstone said, "It is, Your Honor."

"Very well," said the judge. "You may proceed."

Mr. Blackstone then reached down under the prosecution table, withdrew a multi-colored carpet bag, and placed it on top of the polished surface. Opening the bag, he removed a rusty, dirt-covered metal box. With care, he pried open the lid of the box and walked to the front of the room facing the Judge.

"Your Honor, this is the item Mr. Flack and the others were searching for on the day he now admits he murdered Mr. Tanner's parents. As you and the jury have heard, it was found by Mr. Tanner in a hillside cave overlooking the area where Mr. and Mrs. Tanner were killed. Inside the box are a large number of tintype pictures taken during the Civil War. If it pleases the court, the prosecution asks Your Honor to look at the pictures before entering them into evidence."

The judge reached across the front of his desk and took the box from Mr. Blackstone. Setting the opened box in the middle of his desk, he then removed and looked at each tintype. As he did so his face became a mask of disgust. When he finished looking at each picture, he carefully placed them back into the box, angrily slammed the lid closed, and handed the box back to Mr. Blackstone saying, "This evidence has been accepted by the court and will be submitted to the jury for deliberation at an appropriate time."

"Your Honor," said Mr. Blackstone, "the prosecution calls Mr. Franklin, who now admits he is Roy Flack, to the witness stand."

"Mr. Flack will take the stand," said the judge harshly.

Flack, his face a ghostly white, walked hesitantly to the witness stand, raised a trembling right hand as he was sworn in, and sat down.

"You have sworn to tell the truth, Mr. Flack," said the judge, "and if, after your testimony, I find that you have lied to this court, I will rescind your agreement with the prosecution and order you to be hanged without delay. Do you understand?"

"Yes … sir," Flack replied in a weak, strangled voice.

"Mr. Flack," said Mr. Blackstone, opening the box and withdrawing a single tintype.

"I hold in my hand a picture. I am going to give you the picture and I want you to tell the jury what you see."

Flack took the picture and studied it carefully.

"What do you see, Mr. Flack?"

"It's a picture of … a battlefield."

"Describe it to us," demanded Mr. Blackstone.

"There are bodies lying around everywhere."

"Are the bodies lying on the ground civilians or military personnel?"

"Civilian and military; both Union and Confederate soldiers."

"And what is the central figure in the picture doing?"

"Standing behind a man, a civilian, down on his knees."

"Is the man standing a civilian or a military man?"

"Military. A colonel in the Confederate Army."

"And what does the colonel have in his hand?"

"A pistol, aimed at the back of the head of the man kneeling."

"I'm now going to show you another picture, Mr. Flack. And again, tell me what you see."

Flack took the picture and had to choke back a sob. "It's the same picture," said Flack as he struggled to speak, "except the man, who was on his knees, is now lying face-down with his head near blown off. The colonel is standing over the dead man's body while smiling and shaking hands with another man."

"And who is this other man?"

"Me," sobbed Flack.

Again, there was a gasp of surprise and apparent revulsion from the gallery.

"Do you see a sign in the background of the picture, Mr. Flack?"

"Yes"

"And what is the name on the sign?"

"Middleton," said Flack with a quivering voice.

"And what is the name of the Confederate colonel in the picture?"

"Colonel Warren Langston."

"And do you see Colonel Langston in this court room today?" said Mr. Blackstone, as he turned around and spread his arms wide to encompass the whole courtroom.

Flack looked out into the gallery, searching the face of every man. It wasn't until he looked toward the back of the room, and then up into the balcony, that his eyes widened in surprise as he slowly raised his right arm and pointed a shaky finger at a man trying to hide. "That's him," he shouted. "That's Colonel Langston."

Marshal Farnsworth quickly drew his pistol, and fired two shots at Flack.

CHAPTER 21

COURT RECONVENED THE FOLLOWING DAY with Flack once again seated on the witness stand, but this time with the bicep of his right arm bandaged and the arm in a sling. Small red marks on his face also showed the effects of Colonel Langston's second shot hitting and splintering the witness box banister with sharp wooden shards. Colonel Langston had been immediately restrained and unarmed by four burly men hired by Mr. Blackstone as a precaution that the colonel might respond to Flack's identification in such a manner.

"The court will come to order," said Judge Tucker as he banged his gavel on his desk. "Mr. Blackstone, he continued, "do you have any further evidence to offer this court?"

"We do, Your Honor."

"Very well, you may proceed." Then, turning to Flack, Judge Tucker said, "Mr. Flack, I remind you that you are still under oath to tell the truth, the whole truth, and nothing but the truth or my previous warning regarding your punishment will be immediately carried out. Do you understand?"

"Yes, Your Honor," Flack replied meekly.

"Mr. Flack," said Mr. Blackstone, "what is, and what has been, your connection with Colonel Langston, formerly known as Marshal Farnsworth?"

"I was his sergeant during the war. When the war ended, and Mr. Tanner's father disappeared, the colonel ordered me to find Private Tanner and the pictures he took on the day of the massacre. He said the pictures could get all of us hanged, and that Tanner was the only person who knew where the gold was hidden."

"And just who are *all* these people he was referring to?" asked Mr. Blackstone. "Oh, oh, no … no … wait … let's first find out about Middleton, and how all the people there were massacred. Tell us, Mr. Flack, from the beginning, how this massacre came to be."

"Yes sir. Well … we … we all knew the war was ending and that the Confederacy was lost, so everybody was thinking about what they could take with them that might be worth killing or stealing. It was about this time that I was secretly contacted by a man named Ray Gibbons, who Colonel Langston later told me was a Union Army paymaster.

It was Gibbons who told me about the train and the gold, and that I was to pass this information on to Colonel Langston. He also said this information came from a Union Army General that Colonel Langston knew, and that there were to be no witnesses left alive. I guess you know the rest."

"Oh, not by a long way, Mr. Flack, not by a long way," said Mr. Blackstone. "Your Honor, I request that Mr. Flack step down at this point, but made available for further questioning later."

"Mr. Flack, you will go with your guards and remain in irons until called. Mr. Blackstone, you may call your next witness."

"Thank you, Your Honor. The prosecution now calls for Mr. James Holt to take the witness stand."

"Any objections, Mr. Jensen"

"No, Your Honor."

After Mr. Holt was sworn and seated, Mr. Blackstone said, "Mr. Holt, what is your position in the United States government?"

"Sir, I am proud to say that in my position I serve as an Under Secretary for the United States Attorney General, Mr. Thomas Sampson," replied Mr. Holt.

"Yes, a very important job to be sure," said Mr. Blackstone. "And have we met before?"

"Oh yes, you came to my office a week or so ago and asked me about Marshal Farnsworth's congressional nomination as Deputy Chief of Law Enforcement; a nomination initiated by the Attorney General."

"Yes, and as part of that discussion, Mr. Holt, did you tell me that Marshal Farnsworth and Mr. Samson were long time associates."

"Yes, I remember Mr. Samson mentioning that to me, but he never said what that relationship was."

"But you know what that relationship is now, don't you Mr. Holt?"

"Yes, I do."

"And how did you come to learn about this relationship?"

"Well sir, at your urging, you and I went to the United States Army Academy at West Point and examined the attendance records for cadets graduating in the years prior to the start of the civil war."

"And what did we find, Mr. Holt?"

"We found that U.S. Attorney General, Thomas Samson, and Colonel Langston, alias Marshal Farnsworth, were classmates and graduated together. We also found that a plebe, named Ray Gibbons, was accused of rape, but later found innocent after his whereabouts at the time of the rape was vouched for by Senior Cadets Samson and Langston. Ray Gibbons graduated three years later, and, before the war was over he was promoted to the rank of Lt. Colonel and became *General* Samson's paymaster."

"Thank you, Mr. Holt, you have been very helpful," said Mr. Blackstone.

"Your Honor," Mr. Blackstone continued, "at this time I would like to have read into the court proceedings that just before Mr. Gibbon's died of the wounds inflicted by my client, he, when asked, said that he had been sent to kill Mr. Tanner by *'the general'*. Although Mr. Tanner and I had no knowledge at that time who *'the general'* might be, I believe it will become readily apparent to everyone when this trial is concluded."

"The court records will so indicate, Mr. Blackstone," said Judge Tucker. "And my, my, my," he continued in a caustic voice, "this trial is becoming more interesting all the time."

"Thank you, Your Honor. "And if it pleases the court, I again call Mr. Flack to the witness stand."

"And so it will be," said the judge with a smile. "Mr. Flack, get up here and remember that you are still under oath."

"Mr. Flack," said Mr. Blackstone. "You said earlier that Colonel Langston knew Ray Gibbons was a Union Army paymaster. How do you think he knew this?"

"I don't know for sure, but when I passed the message and train schedule to the colonel, he said he knew it wasn't a trap, because it came from a Union Army General who would receive a share the gold for the information."

"So what you are telling this court, Mr. Flack, is that to the best of your knowledge, General Sampson was the instigator of the train robbery and gave the order that all witnesses, both civilian and military personnal who were not part of the conspiracy, were to be killed.

"Yes sir, to the best of my knowledge."

"Your Honor," said Mr. Blackstone, "the prosecution rests and asks the court to find Mr. Flack guilty of the murder of Mr. Tanner's mother and father and the multiple murders involved in the Middleton massacre. It is also requested that warrants be issued for the arrests of Colonel Langston and General Sampson for murder, conspiracy, and the theft of government assets amounting to over two hundred and eighty thousand dollars."

Four hours after the trial ended, Roy Flack was found guilty of all charges and two days later was sentenced to life imprisonment.

CHAPTER 22

WITH THE ARREST OF COLONEL Langston by Federal authorities, the shocking outcome of the trial was on the lips of everyone from San Francisco to the nation's capital. Now at home in the Owens' parlor, Jake, Emily, Beth, and Beth's father were reviewing the events of the trial and trying to come to an understanding of everything that had transpired.

"When did you first know that Marshal Farnsworth was Colonel Langston?" Beth's father asked.

"When I opened the box and looked through the tintypes," Jake replied sadly. "I didn't see him in the first few pictures, but when I did, I recognized him right away. Although he was standin' in the middle of a lot of bodies sprawled on the ground, the most disturbing thing about the picture was the look on his face after he'd executed the civilian, like he was proud of what he'd done."

"Those poor, innocent people," said Beth. "How could anyone do something like that?"

"Only a monster," said Emily fiercely. Her recovery from the nightmare that had so long consumed her now seemed complete. Jake could see that she was a happy, carefree, and independent young woman in love with a man who appeared to be devoted to her.

"Yeah," said Jake, "that's 'bout the only thing a person can say. But the hardest part, at least for me, was knowin' I'd been betrayed by a man I'd come to respect -- a man I thought was my friend, but twice tried to have me killed. A man who I believe hired me as his deputy thinkin' I'd eventually kill Flack and Tolman, so they could never identify him. Maybe he also thought that along the way I might even find the gold."

"But what about this man, Gibbons, who twice tried to kill you?" asked Mr. Owens. "It's apparent that he knew both Langston and Samson, and where to send a message about your conversation with Tolman. Wouldn't Langston and Sampson also want him dead?"

"I'm sure they would have killed him sooner or later," Jake replied.

"So, after finding the tintypes, and knowing that Marshal Farnsworth was Colonel Langston, what were you planning to do?" asked Beth.

"I really didn't know," said Jake. "I knew the tintypes alone could get Langston and Flack hanged, but, more than anything else, I wanted them hanged for murderin' my folks. Then, when Marshal Farnsworth told me he'd be watchin' the proceedings from somewhere in the courtroom, I knew that if we got the tintypes introduced as evidence, we had to somehow contain him. That's when Mr. Blackstone decided to have men sitting near the colonel to arrest him when the time came. But our biggest problem, at least at the beginnin', was provin' that Franklin was Flack, because without that, we couldn't introduce the tintypes as evidence and Flack would go free."

"Sounds like you took a big gamble," said Mr. Owens.

"Yeah, and it was almost a disaster."

"But isn't that when Mr. Culver appeared?" asked Beth

"Yes," replied Jake with a far-off look in his eyes. "Without him the trial would have ended right then."

"So who is he?" Emily asked. "From what you've told us, Mr. Culver admitted he was part of Flack's gang. Why would he come to the trial and confess?"

"Because he owed me a favor that could only be repaid by coming forward with the truth," replied Jake. "When I was sixteen I saved his life after he was shot in a gun fight, not knowing then who he was."

"But he was part of Flack's gang when your parents were murdered," said Beth. "How could you forgive him and let him walk away after the trial?"

"I have forgiven him because he was just a scared kid at the time, and when he saw what was happening he was nearly killed for trying to stop it. Years later, when I found him in St. Louis and asked him for help in bring Flack to justice, he refused, sayin' it would ruin him, his business and his family. So his appearance at the trial was a complete surprise, and one that I will be forever grateful."

"What about Langston, and especially Sampson?," asked Mr. Owens. "Sampson is an important official within the government and is sure to have influential friends in high places."

"Well," Jake replied, "right now, and until there is a trial, they're both being held in federal prison without bail. With the tintypes as evidence, I don't think there is any way they will escape hanging."

"Speaking of tintypes," said Beth, "why did your father take the pictures in the first place and then disappear with them?"

"That's a question I have not answered in my own mind," Jake replied.

"Maybe because, for some twisted reason, Langston ordered him to take the pictures," said Beth's father, "and then, after seeing Langston, Flack and Tolman kill everybody left alive after the massacre, including their own men, your father thought that disappearing with the pictures would be the only way to stay alive and perhaps someday bring the three murderers to justice. I also think your father was a good man and never wanted anybody to know he was ever there."

"I'd like to think you're right," said Jake, "but we'll never know for sure."

"At least Flack is going to spend the rest of his life in prison, or will he, Jake?" Beth asked. "Is it possible he could also be convicted for the massacre murders and be hanged along with the others?"

Jake was quiet for a moment before he spoke. "Yeah, well ... when he agreed to confess everything to save his life, it was for the murder of my folks, and I wasn't sure I could agree. Then I realized it was Langston who had set everything in motion, and gettin' him hanged was even more important that seein' Flack hang. According to Mr. Blackstone, the Middleton massacre is going to be prosecuted as war crime and it is highly probable that Flack could be convicted and hanged with the others."

"So what are you going to do now, Jake?" asked Emily. "With Langston behind bars, are you still a federal marshal?"

"I guess I am until the government decides if ...."

"What the ...! Now what in the world!," said Mr. Owens as he hurriedly started shuffling through the tintypes lying on the table before him. "Something is very strange here."

"Like what, Papa?" said Beth, standing and looking over her father's shoulder.

"Well, I've looked at all the tintypes at least a half dozen times and, except for five, they're all pictures of the massacre."

"What's so unusual about that?" asked Beth.

"Maybe nothing. It just strikes me as ... well, strange."

"So, what's happenin' in those five pictures?" asked Jake.

"Nothing. Nothing at all. There're all pictures of ... well ... scenery."

"Scenery?" said Beth with a look of surprise.

"Yes, scenery. Look, this one is a picture of a saddle-back mountain far off in the distance, and this other one is a picture of a pine tree with its trunk split just above the ground and forming the letter V. And take look at these two. One is a picture of a large rock outcropping with a smaller rock balanced on top, and the other is a picture of a valley with a twisting river running through it."

"What's the fifth one?" Papa.

With a look of confusion, Mr. Owens said, "Well, that's the strangest one of them all. If I were to guess, I'd say that whoever took this picture had to be standing on top of something high up and looking down at the ground. See here, you can just see the hub of a wagon wheel."

"Looking down at what?" Papa.

"At what appears to be a rather large, egg-shaped rock set among some smaller, similar looking rocks."

"So, what do you make of it?" asked Jake.

"I can't rightly say," said Mr. Owens, as he laid the five pictures on top of the low table between the two opposing sofas in the parlor.

"It looks to me," said Emily as she began to arrranged the pictures, "like maybe each one, except for the egg-shaped one, could be looking off in a different direction."

"Maybe my father just liked taking pictures of scenery," said Jake.

"Maybe," replied Mr. Owens, "but I have the feeling that Emily is on to something.

"Look," said Emily as she continued to arrange the pictures. "If you put the one with the egg shaped rock in the center, and place each one of the others on each of the four sides, it could be ..."

"A map!" exclaimed Mr. Owens excitedly. "Yes, yes, I think Emily's right. Why else would your father hide these pictures among the others?"

"Seems a little far fetched to me?" said Jake, frowning. "My pa weren't the kind of man who was into games and such, much less a treasure ...."

"Hunt," said Emily, her eyes wide with astonishment. "A treasure hunt. But what would he be hiding?"

"How about two hundred and eighty thousand dollars in Union gold?" said Mr. Owens smiling. "Think about it. Suppose, after the massacre, Colonel Langston sent your father and a couple of others to hide the gold while he, Flack, and Tolman murdered the rest of his renegade army to avoid having to share the spoils. Suppose also that Langston told your father to take some pictures of where they hid the gold so they could find it later. Then, when your father and the others came back, Langston killed everyone except your father, who somehow managed to escape with the tintypes. The reason Langston didn't kill your father with the others was that he needed your father to lead him to the gold."

"That's a lot of supposin'," said Jake. I've got to admit, though, it does make sense, and if what you're sayin' is right, there were two reasons why Langston was willing to kill anyone who got in his way of gettin' the tintypes. Not only could the tintypes identify him as a mass murderer, they could also tell someone else where to find the gold."

"Oh, Jake, do you really think so?" Beth asked.

Three weeks later, Jake, a United States Army Lt. Colonel, and nine soldiers found the egg-shaped rock, overgrown with weeds, in a farmer's field. After digging for less than an hour they uncovered two large metal boxes containing two hundred and eighty-four thousand, six hundred and twenty dollars in gold.

"Looks like you're a very rich man, Mr. Tanner," said the Lt. Colonel.

Confused, Jake replied, "Now why would you say that? It ain't my gold we're lookin' at."

"No, it's not your gold, Mr. Tanner, but you've just earned yourself a reward from the United States Government for its return."

CHAPTER 23

November 1878

WITH COLONEL LANGSTON AWAITING TRIAL in federal prison, and with no orders to the contrary, Jake continued to perform his duties as a deputy federal marshal. As each day passed, he found himself increasingly anxious for a new marshal to arrive. Anxious because his arrival would likely result in one of two actions: asking Jake to continue as a deputy marshal, or, telling him that his services were no longer required. The latter action, he feared, could perhaps indicate an unjustified criminal association with Colonel Langston posing as Marshal Farnsworth. While he yearned to be free to seek his fortune in Colorado, he also had to admit that he rather enjoyed enforcing the law.

It was a cold, gray, wintery morning when the train from Kansas City slowly huffed and puffed its way into the Dodge City rail station. Jake lounged lazily on the receiving platform while the train's passengers disembarked like ghosts through clouds of steam from the wheezing engine. As was his custom, when time permitted, he studied the face of each man stepping from the train, while at the same time running pictures of wanted outlaws through his mind. More than once, his keen eye identified such a man and possible bloodshed was avoided with a quick arrest. The man, who was now plowing his way through the steam, looked nothing like a hardened criminal. Short in stature and slight of build, the man looked and dressed more like a banker than a fugitive. His face had the appearance of gentleness, and the bowler hat on his head did nothing to detract from his gentlemanly manner. Jake's eyes dismissed the man with only a passing glance and continued their surveillance until the last male passenger stepped from the train. His duty done, Jake left the train station and returned to the marshal's office.

It was mid-afternoon when Jake looked up from reading the daily newspaper to see who had entered his office. It was with noticeable surprise when he saw the gentleman from the train station, whom he had summarily dismissed.

"Am I correct in assuming that you are Deputy Federal Marshal Jake Tanner," the man asked in a pleasant voice.

"I am," Jake replied, smiling as he stood to greet his guest. "How can I help you, sir?"

"Actually, I'm here to help you," said the man as he stepped into the room and walked toward a chair near the desk where Jake had been sitting. "May I sit down?"

"Yes, of course," Jake replied as his smile faded to reflect a wariness about his eyes. "Since you know my name, sir, would you kindly tell me yours?"

"My name," said the man as he sat down and placed his bowler hat on the corner of the desk, "is Jared Thompson, United States Federal Marshal, and I have been ordered by the United States Department of Justice to replace marshal ... well ... let's just say that I'm here to replace Mr. Farnsworth." Reaching into the inside pocket of his dark blue suit, he handed Jake a folded pack of papers saying, "and here is a copy of my orders so stating."

Stunned, Jake accepted the folded pages and began to slowly read the legalize language. His face remained impassive until he began reading the last page, which stated that Deputy United States Federal Marshal, Jacob Tanner, was to be retained for as long as he was willing and able to serve.

Looking up from the document, Jake stammered, "I ... I never... well ... quite pictured it this way in my mind. I thought you might be ... well ... taller and ... maybe askin' for my badge."

"Oh no, no indeed," said Marshal Thompson. "It was I who requested that you stay on. What you have done in solving the Middleton Massacre outrage, and bringing Langston, Sampson, and the others to justice is widely recognized in Washington as nothing less than amazing. Accordingly, I will consider it an honor if you and your wife decide stay in Dodge City and assist me in this new assignment.

"You know I'm married?" said Jake with surprise.

"Actually, I know just about everything there is to know about you," said the marshal as he stood and held out his hand as a sign of greeting. "As I am sure you will soon discover, I also have a reputation that is feared by those who seek to break our laws." Suddenly, within a blink of an eye, Jake saw a gun in the marshal's left hand, and just as quick, it was returned to its holster under the marshal's coat. The smile on the marshal's face never changed and the only part of his body that moved was his hand.

"So, what do you say, Deputy Tanner? Are you willing to stay on?"

"Well ... I ... I mean, me and my wife were thinkin' 'bout going to Colorado and start a cattle ranch. I'm supposed to get some reward money for findin' the gold, and they're offerin' free land to settlers."

"Yes, I can see how attractive that might be to a young couple. So I suggest you take a couple of days to think about it, and then we can talk. Does that sound fair?"

"More than fair, sir, and thank you," Jake replied.

Two days later Jake and Beth sat across the desk from Marshal Thompson.

Although they had already made their decision to go to Colorado, they were hesitant to finalize that decision when faced with the uncertainty and difficulties that must surely lay ahead.

"Have two days been enough time for you to make a decision?" asked Marshal Thompson gently.

"Yes," Jake replied, looking at Beth, "but it has been a difficult decision."

"Can you tell me why?"

"Well, sir, last year Congress passed a law called the Desert Act, a law that allows folks to claim 640 acres of desert land in Colorado for a modest fee. While it's true that I have come to enjoy law enforcement, my dream of owning my own land and making a future for my family is more important."

"So you're turning me down," said the marshal.

"Yes, sir, I'm sorry."

"Well, don't be. It just so happens that I know about the Desert Act and have been to Colorado twice. It's a beautiful area, full of game and strong settlers. But I also know you will face some difficult times getting started. Complicating that difficulty will be the Ute Indians, who are not happy about being moved to a reservation in Utah, and the lawlessness that is already growing as the Indians leave the territory."

"Yes, sir, we know it will be hard at first, but our minds are made up. We plan to leave as soon as possible."

"Then let me make one more offer for you to consider," said the marshal with a mischievous grin. "The Colorado territory is well within my area of responsibility and, as I have indicated, it needs someone besides local sheriffs to curb the lawlessness now going on with more to come. I was going to assign a deputy to this area anyway, so why not you, Jake? You're used to working on your own, and there is no one I trust more than you to bring law and order to the territory. It won't be easy, but I believe you could handle your duties and, with a competent ranch foreman, develop your cattle ranch. And just to make building a cattle ranch a little bit easier, I have on my desk a

United States Treasury Note, payable to Mr. Jacob Tanner, in the amount of twenty-eight thousand four hundred and sixty-two dollars, the finder's fee for the recovery of moneys belonging to the United States government. Of course, the money is yours regardless of your decision, Jake, but I hope you'll continue being my deputy while you build your ranch and help me bring order to a troubled land."

Shocked, Jake turned and looked at Beth, who had remained silent up to this moment. Looking into her eyes, he could see indecision as she mulled the question over in her mind. He knew she longed for the day when he would no longer be a deputy, and not have to face her fears each time he left to bring an outlaw to justice. As much as the idea now appealed to him, the decision was really Beth's to make. He was about to say so when Beth spoke for the first time.

"Perhaps also having an income as a deputy while getting settled in a new land would further ensure our success," she said thoughtfully, "at least until Jake becomes a father in about seven months."

Jake could only stare at Beth with an open mouth.

THE END

COLORADO HIGH

Turn the page for a
Preview of another Jake Tanner Novel

AS JAKE LEFT THE GENERAL store and approached the barber shop, he recognized one of the two prostitutes at the Riverboat Gambler Saloon walking hurriedly toward him on the narrow wooden walkway.

"Mornin', Ma'am," he said pleasantly, as he stopped to let her pass and tipped his hat.

"Oh … oh my, yes … and a good mornin' to you sir," she responded shyly.

Jake took no particular notice of the woman's reaction and continued on toward the barber shop. Inside the shop he took a seat in a chair while the barber finished shaving the face of a man in an obviously expensive suit of clothes.

"I saw you talking and tipping your hat to my whore, Mister," said the man in a gruff, unfriendly voice.

"Yeah, said mornin' to her," said Jake easily as he removed his hat.

"Well, don't ever do that again," said the man angrily. "I can't have my whores walking around town like they were real people saying 'morning' to all their customers. First thing you know they'll get friendly with the men, and then the men will get to thinking they can poke 'em for free. Guess I'll have to teach that bitch a lesson."

"You teach her a lesson, Mister," Jake responded heatedly, "and I'll teach you a lesson. I ain't one of her customers, so let it be."

"She's my whore!" the man shouted as he jumped out of the barber's chair. "And I'll damn well do as I please with the bitch. You interfere with my business again, cowboy, and you'll answer to me."

"I not a cowboy," said Jake, "and this federal marshal's badge on my chest says I don't answer to you or anyone else. So, like I said, let it go, or I'll make your business my business."

"And I'm telling you to go to hell, Marshal," said the man, jamming his hat on his head and storming out of the shop with traces of shaving lather still on his face.

"His name's Pickney," said the barber. "He works his trade out of the saloon and has two of them women doing the favors. He's more trouble than he's worth, and would have been run out of town by now except he has what looks like a gunman watching his back."

After a soothing shave of his own, Jake decided it might be a good idea to check on the prostitute to make sure Pickney didn't carry out his threat to harm her. Entering the saloon, he approached an empty chair at a table where four men were playing poker.

"Mind if I sit for a spell?" he asked.

"Long as you don't mind losing," said one of the men sarcastically while glaring at another man shuffling a deck of cards.

Jake scanned the room casually while losing three hands and winning one. After two more losing hands, the prostitute he met on the street entered the saloon through a back door. She was dressed for the business of the day in revealing attire and had applied several layers of make-up on her face. But even the thick make-up did not hide her already blacking eye and the large purple bruise forming on her cheek. When one of the men at the bar reached out and playfully tried to squeeze her, she stifled a scream with her hands and tried to twist away in obvious pain.

At that moment, Pickney also entered the saloon through the same back door. He was sweating and smiling broadly as he playfully slapped the backs of several men standing at the bar, calling each man by name like a long-lost friend.

Tossing his cards face down on the table, Jake stood and quickly gathered up what was left of his money from the table. The other card players looked at him with annoyance until they saw the angry look on his face.

"I told you I wouldn't tolerate you abusin' the woman," said Jake in a low, menacing voice as he approached Pickney standing at the bar.'

"And I told you to mind your own damn business," Pickney replied while smiling at the men standing around him. But the smile began to fade when he saw the men around him slowly move away .

"I told you to let it go, Pickney," said Jake, "but from the beatin' you just gave the woman I see you ignored my warnin'."

"And I'm telling you that I own these whores, and I'll damn well treat them anyway I want."

Suddenly, Jake's right fist found Pickney's belly, and as the man folded forward, gasping for breath, his left fist smashed into Pickney's jaw. The last blow snapped Pickney's head backward, and he fell to the floor with blood spraying the front of his expensive clothes.

Jake was about to pull the man to his feet and deliver another blow when someone grabbed his arms from behind. Reacting wildly in his rage, he tore loose from the hold and was about to take a swing at the intruder when he realized it was Charlie.

"Easy, Jake, easy. He ain't worth killin'."

Breathing heavily, Jake looked at Charley and said through clenched teeth, "I can't tolerate a cowardly bastard who beats women and kids. Looking down at the now sniveling man, he said venomously, "If I ever see or hear of you beatin' any of these women again, Pickney, I'll give you a real whippin' and run you out of Colorado."

"What are you doin' in town?" Jake asked Charley as they backed out of the saloon while watching to see if Pickney had any friends brave enough to stand up with him.

"The saw mill broke a belt and I came to town to see if you wanted me to go to Delta and find another one," Charley replied. "Good thing I did or that bad man might have hurt you,".

"Yeah, right … thanks, Charlie. Maybe someday I'll tell you why men hurtin' innocent people riles me up so much."

"Whenever you're ready, Jake."

Once outside the saloon, the two men turned and started walking back along the road toward the general store. As they passed the barber, standing in front of his shop, Jake saw him look toward the saloon and then quickly re-enter his shop and put a closed sign on the door.

"You gettin' the feelin' there's trouble followin' us," said Charlie in a clam, quiet voice.

"Yeah, seems like it's my day for trouble."

248

As the two men stopped and turned slowly around, they saw Pickney and another man walking rapidly toward them. Pickney was using his right hand to adjust the gun belt on his hip and his left to wipe blood from his chin with a rag. Walking next to Pickney, with a confident strut that suggested the gun belt tied low on his leg was a problem solver, was a tall, gangly-looking man in a black suit. The wide brim of his black hat shielded the color of his eyes, but there was no mistaking the grim look on his face.

"Looks like Mr. Pickney and his friend want a piece of your ornery hide, Jake," Charlie joked with a straight face.

"Yeah, I heard he had a hired gun hanging 'round to keep customers from takin' advantage of his ladies. This ain't your fight, Charlie, stay out of it.

"Can't to do that, Jake. Cuss me all you want, but I'm stayin'."

Jake didn't have time to argue as Pickney and the gunman approached to within fifteen feet and stopped. Both men made an exaggerated effort to brush back their coat tails while taking a stance with their right hands near the butt of their guns.

All the men had now spilled out of the saloon's swinging doors, and positioned themselves along both sides of the road to witness the confrontation.

"I aim to kill you, Marshal," Pickney shouted boldly."

"You didn't say he was a federal marshal," said the gunman to Pickney in an angry voice.

"It doesn't matter who the hell he is, Morgan, you work for me, and you and me are going to kill him."

"I hell I will. I ain't never killed a lawman, and I ain't about to start now," said Morgan with menacing certainty. If you want him dead, you're goin' to have to kill him yourself."

"Now that's a right smart way of thinkin', Morgan," said Jake. "What about you, Pickney? You can either draw on me or walk away. If you draw on me, you're a dead man. If you walk away, it'll be with just the shirt on your back. Those whores will be free to do whatever they want, but it won't be with you."

"You cocky bastard," raged Pickney as the men on both sides of the street began to snicker and laugh. "I've got a damn good business here, and ain't nobody going to close me down."

"Then best you quit jawing' and get on with it," Jake replied calmly as he moved his right hand down toward the gun on his hip. "I never could abide a low-life skunk that makes money sellin' a woman's favors, and then cries like a baby when he gets poked in the nose."

The laughing of onlookers was apparently too much for Pickney's pride, and he started to draw his pistol.

Morgan, however, knowing Pickney was all talk and no guts, quickly grabbed him by the shoulders, turned him around, and started pushing him back along the road toward the saloon saying "You ain't no match for him, Mr. Pickney."

"Let me go, damn it," Pickney raged as he struggled against Morgan's grasp.

"Well I'll be," exclaimed Charlie as he looked at Jake with astonishment. "Looks like you've got yourself a new friend."

"Seems like," said Jake as he and Charlie turned around and again started walking toward the general store.

Suddenly, two consecutive gunshots split the air and a bullet creased Jake's left upper arm.

Quickly shoving Charlie away, Jake spun around while drawing his pistol and was ready to shoot when he saw Pickney face down on the muddy street. Morgan was standing over him with a disgusted look and a smoking pistol in his hand. "He broke away from me and was tryin' to shoot you in the back, Marshal. I didn't have time to warn you."

ABOUT THE AUTHOR

DOUG ORAHOOD is a retired United States naval officer and California public school administrator. He has published numerous articles in newspapers and professional periodicals and is a contributing author for a California State University textbook. *Retribution* is Doug's first novel in the Jake Tanner murder mystery series.
Doug lives with his family in North Logan, Utah.

Printed in the United States
By Bookmasters